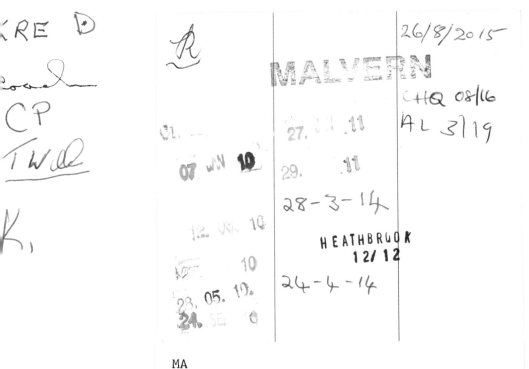

DARK VALLLEY

DARK VALLEY

JACKSON GREGORY

SAGEBRUSH
Large Print Westerns

Copyright © 1937 by Jackson Gregory

Copyright © 1937 by Jackson Gregory in the

Copyright © renewed 1965 by the Estate of Jackson Gregory.

First published in Great Britain by Hodder & Stoughton
First published in the United States by Dodd, Mead

Published in Large Print 2009 by ISIS Publishing Ltd.,
7 Centremead, Osney Mead, Oxford OX2 0ES
United Kingdom
by arrangement with
Golden West Literary Agency

British Library Cataloguing in Publication Data
Gregory, Jackson, 1882–1943.
    Dark Valley
    1. Western stories.
    2. Large type books.
    I. Title
    813.5'2–dc22

ISBN 978–0–7531–8265–9 (hb)

Printed and bound in Great Britain by
T. J. International Ltd., Padstow, Cornwall

CHAPTER
ONE

Twice within forty-eight hours the lone rider, coming up like a whirlwind for dust and speed from somewhere in the farther southwest, had been asked his name — and this was in a country and at a time when it was far from customary to put personal questions to a stranger.

The first occasion had been at the little cow town of Agua Verde. He had tarried there overnight. After stabling his horses — he rode into town on a glorious red-bay stallion, the most superb piece of horse-flesh Agua Verde had ever seen, and was followed by two led relief horses, likewise high-headed, savage-eyed and clean of line — he ate hungrily at the lunch counter, then repaired to the Green Water saloon. Within twenty minutes he had joined four men playing stud-poker. Within another twenty minutes he had proved himself the hardest player of the lot, and all played hard and fast, with an outer though perhaps deceptive semblance of recklessness. The men with whom he played called one another familiarly Al and Smoky and Gaucho and Temlock. The time came when one of them, quite friendly about it, asked:

"An' you, Stranger, what'll we call you?"

The stranger stared at him with a pair of intensely black eyes which were not in the least friendly. He employed the long fingers of a brown muscular hand to sharpen the already needle-pointed ends of a small moustache that was as black as his eyes, and took so long in answering that it began to seem that he wasn't going to answer at all. But finally he said, in an even, low-toned voice which had spoken only when necessary to-night and never above that hushed monotone:

"You can call me Willie, if that'll help any, or even Sitting Bull, or, say, Robinson Crusoe, and you won't even have to smile."

He used gold pieces for counters — fives, tens and twenties — and appeared to have an ample stock; an hour or so after midnight when the game broke up he went off to bed with considerably more gold than he had sat in with. He was out of town and away, none knew where, long before day had brought any other in Agua Verde awake.

The next night late he rode into the mountain town of Fiddler's Gulch. At the "hotel," so proclaimed in the drunken-looking, malformed letters on a split board over the door, he was handed a pencil and a dirty sheet of paper and requested to register.

The way the stranger looked down along his nose at the hotel keeper was like sighting along a rifle barrel. When he demanded curtly, "What the hell?" it was with reason. This was worse than asking a man casually what his name was. Here you were required to set it down in black and white, and it might be used against you.

"Sheriff's orders," he was told by a disgusted landlord. "Ol' Dan Westcott's a-gittin' an ol' man's notions, I reckon. Every hotel in Rincon County's got orders straight from him, an' if you know Dan, or ever heard about him, you'll likely know he's apt to raise seven kinds o' hell with any man that don't do things his way. Me, I tell him things is comin' to a purty pass. It's on-reasonable in the firs' place; it puts a hotel man to a lot of extry trouble; it's aimin' at a free American's con-sti-toot-ion-al rights, an' hell, Stranger, mos' folks can't write anyhow. You can, I'd say?"

The stranger, though he accepted pencil and paper in a way which smacked of reluctance, stood scowling at the two a long while as though hesitating to commit himself in any way; a man might have looked like that if he couldn't remember his name or didn't know how to spell it. Finally he muttered something under his breath and wrote in a hurrying scrawl that it would take a better man than his host to read:

"Bolt Haveril. From Texas."

In his room he lay down with his boots on, smoked and stared frowningly at the cracked ceiling for a couple of hours. He removed his boots only to make his way noiselessly downstairs. No one saw or heard him go.

Later he was seen and talked with by a couple of cowboys on the southern slopes of the Big Bear Mountains, when he hailed them to ask a question. It appeared he had ridden out of country familiar to him; he wanted to know how to get to Dark Valley.

3

They looked him over from the peaked crown of his hat to the spurs on his bootheels; they took full stock of the gallant red-bay stallion he rode, the two scarcely less splendid horses he led, the gun he wore low at his side and the carbine across his saddle, and they told him what he wanted to know. He was still a good fifty-sixty miles from Dark Valley, and he'd think it a lot longer before he got there, as the going got tougher all the way; it was up yonder where the mountain tops were mistily purple against the sky. And the younger of the two cowboys added:

"They don't welcome strangers much in the Valley. Me, if I was you, unless I was a friend of Duke Morgan's, I'd pick me somewhere else to go."

The man who had signed himself Bolt Haveril from Texas, nodded and rode on. The two cowboys continued on their way but now and then turned to look back until he was over the ridge; in Fiddler's Gulch they reported him to Sheriff Dan Westcott. Old Dan asked his questions so shrewdly that by the time they were answered he had a pretty fair daguerreotype of the lone rider. He scratched a leathery jaw, tugged at a snow-white walrus moustache, spat at a horned toad scurrying to cover as though it had read the look in his eye, and admitted complacently:

"I'm sort of glad he's put most of Rincon County behind him, and I'm sort of damn gladder I didn't happen to meet up with him. Pleasant sort of a cuss, wasn't he?"

"Friendly as a rattlesnake," said the younger cowhand. Then, eager with youth, he asked, "He was

4

the feller all right that you was lookin' for — that Mex gent they called Don Diablo. Wasn't he, Dan?"

"Reckon," said Dan, while the older cowboy regarded him curiously, thinking that the sheriff might be ageing after all, as some said, seeing how he inclined to garrulousness today. "Reckon," repeated Dan. "Passed this way yestiddy; stayed here over night 'nd crept out with nobody telling him *adiós*. Signed himself Bolt Haveril, from Texas. Well, at that he might of signed himself Jeff Davis."

"Now what?" demanded the young cowboy. "Seems like he's headed for Dark Valley, an' the lower end of Dark Valley's in Rincon County, ain't it, Dan? Goin' after him?"

"Reckon," said Dan Westcott, and looked sly. He was sly, a seasoned old fox, as all who had cause to know him agreed. "But, being it's late now, I won't start until sunup. Likewise I'm oiling up my old bear rifle to-night, being as it's the longest-range shooting iron in the county, so's when me and this *hombre* meet up it'll be with plenty room between us. And now, as the feller says, seems like I've paid you back in full for all the information I've extracted out'n you, and in case there's any more knowledge you're craving, you know the way to Dark Valley."

"No more cravin', Dan," grinned the young cowboy. "From what I hear, Dark Valley's easy enough to find, but it's something sort of diff'rent findin' your way out ag'in! S' long, Dan. An' while you're oilin' up your ol' bear gun, better brighten up your sights a speck."

"Reckon," said Dan. "S' long."

5

CHAPTER
TWO

Bolt Haveril rode hard all that day, changing his saddle several times with a mind to saving his horses, sparing the bright red stallion especially, but seeming to have no thoughts to spare himself. From every rise he turned to look back, his eyes narrowed, hard, watchful; he was suspicious too of the wild country which he was penetrating so deeply. Most of all his vigilance had to do with the rugged uplands straight ahead, the lofty blue spires which cast their shadows down into the sombre confines of Dark Valley.

One would have said that here passed a man who rode full tilt into some great hazard, who knew it and yet only pressed on the harder for his knowledge. Down yonder, sweeping upward from the gently sloping country on this nether side of Fiddler's Gulch, he had given the impression of a man in rapid flight from something following on behind, dogging him — Sheriff Dan Westcott, perhaps, or in any case the law which he represented. That impression at no time ceased to emanate from his carriage, for he never gave over those searching backward glances, but something else and new was added. It was as though he was not only driven but pulled; as though the impatient haste which marked his flight was a twin with that other haste which made him seem eager to hurl himself along into some bright danger.

It was only dusk in the mountains when he came to the high plateau, knife-edged in steep cliffs on one side, which marked the southwestern rim of Dark Valley. And all at once and for the first time his haste gave place to an idling sort of leisureliness. He stopped and threw down his bed-roll near a creek which, a hundred paces from where he elected to camp, spilled itself down in a feathery cascade some hundreds of feet into the valley below. He rubbed down each of his three horses and seemed to enjoy the task; he watered them, watched one after another roll luxuriously, gave each a handful of oats, staked them out to graze and then proceeded unhurriedly about his own affair of creature comfort.

He made his fire close to the brook. With no breeze blowing, with the air as still as unstable air can ever be, his smoke stood up like a grey tenuous column against the slowly purpling sky; it could be seen for miles. He placed an iron skillet on three convenient stones; he carved thick slices of bacon and set them frying; he dug out of his kit a black iron pot which would hold twice as much as your two cupped hands, and made coffee in it. And between whiles he found time to roll a cigarette and squat on his high heels and sing to himself. He sang like a man crooning a lullaby. You would have thought him at peace. It was all about a little white dove with tender red feet that flew in at his window — first the window of his house, then the window of his heart, for the little white dove came from Her. "*La palomita de mi Morena!*"

The inflection which he gave the Spanish words was pure Mexican. A stranger would have found it hard to decide whether he was Mexican or American. His speech down there in Agua Verde and again with the cowboys on the flank of the mountain sounded like that of an American from Texas. His moustache was of an order popular below the border; when he touched up the ends, as he seemed to have a fondness for doing, now and then he revealed in its entirety a small new moon of a scar, knife-made.

Having dined as languorously easeful on the bank of the stream as an ancient Roman on his cushioned couch, he constructed a slender *cigarillo* of some rich, black tobacco pencilled into a thin white paper, and slouched over to the cliff edge to look down into the valley. Just then he was as Mexican as Santa Ana.

Dark Valley was well named. It was a deep-cleft place which saw a deal more of shadow than of sun, a somehow ominous and sinister long, crooked and in spots dankly depressing gorge, cliff-bound. From where Señor Bolt Haveril stood one could see but the lower, narrower end of it at all distinctly, so did its writhings about rocky promontory and abutment conceal its other portions. A riotous small torrent of a river, obscured mostly by overhanging alder and aspen and mountain red willow, crookedly traced the crooked valley's entire length, to slip away unseen through a dark ravine; it had entered the upper valley, also unseen from here, by spilling down in wild, ever windblown cascades from a higher pass. Here and there the valley was so narrow that two men could have called back and forth to each other from the tops of the cliff walls, but there were also widenings affording pasture lands and even richly fertile small meadows, high in grass and field flowers and, where infrequently cultivated, in garden crops.

Bolt Haveril stood some few brooding moments, his tall black sombrero swung from a finger by its chin strap, the evening breeze ruffling his black hair, his cigarette dangling and his eyes as sombre as the dark valley so far below him. He gave a hitch to his belt, sagging with its low-slung gun, turned his back on all this and returned to his camp site. He pulled off his boots, put down a piece of grimy canvas, spread a grey blanket on that, used his saddle for a pillow, rolled himself into his coverings like a cigarette, pulled his hat low over his eyes and lay still.

In the dawn he awoke and stretched and lay regarding the pale apple-green of a stretch of sky through the pines; he watched it turn to green-gold, then to the gayer, brighter hues of full sunup. Presently into the clear morning sky stood the high column of his camp-fire smoke, frankly unhidden like last night's. Breakfast unhurriedly done, he took up his carbine and, before saddling, turned back on foot the way he had come yesterday.

And now again he moved guardedly, like a man sensing danger all about him. Some three or four hundred yards along the return trail was a nest of big boulders through which he had ridden last night.

Stooping his tall form and running swiftly across the open space intervening, he came to a stop behind the rocky barrier and peered forth down trail as though not only suspicious of pursuit but inclined to be confident of it. Keeping his rangy body pretty well concealed, though the high crown of his sombrero and the nose of his rifle did briefly show themselves over the top of a boulder, he prepared to wait, as patient as a cat that has already smelled its mouse.

The mouse in this case, however, was a fox — a long-legged, two-legged, grey old Rincon County fox known across a pretty wide sweep of territory as Sheriff Dan Westcott. He showed up, advancing cautiously and on foot himself, quite like Señor Bolt Haveril in that, on the farther rim of an opening in the Bear Mountain timber like the one across which Bolt Haveril had so recently advanced, and he too came to a halt behind the convenient barricade offered by a fallen pine. That he had seen the smoke of Bolt Haveril's fire was unquestioned; Dan Westcott was far too vigilant, far too shrewd-eyed to have missed it.

The two men spied each other at almost the same instant. The sheriff, with his long-range rifle raised threateningly, shouted a shrill command:

"Hi there, you! I got the drop on you! Come out peaceable or I'll blow your damn' head off!"

"*Que quiere usted, Señor?*" the other called back to him. "W'at you say? Who you want?"

"You, damn you, that's who I want! A feller that they call Don Diablo, down beyond Laredo."

The man in the big sombrero behind the rocks laughed at that.

"Me, I'm Bolt Haveril, from Texas," he called back. "American, not Mex. You got the wrong man, pardner."

"Like hell, I have!" shouted old Dan. "You're Don Diablo, real name Juan Morada, all right, and you're coming along with me —"

The carbine, as steady as the rock itself on which it rested, made answer for its owner and cut the sheriff's words short off. It was a neat piece of shooting, all things considered, for the early light was tricky among the pines and there were splotches of sun quivering among shadows which seemed to breathe like live things; though the bullet left Dan Westcott unscathed it carried his hat off his head with a hole drilled through the crown.

A yell burst from the old sheriff as he leaped to better cover:

"You danged long-eared jackass! You come damn' near nailing me that shot, don't you know it? Now — now jus' suppose you take this!"

Thereafter no words were squandered. Dan Westcott cut loose with a string of bullets which screamed as close to the man behind the rocks as any man could listen to with the least pleasure. There had been a flash of white teeth, a broad and even good-humoured sort of grin with a touch of sheer diablerie about it when Bolt Haveril had shot off the sheriff's hat; there was no more grinning as Dan's flying lead came so uncomfortably close. For ten minutes the two alternately held their fire, to peer out guardedly, and

11

blazed away. At the end of that time, with a good dozen shots fired on each side, the duel came to an abrupt end.

Neither man made any attempt to assure himself that any of his many bullets had done the work for which bullets are made. Old Dan Westcott said to himself smugly, "Well, that job's done," and on all fours crept back among the pines, getting to his feet only when safely away, hastening back to his horse and riding again southward. He didn't so much as turn to look over his shoulder.

The other man emulated Dan Westcott. He went to his horses, saddled and made his pack, mounted and rode north toward the upper end of Dark Valley. He went slowly, frequently abandoning the dim trail to ride circuitously through the trees and buck brush, and was again the man of yesterday in that he was forever peering into shadowy places, glancing back over his shoulder, keeping a hard brown hand close to the grip of a belt gun. Always he kept Dark Valley at one side, a sheer-dizzy drop below; at times he rode close to the cliff tops, at other times, seeking the more solitary and more devious way, he was as far as half a mile from it. When he had travelled a little more than half way between points marking the valley's lower and upper ends, he gave over looking behind him; he said curtly to the red stallion:

"Well, Daybreak, we ought to be out of Rincon County by now and getting into Juarez County. Happens every county has got its own sheriff; it's Dave

Heffinger up this way. They say he favours a sawed-off shotgun loaded to the muzzle with buckshot."

He rode so slowly that the stallion Daybreak, supercharged with fierce energy, was in a lather from chafing restiveness; he champed his restraining bit and, save for the firm hand on his reins, would have jerked his head around many a time to snap with bared teeth at his master's leg. The other horses, the smoky roan and the sorrel, were also fretful from restraint, wetter with perspiration than if they had their morning run. But the rider fought the three of them down to slow progress and gave every appearance of treating Juarez County and its lawful overlord, Dave Heffinger, with respect equal to that he had observed toward Rincon County and Dan Westcott.

He came abreast of High Gap, the main pass leading down into the sombre deeps of Dark Valley, and to the first fence he had seen. Here, too, he came of a sudden on a road that was less a road than a winding clear-way through the pines, gouged with two wheel ruts. He gave no evidence of any intention to turn into this road, down toward the padlocked gate vaguely glimpsed through a screen of laurels, but was pushing on toward a brushy mountain flank above when a shout rang out, commanding him:

"Get your hands up, Don Diablo! I've got you covered with both barrels! If you start filling your hand I'll blow you clean to hell!"

Instead of filling his hand or doing the other thing, namely lifting both hands, empty, Bolt Haveril promptly elected a third line of action. As he dropped

13

his carbine he pitched headlong out of the saddle, and the hidden shotgun roared — both barrels together making a reverberating thunder in the rocky defiles of the mountains. Yet it remained that a second time that morning Bolt Haveril went unscathed. He struck the ground rolling and was still rolling when he brought up against the padlocked gate under the laurels. As if of its volition an old walnut-gripped forty-five had got into his hand; he saw a puff of white smoke drifting lazily away and started shooting.

And then an odd thing happened, the sort of thing which folk, for lack of a better name, term a coincidence. He caught a glimpse of a man's hat — a new pearl-grey Stetson this time — and, though the man who wore it got safe away that day without a bullet through his head, still the hat of Dave Heffinger, sheriff of Juarez County, was ruined. And a second time a sheriff let out a yell, this one throaty with rage.

The man crouching at the gate permitted himself a grin, one that twitched a pointed black moustache in such fashion that the small new moon of a scar flashed into full instead of semi-eclipsed evidence. But the grin vanished as swiftly as it had flashed into being. Close behind him, not three swinging paces away on the other side of the gate, was a third man, and he spoke now in a measured, deep-toned and peculiarly surly voice:

"Well, Stranger? What's the trouble?"

Bolt Haveril didn't turn. His eyes were still concerned with the patch of buck brush and the scattered rocks over which the white puff of smoke had drifted. But he answered.

14

"Trouble?" he shot back, and sounded no less surly. "Look at my horses! Stampeded, the three of 'em! And you, whoever the hell you are, if you think I like walking, you're crazy!"

The newcomer into his scheme of things snorted. Just then came another shout from the man lying hidden in the buck brush.

"Throw your gun, you down there by the gate and come along with both hands high, or you're a dead rooster. Me, I'm the law up here, and I c'n see you and —"

Bolt Haveril lifted his gun, but the man behind him said commandingly, "Hold it!" and then raised his voice to call out, "That you, Heffinger?"

"You're damn right it's me!" Heffinger shouted back at him. "And you, Morgan, keep out of this. Which Morgan are you, anyhow? Duke?"

"No. I'm not Duke Morgan —"

"Budge Morgan, then! Anyhow —"

"You listen to me, Dave Heffinger!" roared the unseen Budge Morgan. "You're getting too damn' close to Dark Valley and you better know it! Ain't you got it through your head yet that the end of your prowling territory's more'n a mile off from this line fence?"

There was a silence. Then the sheriff said angrily:

"One of these days, Budge Morgan, I'll have me your hide, along with some more Morgan hides, nailed to my barn door!"

"You'd never last long enough to see my hide dry out in a summer sun, Dave," retorted Budge Morgan. He in his turn grew silent a moment; then he called out to

15

ask: "Who is this *hombre* anyhow? What do you want him for?"

"Hell!" shouted Heffinger. "He's that dirty greaser that thinks he's king down on the border, Don Diablo, that's who!"

The gun in the wanted man's hand cut loose with a string of bullets.

"You're a liar, Heffinger," he yelled as he fired. "Me, I'm Bolt Haveril, from Texas."

A hand reached through the gate and tapped him on the shoulder.

"Leather your gun and keep your mouth shut," said Budge Morgan. "Me, I'll step out and have a word with this damfool sheriff. He's off his stamping grounds and he'd better know it."

CHAPTER
THREE

Budge Morgan put a key into the padlock, opened the gate and went swinging along long-stridedly, a big, black-bearded ruffianly looking man, to a meeting with the sheriff of Juarez County. Bolt Haveril stood up; his own peculiar brand of satisfied smile brought the white crescent of a scar out into the clear like its prototype escaping from under a black cloud.

This time that sudden flashing out of the little new moon might have construed a romantic omen. He heard a voice, one that had never rung its charges in his ear before, close behind him; and, instantly, if for only an instant, forgetting both Morgan and the sheriff, he whirled about. It was a hushed voice, a girl's, faltering and faint in his hearing yet disturbingly musical.

"I — I don't know who or what you are," she said hurriedly, scarcely above a whisper. "There's no time for me to ask, for you to answer, for me to tell you anything. The others are coming — I know they won't let you go away without taking you to Duke. If you are in the valley to-night — try to meet me, late, at the bridge below the waterfall —"

It was a plea and a command. He got scarcely more than a fleeting glimpse of the girl, so swift was her withdrawal, but his senses were very alert at that moment and registered details sharply. The outstanding impression was one of a new kind of endearing beauty all enwrapped in the mysterious folds of contradictions. Just as at one time she both begged and dictated, so did she somehow convey to his understanding that she was desperate yet courageous, in despair yet striving to weave despair itself into the texture of hope, that it was in her to be as haughty as a lovely sylvan princess and as soft and yielding as the princess's milkmaid. Then those "others" of whom she spoke, more men from the Morgans' valley, came around a bend of the dark, steep, winding road under the laurels, and he lost sight of her. Lost thought of her, too, as he turned to confront the three stalwart, massive-shouldered young fellows — Morgans all, he judged them, from their build and carriage, from the coarse black hair and dark skin, from the not unhandsome features, from the savage blue eyes. They were demanding of him all at once:

"What's up? — What's going on here? — Who the hell are you?"

He sighted down along his nose at them; all were inches shorter than himself and also he stood on higher ground with the road coming up from the shadowy ravine so steeply to the gate. They were armed and looked truculent; he had his gun in his hand and merely looked dangerous. He answered, not in the least hastening, tending rather to linger on his few words almost with an insolent drawl:

"Me, I'm Bolt Haveril, from Texas. Right up there in the bushes is the sheriff of Juarez County. He mistook me for some old *compañero* of his and cut loose on me. A man you might know — calls himself Budge Morgan — has stepped up there to chat it out with him." While speaking he showed them how a man could roll a cigarette with one hand, a lovely, lost, and all but forgotten art. "Got a match, one of you boys?" he asked.

Then he saw the girl where she stood partly screened by the leaves of the laurel tree on the roadside bank; her face remained a disturbing mystery under the wide droopy brim of her straw hat. One of the newcomers at the gate saw her an instant first; it was his words to her that drew Bolt Haveril's eyes her way.

"Oh, hello Lady," said one of the three. "You here? Come along with Budge?"

"Yes, Tilford," said Lady. "We heard the shots and hurried."

Another of the three asked swiftly:

"This man here, who is he?"

"I don't know, Camden," she answered. "I don't know anything about him."

"We'll know a lot *pronto*," said Camden Morgan.

The third man spoke up sharply; he was the youngest of the lot but so much like them that Haveril made sure the three were brothers. This one said suddenly:

"Budge, he's up there having it out with that slinking damn sheriff. I'm going up there. What's he saying to Dave Heffinger anyhow? Budge is getting too big for his breeches; if he thinks —"

"Keep your shirt on, Rance," said Tilford Morgan, and clapped a big hand restrainingly yet in no unfriendly fashion on his brother's shoulder. "We've all got orders right now to take orders off Budge; it might come in handy to remember that, Kid."

"Hell with orders and with Budge too, and with you, Til, if you try to tell me where to head in!"

He jerked away but, as Tilford only laughed at him, stood where he was. Orders in Dark Valley came straight from Duke Morgan and meant something. So Rance stood glowering and appearing to hesitate, yet not really hesitating at all because he was not yet the man, and perhaps never would be, to clash with the valley's dictator, his father, Duke Morgan.

Bolt Haveril had regarded the trio interestedly all this while, though now and then sparing a glance to the girl who had not stirred from her place under the laurels. Now, however, his attention was drawn from these to yet another man coming up along the overshadowed roadway, appearing around the bend in the road about which the others had come. From this man's appearance he judged that here at last was a man who was not a Morgan.

He was younger even than Rance Morgan, darker than any of them, unlike them in build, too, being very slender, with slenderness's catlike grace. He wore his dark hair long; his face was fine and narrow, an ascetic face if a face can be that and frankly evil. There was a sort of sleek, sneering elegance about him; his boots were of carved reddish-brown leather, oiled and polished and kept free of dust; his belt was heavy with silver *conchas*; his gun was pearl-gripped; the big white silk scarf about his lean dark throat was knotted with foppish care.

Yet a Morgan he was, though those other Morgan men chose to consider him only a half-Morgan; that was because, though Duke had sired the lot of them, the youngest, Sid Morgan, was by another mother. She, when twenty years ago Duke Morgan had stolen her from her border home, bringing her into his valley to become his second consort, had been one of those startlingly lovely little animals of mixed Mexican-Indian blood who at wide-eyed fifteen are like little mystified dark angels. Sid Morgan, though as much Morgan as any of them, was also the son of the Southern Teresita.

He appeared to see the girl first of all, half hidden as she was in the laurels' shade. He greeted her with an odd taunting sort of gaiety as vicious as the swish of a whiplash, having the trick of speaking his words laughingly yet nonetheless with a sting in them, calling to her in a voice as musically soft as ever sang sentimental ditties to a Mexican guitar:

"Oho, my little Cousin Lady is here already too! To be in at the kill? To see the dogs pull the gallant stag down? Or why, Lady? Maybe to make pretty eyes at some new and handsome stranger?"

As Lady stiffened, to regard him through narrowed, darkening eyes, there was nothing of the soft, yieldingness of the milkmaid about her. Her lips, berry-red from youth and health and vigour and the outdoor life she led, opened for a swift retort, but she checked herself, lowered the dusky fringes of her lashes like one drawing down the window shades against an unwelcome sight, and thus did her best to eliminate Sid Morgan from her scheme of things.

He stood a moment chuckling and regarding her as though she amused him mightily, then lounged on upgrade and to the gate.

"Is this the *hombre* all the shooting was about?" he asked, turning the impertinent scrutiny of his now lazy and always mocking eyes on Bolt Haveril.

No one answered. Bolt Haveril, as watchful as a cat, not to miss so much as the flick of an eyelid of any of them, saw in a flash that all was not loving harmony in this mountain fastness of the Morgans. This languidly swaggering boy hated the girl with all the passionate hate of his badly mixed bloods. She loathed him. And, now that he spoke to the trio at the gate and none answered, Haveril saw that between them and the dark, slenderly devilish Sid Morgan there was a bristling resentment like a high, spiked wall.

Under Sid Morgan's almost paper-thin nostrils was the sketch of a tiny black moustache; it looked like a brief line drawn by a heavy-leaded pencil. He fingered it thoughtfully, was contented with a moment's silence, then spoke again. This time he addressed one man in particular, singling out Tilford Morgan, saying quietly:

"Tell me, Til. Is this the man all the shooting was about a couple of hours ago, and again just now?"

"Seems like it," answered Tilford, as curt with Sid as he had been genial with Rance.

"Who was shooting it out with him the first time?" Sid asked. "Old Dan Westcott?"

"You know as much as I do about that, Sid," said Tilford.

"And just now?"

"He says it's Dave Heffinger."

"Where's Heffinger now?"

"Up there in the brush somewhere, I guess."

"Where's Budge?"

"With Heffinger. Talking to him."

"Dave Heffinger's got his nerve," observed Sid Morgan, still fingering his thin black line of down, still thoughtful. "You'd think by this time he'd know better than to stick his nose into goings-on this close to the Valley."

This was no direct question and Tilford let it go without remark. Sid turned his attention to Bolt Haveril.

"Who is this *hombre*?"

"He says he's Bolt Haveril, from Texas."

Sid addressed Bolt Haveril then, speaking swiftly and in Spanish. What he said was, "You're Don Diablo, that's who you are, my fine friend; and right now, on the jump to save your hide, you are between the sheriff of Rincon and the sheriff of Juarez, like a nut that's going to crack wide open in the jaws of a nutcracker."

"Talking to me?" returned Bolt Haveril coolly. "Put it in English and maybe I can understand you."

Sid had, as one would know to look at him, a peculiarly nasty, sneering sort of quiet laugh.

"Don't understand Spanish, huh? Not a Durango Mexican to begin with, lately a border bandit?"

"Me? American, Texan. A ranger down on the Rio Grande."

Sid could be smilingly thoughtful.

"You look like a Mexican, all right."

Bolt Haveril shook his head and seemed as thoughtful as Sid had ever been.

"You get fooled by the looks sometimes," he said gravely. "Me, I've seen a thing that looked like a cross between a skunk and a snake, but it had two legs and a fuzz that looked like some day it might grow up to be a moustache, so maybe the thing was some kind of a human."

"If you want to get killed," cried Sid hotly, "if you want to start anything —"

"You came mighty close calling me a liar just now," said Bolt Haveril. "Most places, a man does that just to start a fight so I get the notion that might be what you're craving. Me, I'm peaceable by nature, likewise accommodating. Whatever you say, Sid, goes with me and goes fine."

"You're crazy! With the four of us here —"

"Shucks!" That revealing grin of Bolt Haveril's showed itself fleetingly. "Why, man, I'm betting you ten to one, and you name the money, that not a one of these boys would interfere — not, anyhow, until they allowed plenty of time and chance to see you wiped out!"

A dark flush came into the boy's face; his right hand was nervous and restless and perhaps tempted and eager and hesitant, all at once. Finally he lifted it, fingering his upper lip.

"Even if you had the luck to kill me, you fool," he snapped angrily, "do you think they'd let you go? You'd be dragged before my father, Duke Morgan — you'd be better off dead before that! I am his favourite son —"

"You're a liar, Sid!" cried Camden Morgan. "And if that is a fighting word and you want to take it up, grab your gun and I'll shoot six holes through your rotten heart!"

"Cam, damn you, shut up!" roared Tilford, and glared at him, then turned to glare at Sid. "You, too, Sid. What's eating you, anyhow?" Then he added, his gust of rage blown away: "Cam, you and Rance poke along up there where Budge is. Ask shall we head back with this man that calls himself Bolt Haveril —"

"From Texas," Bolt Haveril reminded him.

"Or will we wait here?" continued Tilford. "Ask him too about Haveril's horses. There were three of them."

Camden and Rance went out through the gate and up the wheel track, soon vanishing in a brushy cleft on the mountain side near the spot whence the sheriff of Juarez County had discharged buckshot and anathema. Bolt Haveril leaned idly against a gate post, tracing patterns in the dirt with the toe of his boot and wiping them out again, while Tilford Morgan and Sid regarded him curiously or stared off toward the place whither Budge, then Camden and Rance had gone. Once when Bolt Haveril glanced up from under the sheltering brim of his hat, toward the laurels, he made out that the girl — "Lady," they called her — had stolen away.

Then at last returned the three Morgans who had passed out through the gate, Budge riding the stallion

Daybreak and already aware that he bestrode a devil-horse always alert for the chance to throw a man and savage him, Cam and Rance leading the sorrel and the smoky roan. When they reached the gate, Bolt Haveril moved to intercept the first of them, Budge on Daybreak.

"I can't remember that I asked you to break in on my little argument with the sheriff," he said as his eyes and Budge Morgan's came to a studiedly expressionless meeting. "But I can say I'm grateful to you and the other boys for rounding up my scattered ponies for me. And now if you'll light down, I'll fork and be on my way."

"Shucks, you couldn't do that," said Budge, sounding affable, yet with no softening of rigid features, no glint of geniality in his eyes. "Not without dropping in on us long enough to say 'Howdy,' anyhow. Come along with us; Duke will be glad to see you, Don Diablo."

"Me? I'm Bolt Haveril —"

"From Texas!" put in Tilford, and laughed.

"Sure," said Budge. "Sure. Come ahead, Haveril. I've invited you to drop in on us. You don't figure we're not good enough for you, do you?"

"I'm sort of in a hurry —"

Budge laughed this time.

"Shucks," he said, more affable than ever.

"If you're in a hurry you'll make time by going slow a little while — long enough, say, to let Dave Heffinger clear out of your way. You don't want to make us mad, do you? After, like you say, we went to all the trouble of surrounding your stock, you wouldn't want to make us sore, would you, Haveril? Besides, Duke would be disappointed —"

"If you don't keep a pretty tight rein on Daybreak he's apt to jerk around and bite a leg off for you," said Bolt Haveril.

"Seems to me I've heard about this horse," said Budge. "Or a horse a hell of a lot like him, only they didn't call him Daybreak. Colorado, that's what his name was. Funny name for a horse; means Red Colour, don't it, Sid?"

"You better not keep Duke waiting all day," said Sid.

"Sure, that's right," nodded Budge. "Come ahead, Haveril, and say 'Howdy' to Duke." He retrieved his carbine from a patch of brush.

"I've heard about Duke Morgan," said Bolt Haveril. "Sure, I'd like to say 'Howdy.'"

Budge rode ahead down the steep winding road on the horse that was called Daybreak — or Colorado — and after him walked Bolt Haveril with a Morgan at each elbow, with Cam and Rance following with the led horses.

Tilford had not forgotten to close the gate, replace the heavy chain and snap the padlock back into place.

CHAPTER
FOUR

The earth smelled wet along the narrow wagon track, winding into the bottom of the ravine, like a tunnel based in rich black soil and overarched by mountain laurels. This road was a serpentine open way with dankness flanking it, with ferns encroaching, with a thickness of timber on either side like a wall of tropic greenery. Then there was the river, racing green and black water trimmed in glistening white froth, to cross over a puncheon bridge. There was the North Waterfall on the right, coming down like a mad thing from the cliffs, and spilling into a deep, dark, troubled pool; and all of a sudden there was the forest-ringed clearing with the log-and-rock houses set in its middle like a child's clumsy toy town on a green velvet carpet. In the background the wild azaleas and dogwood, bursting with springtime, were in frolicsome blossom.

One of these Morgan houses stood boldly forth from among the others, big and square and massive, its sturdy walls green with moss, its ample porch bright and warm with the sunlight. A man, big and square and massive, as boldly self-assertive as his fitting habitation, stood leaning against one of the rough log pillars supporting the porch roof and awaited the nearer approach of the small procession.

Anyone who had ever heard of these wild Morgans must have known at the first glimpse of him that this was Duke Morgan.

Budge Morgan, high up on Daybreak, made a careless sort of gesture and rode on around the house and to the barn barely glimpsed from here through the pines; Camden and Rance with the two led horses followed him. Bolt Haveril, with Tilford at one elbow and Sid at the other, went straight on to the broad puncheon steps leading up to the porch from which, with never a word, Duke Morgan looked at him.

"Howdy, Duke," said Bolt Haveril, leaning his carbine against the porch. "Passing by, I just dropped in to say 'Howdy.'"

"Howdy," said Duke Morgan.

Bolt Haveril had to put back his head to look up at Duke Morgan; that was because of the porch being three feet above ground and because of Duke's towering height. One might have guessed that Haveril didn't like looking up to any man. He went up the steps to Duke's side.

Customarily men shook hands, Western style. Neither of these two made the first gesture toward any such thing. For a little while, with nothing further to say, they looked at each other. Neither hid his interest. Each strove with utter frankness to make what he could of the other. And Tilford and young Sid, still on the ground below them, filled their eyes with the picture the two constituted.

The shadowy hint of a frown puckered Bolt Haveril's black brows; that was because even yet he had to look up at Duke Morgan. Bolt Haveril's lean, hard, flat body stood better than six feet, too; but he found in this middle-aged patriarch of the Morgans one of the biggest men he had ever seen. Duke was a good two or three inches taller, a good two or three inches thicker and broader, a stalwart black-bearded giant with hands that might have served as sledges. Nor was the feeling of "bigness" about him altogether physical; big, too, in forceful character was the man, and you recognized that fact as soon as you saw how he carried himself and looked into his steady, intelligent blue eyes. To be sure that forcefulness of character which made him leader and head man here was sprung directly from the primal fact that nature had bestowed on him a body which could literally crush any other human body he had ever encountered. He was like a man cast in a grizzly's outer semblance.

"You're Juan Morada," said Duke.

"I'll begin to think so myself, pretty soon," said Bolt Haveril.

"What does that mean?"

"Nothing much. Only everybody this morning keeps telling me who I am. And they all say the same thing. Maybe I pitched out of the saddle yesterday and landed on my head."

"Trying to be funny?" asked Duke.

"Not half trying."

"You're Juan Morada. Down on the border they call you Don Diablo. You're on the jump with a bounty on your hide."

Bolt Haveril's lip twitched. The little new moon shone fleetingly forth as from behind a black cloud.

"Hunting hides now for bounties?" he said in a sneering sort of way. "I must have made a mistake. You're not Duke Morgan after all?"

"What's the idea, Don Diablo?" demanded Duke.

Sid Morgan spoke up swiftly.

"He claims he's not Don Diablo at all, but a Texan named Haveril — Bolt Haveril."

"I never spent so much time before talking about who I happen to be or don't happen to be," said Bolt Haveril. "Now, with this settled, what the devil do you think you want with me, anyhow?"

Duke Morgan all the while regarded him stonily, his blue eyes hard and bright and noncommittal. Then Budge Morgan, already returning from the stable where he had left Cam and Rance with the horses, came around the corner of the house. Duke, without speaking, asked him his question with a sideways slash of the eyes towards Bolt Haveril and an uptilt of the square-bearded chin.

"Sure," said Budge. "He's the right gent all right. I had a talk with Dave Heffinger. Both Dave and old Dan Westcott tried to collect on his hide out there. Heffinger swears he's going to get him yet and hell take the Morgans. He's Juan Morada, the feller they call Don Diablo."

"Why should he try to lie out of it?" demanded Duke.

"Why shouldn't he? He don't know us, does he? And he knows he'll swing sky-high once they get him. Who wouldn't lie out of it?"

Duke nodded in his ponderous way. His voice, always a profound bass, seemed now to come from some cavernous sort of place down deep in his lungs. He spoke to Bolt Haveril, saying:

"I don't know what your game is, young feller, but I'd be seven kinds of a damn fool if I mistook you, and you'd be worse than that if you thought I'd fail to know you. There's the description of you that has been posted on a good many 'Wanted' signs. There's a scar at the corner of your mouth. And, as much as anything else, there's that stallion that's got a longer reaching reputation than most men's. El Colorado, they call him. And —"

"I got that stud horse from another feller," said Bolt Haveril. "His name's Daybreak. Maybe I sort of look like Juan Morada; shucks, that's nothing; lots of men look like lots of other men, when somebody just tells you about it and you don't see 'em stood up alongside one another. As for a man having a scar on him —" He laughed softly. "If I wasn't laughing already," he said, "I'd ask you, don't make me laugh."

Duke began to look puzzled. Also the bright hardness of his eyes took on the glint of anger.

"I don't understand what's got into you, Morada!"

"Better call me Haveril, Bolt for short."

"You've got more sense than to try to double-cross me, haven't you?"

"Me double-cross you?" Haveril looked the part of a hurt innocent. "How could I and why should I? Since when have the two of us known each other? I never clapped my eyes on you until now, and you never saw me, and there's no kind of business between us and —"

"I've said once I don't know what the devil's got into you," said Duke Morgan, his deep bass rumble like distant thunder threatening an electric storm. Then for a moment he checked himself and glowered at Haveril with a new sort of expression, his chill blue eyes probing like blue steel drills. He added curtly, "If it's just that you don't want to talk before these other men, say so."

Bolt Haveril didn't say anything in reply; that was because just then young Sid ran up the steps and into the house as though in some sudden hurry, and because on Sid's face there was such a devilishly cruel look.

"Well?" snapped Duke.

Bolt Haveril started and his gaze returned to a meeting with Duke Morgan's.

"I was passing by," he said imperturbably. "I had a run-in with a couple of sheriffs; I guess these boys know all about it. Maybe they can tell you old Dan Westcott ran off with his tail between his legs and a bullet in his shoulder; maybe they'll tell you I shot Dave Heffinger's hat off his head, coming just that close to getting him between the eyes. I'd have finished my chore with him in five minutes and been on my way, but Budge here invited me most cordially to drop in for a pleasant hour."

"Go ahead," said Duke. "If you talk long enough you might say something."

"Might," said Haveril and appeared to meditate. What he was wondering about was that sudden darting into the house by Sid; he kept his ears on the stretch for the slightest sound, and the eyes under his sleepily lowered lids were watchful. He added slowly, "If you're so dead set on the two of us doing a lot of talking, Duke, why don't we go somewhere and sit on a log by ourselves?"

Rance, returning from the stable the way Budge had come, called to his father:

"Hi, Duke! We opened up this *hombre's* bed-roll like you said; he's riding pretty heavy with money. Gold twenties, a lot of fives and tens, and some greenbacks. The paper money's stained with something; might be blood."

"And the gold twenties, some of them, anyhow," rumbled Duke questioningly, yet in the tone of one who anticipated an affirmative answer, "were earmarked, huh?"

"Sure," said Rance. "Pretty near all of 'em have got your mark under the eagle."

Bolt Haveril, merely listening, had not said a word. Now he spoke up quietly.

"Funny tricks you boys seem to have up here," he said. "Do you poke through every stranger's bundle to see if you can find a few pennies? Times must be hard up this way, or else the Morgans are going to seed."

"And even with that money on you," said Duke, "you'll still say you're not Morada?"

"Me, I'm Bolt Haveril. From Texas. That money? I got it from another fellow. The stain on the bank notes? Didn't it look kind of like black coffee stains? And, by the way, what are you doing with it? Leaving it where you found it or trying to make off with it?"

"I'll have a look at it," said Duke Morgan, and started down the steps.

He said something else too, but did not finish what he started to say; he broke off in the middle of a word as certain sounds, bursting out suddenly, startled all who heard them. The sounds were a savage growling like an infuriated wolf's, a piercing scream of terror, a man's laugh so devilishly cruel and mocking that it could have come from no one other than Sid Morgan.

Then for an instant there was a flurry of action, of which Bolt Haveril could make little, since it took place just beyond the far end of the long porch where it was smothered in vines and small shrubbery. He saw only vaguely the blur of swift shapes as he heard the growl and the scream and the laugh; but two seconds later, as he ran down along the porch and as those shadow-shapes burst out into the clear, he got the whole story in a flash — and in that same flash Bolt Haveril came very, very close to snuffing out two lives with the gun already in his hand: the lives of a big wolfish, fang-dripping dog and of the evilly laughing Sid Morgan.

Sid, when he had run into the house and through it and out at the rear to get the dog chained there, had already seen the girl. Lady, her interest or curiosity or need be what it might, was crouching in the shrubbery at the porch's end, eavesdropping. Sid, coming swiftly and noiselessly around the house, holding the end of the ten-foot chain, had set the gaunt, red-eyed beast on her.

Later Bolt Haveril learned that the one thing on earth that Lady most feared, and with reason, more even than she feared and hated Duke Morgan, was Sid's watchdog Stag. And now that she leaped up from her hiding place and ran screaming, Stag lunged after her with such unexpected swiftness and power that he ripped the end of the chain out of Sid's hand — and Sid stopped laughing then.

Stag, his great bounds carrying him high in the air and far out, overhauled the flying girl. His hurtling body catapulted against hers, throwing her off balance so that she stumbled and fell. Before she could rise, if indeed she was not paralysed with fear beyond stirring, the bristling dog, head up, jaws slavering, stiff reddish hairs along neck and far down the backbone standing straight up, growled again and bared his teeth. Just then Bolt Haveril was about to shoot, meaning to pick off Stag first before he could tear the girl's throat out, to drop the now rigid Sid next. But before his gun was all the way out of its holster the whole episode was as good as over, strangely yet definitely ended.

A queer, liquidly musical call, flutelike yet weirder and wilder than any flute — certainly a human note, though it was not like a man's voice, exactly, or a woman's or a child's — came from no farther away than the river bank. At the first sound of that call, Stag jerked his head about, stiff at attention, and though his teeth were still bared his red eyes roved elsewhere.

Then the call came again, louder, clearer, more insistent — and the big dog began whining. Bolt Haveril, amazed at all this and wondering what sort of creature it was that could check the dog at the moment of his kill, hurried back to the steps and down to the ground. He saw, emerging from the shadows thick along the river, a queer slight figure altogether as wild looking and weird as were the fluted notes with which he had talked to Stag.

"It's Crazy Barnaby," muttered Budge. "Damn lucky he was on hand; damn lucky for Lady — she'd be dead now else; lucky for Sid, too; Duke would have killed him."

Crazy Barnaby coming on, a dark, haunted-eyed boy in his latest teens, an unkempt being whose clothes were mostly rags, whose long black hair fell to his shoulders, in whose dark, stained hands was a rude staff crowned with three tiny silvery-tinkling bells, called again to the dog — more softly now. And Stag, never again glancing at the prey he had brought to earth beneath his heavy paws, whirled and whined like a pup and then made off in a straight line, jerking his jangling chain after him, to Crazy Barnaby.

Bolt Haveril, as he slowly leathered his gun, took in with the frankest of interest all that was going on about him. He saw Stag leap upon the queer slight figure coming up from the creek. The dog set both paws against Barnaby's shoulders and licked his face, and Barnaby patted Stag and put an arm about him and fell to laughing like a child, then to whispering something in the dog's ear. That ear came stiffly erect and Bolt Haveril was troubled for some small fragment of a second with the utterly preposterous suspicion that Crazy Barnaby was whispering secrets and that Stag, harkening so intently, understood every word!

But he forgot the thought and lost sight of the two figures as at last Lady rose and faced Sid. Her face was as white as a sheet; her eyes were still large with terror; you knew that the pained heart was all but bursting within her bosom heaving now so wildly. She did not say a word. It was, Bolt Haveril judged, because she couldn't speak yet. But words were scarcely necessary; as the fear ebbed out of her eyes a blazing anger, riding on a full tide of hate, surged into them.

"She'd kill Sid if she had a chance," thought Haveril, and wondered at the two of them that they could hate each other like this.

Rance Morgan was the first to speak up; he turned toward his father, saying hotly:

"Damn it, Duke, Sid ought to be shot for that. Stag came close to killing Lady; Sid wanted to have her killed —"

"Shut your mouth, Rance," said Duke Morgan. Then he turned upon Sid, a Sid no longer laughing but beginning to look frightened. "Sid," said Duke, "if Lady had been killed just now, I swear to God I'd have killed you by slow torture. You know I mean that, don't you?"

Sid moistened his dry lips, and nodded.

"I didn't know Stag would jerk away like that —"

"Shut your mouth," said Duke. "Right now, Lady, alive and kicking, is worth more to me than you'll ever be. Well, I'll let you live. But —"

Had he finished he would no doubt have said something like this: "But I'm going to come so close to beating you to death right now that you'll never make this mistake again." He made a sudden lunge toward his youngest son, meaning to take him unaware; but the foxy Sid, with eyes never so alert, read his father's purpose before the big body even stirred, and like a frightened rabbit Sid Morgan took to his heels, dashing around the corner of the house, vanishing in the grove.

Budge and Rance and Tilford burst into uproarious laughter. For an instant Duke stood frowning, then he too began to laugh.

"He'd better run," he chuckled. "He's a smart kid, is Sidney." Still chuckling he spoke to the girl. "Well, Lady, it was a dirty trick Sid played on you, wasn't it? At that, I'll bet you're half to blame. Why can't the two of you be sweethearts, 'stead of cat-and-dogging each other?"

The girl did not answer him. She didn't look at him or at any of the other Morgans. She walked down the mossy path through the tall ferns toward a half seen log cabin set apart from the other houses. As she departed Bolt Haveril caught one flash of her eyes as they turned upon him. Then she was gone, down there among the tall ferns and alders, and he found that the morning had brought him ample to think upon — these wild Morgans with their outside feuds and their inner hates and jealousies; an unkempt boy who looked like a witch's son and whispered secrets in the ear of a blood-lusting dog called from its quarry; his own predicament — and, somehow as emphatic above all these dark considerations as a bright young new moon over a dark forest, the remembrance of the look on Lady's face, first at the gate, now here, and her first words: "To-night, late — at the bridge by the waterfall . . ."

CHAPTER
FIVE

The Morgans, whenever they spoke of their lofty, cliff-guarded demesne, called it simply the Valley. For them there were no other valleys; this one, which they loved with a fierce, passionate ownership-love, sufficed. For them there was the Valley with those who dwelt therein, the Morgans; the rest of the world was vaguely "Outside". The Outside covered everything from the Mexican border to the Canadian, from the Pacific to the eastern plains that melted away at last into the Atlantic. Here you had the Valley, the Morgans; elsewhere, the Outside, the Outsiders. And since time out of mind — since at any rate the first Morgan, Duke's grand-uncle Jeff Morgan came here — there was little commerce between the two.

When now and then the Morgans found it necessary to ride out of their Valley, or when some uncurbed impulse prompted the brief sortie, it was the usual thing for at least a half dozen of them, often a dozen or even a score, to ride together; and more often than not their excursion was one of high-handed lawlessness. They went forth like a pack of wolves; they ravished and robbed and looted; hot with liquor when they started, they were red-eyed drunk when they came storming back. All this was known for a hundred miles in all directions from their snug little mountain kingdom; that they were permitted from year to year to go on their way was due to several factors: First, they were Morgans and had lived thus since the first white man, a Morgan, led the hunters and trappers westward unto these high places. They were based in habit and in tradition.

Further, in the Valley there were thirty or forty of them, all Morgans or men with some dash of Morgan blood in them; and though many a time hatred and jealousy flamed up among some of them and they fought like mountain lions, yet always they banded together against an invasion of the Morgan privileges and prerogatives. They boasted that they were here a long while before the Outsiders, of late grown milksops, started electing them their sheriffs; that never had a sheriff once penetrated the Valley save as a friend and on invitation from the Morgans.

Still further, making their bold tenure here a thing which seemed assured to continue with its swagger, their strength was not alone restricted to their intrenchment in this all but inaccessible fastness. Among the Outsiders, where they were universally feared, they had a pretty fair sprinkling of friends. These were for the most part the undesirables of the back country, the parasitic element which inhabited the mountain places of disorder, the saloon and gambling houses; there were, too, men who had their small, unkempt ranches and appeared to live without toil or any great reward; there were the hunters and trappers and goldseekers who came and went their devious ways, sometimes in peace, sometimes ruffling the high serenity of the brooding wilderness country. Some of these were Morgan sympathisers; some of them came, perhaps twice a year, to the Valley, to stuff their hides full at the roistering barbecues, to drink themselves skin-tight on the heady Morgan whisky, to ride away provisioned and with money in their pockets.

For the Morgans, after their own interpretation of the word, were kingly. Freebooters and robbers, they occasionally opened a strong hand and let gold pieces trickle through the fingers for smaller men to glean. These smaller men earned and were worthy of their hire; among the Outsiders they were little more than Morgan spies.

And so it was that at the trading post where a settlement was already starting, and at Red Luck Ravine where a rough and ready little town grew up at a crossroads in a mountain meadow, when a number of men chanced to gather they did not always speak everything that was in their minds. For there was always apt to be some hanger-on for whom no one could altogether vouch, a man who might be a Morgan Outsider. Certain it was that only last spring a fiery old cattleman, Ed Daly from Rincon Alto, rather over-indulged in his constitutional rights of free speech, was utterly indifferent who his audience might be, said things about the Morgans which everyone knew to be true, passed along in his tirade to making a few threats — and a week later the Rincon Alto was raided, its stock scattered, its buildings burned, Ed Daly badly hurt and two of his strapping tall sons dead with bullets through them. The raid took place on a dark night; the raiders were masked; no one could swear that they were Morgan men and everyone knew that they were none other.

Nor was any man dead sure which of the dozen who had listened to the old cattleman's denunciations and threats had been the one to carry the tale to the Valley. It grew to be the custom hereabouts, when two men spoke together and when a third joined them, for them to fall silent.

Dark Valley was an abiding place of eternal shadows. And here of late a shadow within the valley grew so tall that it towered against the sky. Dark Valley was a priceless, lovely heritage for the Morgans to swagger and royster and wax great in, for them to love as they loved nothing else on earth, for them always to have and to hold — unless somehow it slipped out of their grasp. And now, among the shadows of the Valley the tallest, blackest, gloomiest shadow of all was the fear that the century-old tenure was in danger of breaking.

When infrequently an Outsider came uninvited to Dark Valley he stopped and rapped for entrance, in a way of speaking, at one of the three barred doors giving access to the Morgan demesne — the gate through which Bolt had entered, South Gate at the far lower end, and Middle Gap Gate. Slung to a cross pole over each gate was a big bell. Rumour, fast taking on the old lichen-tone of legend, said that the three bells once swung in a lonely adobe church, long since melted back into mother earth, called the Little Santa Anita. Long dead Morgans, if the tale had it aright, had wrecked the church because its priest refused to do their bidding in some unholy travesty of wedlock they had demanded, and had brought the bells here to serve them as they did now.

Bolt Haveril heard the reverberating, not unmusical clamour of a bell, and did not in the least know what it purported since he had failed to mark the bell itself above the gate and half hidden by the over-arching trees. The notes swelled out sonorously, filling the long narrow valley, echoing against the cliffs, carrying word to every Valley dweller that someone at the North Gate came upon some matter of urgency.

Duke Morgan, having laughed away the episode of his fiend of a young son having set the wolfish Stag on Lady, had started toward the stable to have a look at what the boys had found in the newcomer's bed-roll. Now, at the swelling bell notes, he halted and stood frowning in a concentration of effort to read some particular significance into the sound. In the end, however, he turned, still scowling, toward Budge, demanding:

"Who's that? It wouldn't be that fool sheriff coming back, would it?"

Budge strode away, down toward the bridge. A man met him there, coming from the gate. The two spoke briefly, then Budge returned to report.

"It's Rick Mooney." When the Duke, having forgotten the name, continued to frown and stare, Budge completed his explanation: "He's that yeller dog, Duke, that used to work for old Ed Daly over at Rincon."

Duke remembered, grimaced and spat.

"Let him in. Bring him to me if he's got anything I want to hear. If he's just trying to horn in again on past performances, cut his ears off and boot him to hell out of here. I'll be at the barn."

"I'll come along with you," said Bolt Haveril. "If you're headed for a look-see at what's mine, I might as well be handy."

Duke shrugged heavily and went on; it seemed natural enough that this fellow, whom he took to be Don Diablo, would wish to be on hand while others looked into his pack. There was nothing to make him suspect that Bolt Haveril's entire interest was given to the bell ringer, the man who came with urgent word from the Outside and who, did his message prove to be important, was to be brought straightway to Duke Morgan.

But there were those who knew where Bolt Haveril's interest would be sure to centre at a moment like this — Sheriff Dan Westcott of Rincon County and Sheriff Dave Heffinger of Juarez, who were at the moment listening to the same bell notes and nodding their greying old heads together over them.

"It's sort of like a funeral bell for them hell-bustin' Morgans, only they don't know it," said old Dan Westcott. "They wouldn't, not bein' dead yet, but —"

"Not dead by a damn' sight, Dan," muttered Dave Heffinger, and shook his head soberly. "And it strikes me there's apt to be funerals for me'n you both before the Morgans are turned under."

"Shucks, Dave, that's no way to talk," snorted Dan. "But come along; let's get going."

They had met by prearrangement in a dense bit of woods less than half a mile from the spot where Dave Heffinger had ambushed Bolt Haveril. The older man, after his duel with the lone rider, had in reality but made pretence of a retreat south to his headquarters in Rincon County; he had merely withdrawn to his tethered horse and had arrived where he now was by riding a short unseen arc through the timber.

From their vantage point they had taken in a good deal of what had happened. They had watched the induction of a certain stranger — be he what he claimed, Bolt Haveril from Texas, a rancher, or the ill-reputed Juan Morada, Don Diablo of the border — into the Morgan valley. They had pursed their lips and fingered their chins and done their bit of placing their mental bets on the outcome.

They mounted and rode, of one mind to come into Red Luck as soon as possible. As they started, Dave Heffinger pulled off his hat, spun it on a horny forefinger, regarded it dismally and remarked:

"I can't say, Dan'l, as I've got to regard all your friends as my friends. That damn young pup mighty near drilled me between the right eye and the left eye. If I hadn't heard the bullet coming, and dodged —"

Dan cackled at him, and then pulled off his own hat.

"Look at it," he said, and managed a sort of giggle unbecoming his years and official status. "Shot me,

46

Bolt did, just like he did you. And I'm here to tell you, Davie boy, of all the shots I know, Bolt Haveril's the nearest. He can trim your eyebrows and never burn your hide."

"All I know," grunted the sheriff of Juarez County, "is that he's done gone and spoiled a good hat for me."

"It lets the air blow through so as to keep you cool," chuckled Dan Westcott, and they rode.

In due course, following a circuitous and little travelled trail, they came to Red Luck. That is to say, they arrived at a small nucleus where ganglions of the whole mountain country centred. It was not so much a town as a cluster of houses at a crossroads. There was the blacksmith shop with the little frequented hotel as an adjunct, the place where the stage stopped to take on or discharge a passenger or two; there was the lunch counter across the road; there was most of all the saloon where the thirsty and adventurous drank doubtful whisky and danced with undoubtable girls. The two sheriffs headed straight, like homing pigeons, for the saloon. The Barrel House it was called, not without reason.

There was a small back room which reeked of privacy. They sat and drank their whiskies straight.

"Now," said Dan.

"Yep, just about now," agreed Dave, and downed his drink like a man who needed it. He looked fidgety; he was nervous; he didn't try to conceal from an old friend who knew him from the crown peak of his sombrero to the bottoms of his lop-sided boot heels that he was worried. "Spill it, Dan'l."

"You've got most of the story already," said Dan Westcott.

Dave Heffinger dabbed at his wet lips with a bright red bandana.

"Have I?" he said laconically. "I got a short letter from you, Dan'l, which left out about twice as much as you said. I played out my hand the way you told me to; I had me my run-in with this friend of yours; he shot me through the hat and I stood for a good cussing from Budge Morgan. Outside of that, if anybody asks me, I can just say I don't know."

"It's like this," said Dan. "First off, you know how things stand in Dark Valley, and what Duke Morgan's game is."

"Sure," said Heffinger. "I got that."

"*Bueno.* Now young Haveril cuts in. That's who he is all right, Bolt Haveril, from Texas, like he says." He indulged again in his good-humoured chuckling noises. "He's a big rancher down there; he runs stock over a hundred thousand acres. Likewise and also he's more than that. He got himself made a deputy sheriff."

"Just for fun?" said Dave.

"More than that. He had him a notion to go out and get Don Diablo. Now he's out to pull the Morgans down."

Heffinger stared into his empty glass, then cursed into it. Dan Westcott saw that it was promptly filled.

"I've been sheriff up here seven years, Dan," said Dave. "You've been sheriffing down in Rincon County for twice that long and mebbe more. All this time I've wanted to get my rope over the Morgans' horns, and

48

you know it. No can do. You, too; you've tried and couldn't nail them. Then how come this young hop-o'-my-thumb Bolt Haveril thinks he can cut the mustard? And being deputy sheriff down in Texas won't help him; this ain't Texas!"

"He's young," said Dan. "So he's hopeful. That's the way young fellers are. Remember, Dave? What's more, there's what I wrote in my letter; there's a Morgan girl in the Valley, they call her Lady, and her brother got clear of the Morgans somehow and spilled all the beans to Bolt. And when he got himself shot up, knocked over by that feller Don Diablo, why Bolt did some figgering, and stepped up here to fix things. That's clear enough for a child of three to understand, ain't it?"

"What a child!" groaned the Juarez County sheriff and drank deep. "I've seen just enough sense in what you've said to play along with you, Dan'l; but I'm damned if I understand."

"You're damned anyhow," said Dan complacently. "But here it is: we've given Bolt a proper send-off in the Valley; the Morgans are dead sure he's a *mal hombre* and that the law's after him, seeing they heard and watched when Bolt and me had a gun fight, and also when you and Bolt did the same. And he's in the Valley, where most folks can't get very easy. Next, we've started a ruckus out here, and we know from hearing the Morgan bell ringing that word of that same ruckus has been carried into the Valley. Come night time, the Morgans will be swarming out of their snug places like a swarm of hornets you throwed a rock into. Then, says Bolt Haveril, he'll grab the girl somehow, one way or another, and get her out of there. That done, where'll the Morgans be?"

"Where?" asked Dave, as one who wanted to know.

"Morgan Valley," said Dan, "belonged to Thad Morgan. He had two kids; one was the boy that broke free and got shot up down in Texas by Don Diablo, with this Don Diablo getting his orders straight from Duke Morgan; the other is the girl they call Lady. Like I say, the boy, Bob, got away. If Bolt Haveril gets Lady out before she is of legal age and can sign her property rights over, well then the Morgans haven't any more claim on the valley than you have. Or me. And though they might squat tight and make trouble for a year or two, they know damn well they'd go out on their ears. Got it, Dave?"

"Hell, yes," said Dave. "Only what makes Bolt Haveril, the young hat-shooting hellion, think he can do what you and me have tried to do for years? He'd do it in five minutes!"

"He's young, like I said," sighed Dan. "I know the kid. I knowed his daddy. I hope he don't get filled up with Morgan lead — but I've got my doubts. Duke Morgan ain't only a wolf and a tiger and a bear and a skunk and a rattlesnake, but he's also a damn fox. Bolt had better look out."

"And it's all set to happen *pronto?*" said Dave.

"Yes. *Pronto.* To-night, mebbe."

"Most likely there'll be hell popping soon," said Dave resignedly.

"Just you sit back and listen for it," said Dan Westcott, sounding comforting. "You're apt to hear her

50

pop any minute now. We've took the lid off and Bolt Haveril has dropped the match in the powder barrel, and all we got to do, Dave, is wait — and while we're waiting, have another drink? Good whisky, ain't it?"

"It sure is," said Dave.

So they waited.

CHAPTER
SIX

The man Rick Mooney, shoved across the board of his destiny like a silly pawn, came to Dark Valley and rang the bell of North Gate because Bolt Haveril had so decreed. Yet it remained that Bolt Haveril had never heard of a man named Rick Mooney, and Rick Mooney had not the vaguest idea that an individual named Bolton Haveril existed.

All that Rick Mooney knew was that he had an earful of news which should be spilled immediately to the Morgans; he'd stand in closer than ever with them; they'd hand him money generously; they'd clap him on the back and somehow give him the feeling that he was a big gun. That made his pigeon breast stick out inches; it put warmth into the cold marrow of his spine.

And all that Bolt Haveril knew was that he was out to bring young Bob Morgan's sister out of captivity, and with the same sweeping gesture cut the legs out from under the proud Morgans. Hell had waited for them long enough. So, with the co-operation of two sheriffs, he had arranged that to-day there should be such word brought to the Morgans as would send them buzzing forth from their valley. Whether the messenger was one man or another did not in the least signify. But after the bell had rung and he had heard the few words which had passed between Duke and Budge Morgan, he knew that the messenger had come and that it behoved him to hear what the message was and to take stock of what Duke Morgan had to say and meant to do.

And he heard the whole of it, since Rick Mooney, when he arrived, was so full of it and so excited that he blurted it out as fast as his profane tongue could waggle. He was brought to the barn where Duke Morgan and Bolt Haveril had already gone.

Duke Morgan stooped over the small heap of gold coins and bank notes displayed on Haveril's tarpaulin. He took up one twenty dollar piece after another, studied it, dropped it back when done with as though it had become after his scrutiny no more than a pebble. He straightened up and glared at the stolid, watchful Haveril.

"I marked that money when I sent it down to the border," he said in his angry rumble. "I didn't trust Juan Morada then and I don't trust him now. But there's no sense your lying any more. I paid you to nab that damn young fool Bob Morgan; I paid you to save him for me and see to it that I got him back alive. And I paid well."

Bolt Haveril shrugged and the faintest hint of a smile touched the hard line of his mouth.

"Well?" demanded Duke. A deeper hot colour had come into his face and the veins on his forehead stood out full of blood.

"If you want to claim that money, go ahead," said Haveril as though the matter were a small one and beneath him. "You've got it here, you've got the odds against me —"

"Hell take the money!" roared Duke, and kicked at it with his heavy boot. "It's Bob Morgan I want."

Then it was that Rick Mooney, convoyed by Budge and Tilford, came hastening, almost running.

"Duke!" he called. "There's hell to pay Outside. They've rounded up every one of your friends they could find — they've got seven of 'em in a herd — they swear they're goin' to hang every mother's son of 'em, an' hang 'em *pronto*. They're in Pocket Gully —"

Duke stared at him as though he wouldn't believe this, and for the moment forgot all other matters.

"Who told you?" he demanded curtly. "How do you know? What friends of mine are rounded up? And who did it?"

Rick Mooney couldn't tell his tale fast enough.

"Nobody told me. I know because I was one of them. I got away in the dark, just before day. I had a hell of a time getting here; on foot all the way, an' Gawd, my feet hurt me! They've got the two Bedloe boys an' old man Adams an' his son Jimmie, an' Injun Joe an' Slim Conroy an' Doc Savage."

Duke Morgan's amazement matched his fury.

"Who did this?" he asked thickly. "How many of them were there — and what in hell's got into them?"

"I don't know who they are, Duke! There was only a half dozen of 'em, I'd say. They had their faces covered, an' they was even careful how they talked, talkin' mighty little an' sort of mum'lin'. They caught me when I wasn't thinkin' of anything like that, in the dark

54

jus' before I got into Red Luck. I guess they jumped the other boys the same way, one at a time. Then they herded us over into Pocket Gully an' hawgtied us where the ol' stone corral an' the rock house is. They lef' two fellers ridin' herd on us, the others ridin' off to round up Brocky Winch an' the Tomkins outfit. Me, they hadn't done a very good job tyin' me up; it was dark, only for a little camp fire at the far end of the corral; I got loose an' snuck into the brush an' I been wrigglin' an' hiding' like a snake an' runnin' an' limpin' ever since."

It looked as though the distended veins in Duke's forehead must surely burst. Yet instead of flying to new heights of gusty rage the man steadied himself and spoke in a strangely gentle fashion, almost under his breath.

"So they're going to hang those boys, huh? *Pronto?*" His enormous chest swelled to a long, slow intake of air; only after his breath was expelled as slowly as it had been taken in he added, "Then I reckon the hanging's all over by now, huh, Mooney?"

Mooney shook his head.

"Like I say, they didn't talk much. But there was one feller who gave orders. He said as this was to be a public party. Nobody was to be hung until they'd gathered up all the Morgan Outsiders. Then the whole crowd was to be hung the same time. There was goin' to be invitations; men was to come from Red Luck an' Rincon an' the ranches an' all over. They figgered on the party for daybreak to-morrow mornin'."

Duke turned to Budge.

"Get word through the Valley, Budge," he said. "We're doing us some riding, every damn man of us."

Budge made that airy gesture of his, half salute, and turned away. Duke called him back before he had gone three swift steps.

"Hold on!" said Duke. "I'm talking before I think." He steadied himself. "No hurry, Budge," he went on. "They've either hung 'em already or there's time aplenty. What's more, we'll leave some of the boys here. Who knows what's in the wind? Maybe, if they think they can clean up on our friends Outside, they'll even think of riding in on us here. Put good men on guard at every gate. We'll ride about twenty strong, leaving the rest here with their eyes peeled and their guns oiled."

"They'll know Outside that Rick got away," muttered Budge, "and that he most likely headed straight to the Valley."

"Let 'em know and be damned!" roared out Duke, letting his ready rage sweep him away again. "Let 'em hang every man jack that's a friend of ours, and I swear by the Lord we'll hang ten of them for every one they swing for us." And he ended with such an outburst of sulphurous profanity as to make Bolt Haveril, used as he was to outspoken men, lift his brows and stare.

Then a mellifluous voice, strange and new in Haveril's ears, poured itself like oil over the violence of Duke's subsiding wrath.

"Peace, Brother; peace!" said the voice. "When the day of wrath dawns, it is the Lord whom you blaspheme who shall hurl down the thunder-bolts of

56

His vengeance. So, peace, Brother, and still thine iniquitous tongue."

Bolt Haveril turned to look at the speaker who had come up so silently, and saw a very large bodied, very fat, paunchy man with a beaming florid face, with jowls that hung down, with small wicked eyes like a pig's. The man was dressed all in black with a round black hat and white collar, dressed like the preacher he said that he was. The "Reverend" Thomas B. Colby, he called himself. Were a Morgan to be buried, he officiated, hurling such curses at the Morgan Killer or at the natural death which had snared him as to make a man shudder; were a Morgan to be married, it was he who performed the travesty of a ceremony, though the girl shrieked and begged on her knees to be spared. Of all the Morgan crowd this "Reverend" Colby was perhaps the wickedest, a great fat tub of a man who, were a pin stuck in him, would ooze blasphemy rather than blood.

"Tom Colby," said Duke angrily, "some day I'll forget how to take you as funny and will butcher you and feed you to the hogs."

"Tut, tut, Duke," chuckled Colby. "You talk sacrilege, to set your hand against a minister of the Lord."

"A minister of hell," snorted Budge Morgan, who had small liking for a man whom Duke tolerated because, most of the time, he enjoyed him.

That pleased and flattered Tom Colby, and his fat jowls puckered in one of his broad, buttery smiles. He was opening his wide, oratorical mouth for some further ribaldry when Duke, staring beyond him at someone approaching, burst out in a new and curious tone of voice:

"Now what? What's all this?"

It was the girl, Lady, joining them. What Duke had noticed and what the others were quick to remark was the newly donned cartridge belt about her slim waist, the heavy gun at her side.

Her eyes were unafraid now and darkling with anger.

"If Stag over shows his teeth at me again, I'm going to kill him," she said, speaking quietly yet with an obvious pent-up force of determination. "I warn you, Duke Morgan. And — and Sid too! If he dares —"

Duke stared at her a moment, then only laughed at her and turned his back. She came closer and stood listening, looking curiously at Rick Mooney, at Budge and Duke, at Bolt Haveril.

Bolt Haveril, pretending to ignore her, pretended something else also. After all his whole game here, if he meant to achieve his purpose the swiftest way, must at least for the moment rest on pretence, and his simulation needed to be the best. He managed to seem all eagerness when he spoke up, demanding of Duke:

"When you ride, Duke, let me in on it! It's apt to be a nice, lively little party, and wouldn't you say offhand that an extra man would come in handy?"

"From what I've heard of Don Diablo," grunted Duke, "he's just the sort of man I'd like to have with me on a ride like to-night's — if I only knew he *was* with me."

"Fine, Duke. Only, anyhow until we get to know each other a mite better, why not call me just plain Bolt Haveril?"

58

Lady's eyes were upon him, puzzled, hopeful, apprehensive. Duke's eyes fairly gimleted into him. Then Duke beckoned to Budge and started away; fat Tom Colby waddled after them and for a truly eager moment Bolt Haveril thought that he was to have a few words alone with Lady. But Duke paused to call back.

"Come ahead, Morada. Grab up your gold and anything else you want to have with you, and I'll show you to a cabin where you can hole up while you're in the Valley."

"Tell me what's happened this morning, Duke?" called Lady. "What did this man Rick Mooney come back for? And where is it you're riding?"

"You want to know too damn much," he grunted at her. "Run along and play with your friend Crazy Barnaby. Come ahead, Morada."

So Bolt Haveril didn't so much as look at Lady again, but took up his bed-roll with its gold coins again in their little canvas bag, and followed where he was led, to a sturdy, one-room log cabin.

"You can bunk up here," said Duke. "In a few minutes I'm riding down to the Lower End; the boy'll have horses ready and you can come along. Most folks would give their ears to see what the Valley looks like from the inside."

"Fine, Duke," said Bolt a third time.

Bolt Haveril saw most of Dark Valley that day and marvelled at it, finding it incredibly beautiful, locked away from the world by those tremendous cliffs which in many places towered sheer a good six or seven hundred feet. Before seeing the place he had wondered at it being so hard for one to escape save through one of the three always guarded passes; now he realized the utter impossibility of a man getting out on horseback, for no horse was ever foaled that could have accomplished the thing. A man on foot? But even that looked next door to impossible.

He saw many of the Morgan men and several of their women folk and a few small boys and girls. The Morgan men were pretty much all alike; he'd know one of them if met a thousand miles from here, stamped with force and vitality and lusty vigour and arrogance. The women, too, were alike; they were Morgan chattels, had been dragged here by the hair of their heads, and for the most part were subdued, timid things. The children were all growing up wilful, headlong Morgans.

Dusk came early in Dark Valley and Duke Morgan and a score of armed men gathered by Budge prepared to ride. Up to the last minute Bolt Haveril did not know whether he was to go with them or remain behind. All afternoon he had matched his wits against Duke's. He knew that his seeming eagerness to go with the marauding party into Pocket Gully mystified the Morgan leader, that he had aroused Duke's suspicions. Duke went aside and talked a long while grumblingly with Budge. Then he came striding back to where Bolt was saddling Daybreak.

"You stay here, Morada," he said.

Bolt glared at him as though turned surly.

"No. I'm riding with you."

"You stay here, hear me!" thundered Duke. "I'll talk to you when I get back. You stay here. I don't want any stranger along to-night, and I don't care whether you're Don Diablo or the devil himself. Get funny with me and, damn you, you'll stay here tied up hand and foot."

Then Bolt Haveril, having had his way, shrugged, yanked the saddle off Daybreak's red back and went with it into the stable. The party, with Duke at their head, rode away.

CHAPTER
SEVEN

That he was being spied on was at first a mere suspicion, then an utter conviction before Bolt Haveril could have told you what it was that had forced the realization upon him.

Before the Morgan men had ridden away they had had their hearty dinners, most of them in the big stone and log house where Bolt had first seen Duke. Bolt had dined with them, as hearty as any, and from the porch had watched them spur up the shadowy road to the gate. He had not seen Lady again; there had been no women folk sitting down with them at the long table with its heavy flanking benches. As the departing hoofs made a dull thunder on the turfy track, he had marked the several men who held back. They were going to keep watch to-night — and after a while he told himself that they would have had their orders from Duke Morgan to keep watch on him.

As it grew dark he sat on the porch of the cabin allotted to him and smoked his cigarette. He thought: "To-night, if ever, is my chance; but it's not going to be any wide-open chance at that Duke, even when he's boiling mad, can keep a cool spot in his brain." He thought also: "Somebody's no doubt squatting out there under the pines watching me." So he drew deeply at his cigarette, making the burning end glow a hot red.

When he had finished that first cigarette and flung the still glowing stub down into the yard to make a small bright arc and die out, he sat still a long while knowing himself to be invisible to any prying eyes. Late to-night Lady would expect him down at the waterfall. Of course it would have to be late, he knew that she too was watched more and more narrowly with every passing day.

After a thoughtful, watchful while he rolled the second cigarette and lighted it leisurely, letting the mite of his match burn off the free sulphur, holding it so that it illuminated his face. Again he smoked, sure that he was being spied on.

At length he rose and went into the cabin and closed the door. The first lighted match showed him a single small window, high up and shutterless. He found a candle on a shelf and lighted it. Then he stretched luxuriously like a tired man, methodically spread out his blankets on one of the two bunks, pulled off his boots and lay down; only then did he reach for his candle and blow it out.

And now to wait. Now to throttle down that headlong impatience which was an integral part of him, and to command a patience which must last for hours. The devil of it was, he pondered, that he couldn't watch the hands of a clock; he'd have to guess at a couple of passing hours, with every minute as long as ten. But even that thought prompted a flicker of a grin there in the dark; if some fellow squatted outside trying to keep tab on him, that chap would find the time every bit as long.

Before the first thirty minutes were over he heard a board creak; someone had tiptoed up to the cabin porch. After that faint, tell-tale sound the night was very still again, profoundly hushed save for the chorusing of frogs in a reedy pool down in the meadow and the shrill singing of insect life. Whoever had come up on the porch, he judged, was still there; sitting on the steps, no doubt.

It must have been a full hour later when, fainter than the first time, there came the creak of a floor board. Thereafter silence as before.

Bolt slipped swiftly from his bunk, took up his boots and went to his window.

"He's gone," he thought. "Maybe for the rest of the night, figuring his job's done; maybe just for a drink or something, meaning to come back. Anyhow, here goes."

Looking out through his window he couldn't see anything moving, so dark was the night; there was just the black wall of the pine grove. So, with his boots in one hand, he wormed his way through the small square opening and came down on the porch as light as a cat. A moment later he was on the ground, drawing his boots on. Then he slipped around to the rear of his cabin, groping his way gingerly, and with the greatest stealth withdrew into the copse of young trees at the rear.

When he saw a faint dim light he came to a standstill; presently he made out that it was the yellowish glow from a lamplit window in one of the detached cabins. He moved along again silently and in another quarter glimpsed another lighted window. One would think it late enough for all these folk to be abed; yet to-night there was a feeling of uneasy restlessness in the Valley.

Giving Duke's big house a wide berth lest he stir up Stag chained at the back and so start up a din of barking, he moved noiselessly toward the first lighted cabin he had seen. It was a low, squat thing, its door sill not six inches from the ground, but larger than he had at first judged, an affair of perhaps three or four rooms. Only one room was lighted, and its window, shutterless like his own, was open. Some sort of a flimsy curtain hung over it, but he could see through it dimly, and he could hear what was being said.

There were two people in the room. One of them, a woman, was the most restless creature he had ever seen; when he heard her hurried tones and got even that vague view of her he set her down for the Valley's outstanding virago. When he saw that it was Sid Morgan with her and after he had listened a moment, he knew that this was Teresa, Duke's second and last wife, Sid's mother. She was small, withered, crooked. She moved with a dragging limp, using a cane. Her face he could not see.

"If he is Juan Morada, why did he come here?" she demanded shrilly.

"How do I know?" grumbled Sid. "You and I don't know everything that's between him and Duke. Maybe he came to get Lady for himself, *quien sabe?* Maybe he's got Bob Morgan tied up somewhere, or maybe he

65

killed him. If he could grab Lady — well, he'd be cutting the ground out from under Duke, wouldn't he?"

"*Um*," said the woman irritably. "You use your maybe's like beads on a string. What if he is what he says he is, just a rancher from down in Texas?"

"Then why would he be up this way? And why would he have Don Diablo's horse and the gold that Duke sent down to Don Diablo? And then there's that damned scar at the corner of his mouth — and Duke, not an easy man to fool, is sure it's Morada."

"So Duke is not easy to fool?" She laughed tauntingly. "Have I not fooled him more than once? — But never mind all this: are you sure the man is in bed asleep?"

"I want another drink; I'm dry," said Sid. "Yes; I've been squatting there at his door all night."

"And you'd better go back and squat some more," she told him dryly. "Duke left you here to watch; he trusted you with what may be a pretty important thing; if you failed him in this he would kill you."

"I'm going," grumbled Sid.

Bolt Haveril withdrew, silent, yet making what haste he could.

As he went he saw a lighted lantern, swung low, revealing a man's boots as the man made his way to the stable. Wondering who this was and what errand carried him out there so late, Bolt followed. As he did so he realized that soon the black velvet dark down here in the Valley would be thinned by a moon which always looked in here tardily; upon the cliffs and mountain

66

tops in the east there was already the soft glow of moonrise.

The man going into the stable hung his lantern high on a peg, and Bolt saw who it was — Crazy Barnaby, but without his staff and bells this time. As the youth went deeper into the big barn, Haveril stood at the side of the door, watching him curiously. The boy went straight to the stall where the red stallion, Daybreak, was tethered.

Instinctively Bolt Haveril came close to shouting a warning. It would be like Daybreak to rip the shoulder off an unwary man with those savage teeth of his, or to lash out wickedly with shod hoofs and do his killing with them.

But Barnaby was the last man on earth to require any such warning. He stopped before he came too close, and stood there quite motionless, looking at Daybreak. And Daybreak, pulling his head back over his high red shoulder, half turning in his stall, looked at Crazy Barnaby.

Bolt Haveril felt a queer prickle in his flesh as he watched; he remembered the affair with the wolf-dog Stag. After an extended silence in which neither the boy nor the horse moved a muscle, Barnaby began talking to Daybreak. He didn't use words but just made soft sounds which seemed to start low down in his brown throat, queerly soothing bass notes, which changed into almost whining yet musical utterances upon his lips. There followed those same sorts of liquid, weirdly blood-ruffling calls which had spoken to Stag.

Daybreak pricked forward his ears, lifting his head higher and higher. Barnaby laughed softly and drew a step nearer. Daybreak shook his superb body; it was like a shiver rippling through him from head to tail, from hoof to crest. Barnaby came another step closer, still talking to the horse with those strange wordless syllables.

Daybreak whinnied softly, and Bolt marvelled that the big stallion's whinny was next door to a whimper. Barnaby laughed again, confidently now, and stepped to the stall and began stroking Daybreak's glossy hide, Daybreak's deep indrawn breath was like a man's sigh. Bolt Haveril gasped, never more amazed. Plainly he could leave Barnaby and Daybreak alone here to cement their new friendship. He stepped back and into the deeper shadows.

Before he came within sight of the waterfall itself he heard its rush down the cliffs and the splash in the deep pool below. He wondered whether Lady were there already waiting. The glow on the east's jagged horizon was brighter now; suddenly a finger of moonlight thrust through the pines on the upland and pointed out to him the flashing spray of the white-maned cascade.

He advanced cautiously. He did not cross the bridge, judging it would be guarded, but kept well away from the little turbulent river until he was almost under the cliffs, with the flying spray, tossed lightly by the rising night wind, in his face. Here again, under one of the bigger pines, his body viewless against its trunk, he stopped.

Yes, Lady was waiting. She, too, had chosen this spot. She could have put out a hand to touch him. Instead she whispered softly, to make sure:

"You — who are you?"

At first it was difficult to make out even the vague outline of her form. Then he saw the white oval of her face and, when he moved a step and she turned toward the moon, he stooped close enough to catch the subdued glimmer of her eyes.

"I feel as though there were spies behind every tree," he said hastily. "Sid is on the prowl and —"

"I know! I followed him. I saw him watching at your cabin, then going away. I saw you come out the window, and I came hurrying here to wait. All the gates into the Valley are watched closely to-night; and there is a man hidden right down yonder at the bridge. I was afraid you —"

"Listen! We've got to talk fast. I know a lot about you and the trouble you're in, the danger that's coming closer to you every day —"

"Bob told you! You've seen my brother Bob!"

"Yes. Bob and I got to be friends right off. He told me everything. He — well, I guess you might almost say he sent me —"

"Where is Bob?" she asked anxiously.

"Where I first met up with him. Down in Texas, close to the border."

"He didn't come back with you, not even part way!" Suddenly she clutched his arm with fingers which gripped tight yet began to shake. "Something has happened to Bob! He has been hurt. He — he is dead!"

"Sh!" he commanded, and put his hand down firmly on hers. "Take it easy, girl, or you'll do us both in. Bob's all right, I tell you."

"But something *did* happen to him? He has been hurt, or sick?"

"He was hurt, yes," he conceded reluctantly. "But I tell you it's nothing bad; he's going to be all right. And I'm here to take you back to him, back down into Texas, the fastest way I know."

The moon, inching up to a wider gap in the trees, showed him her eyes again; they were round with excitement, with eagerness, with fear for her twin brother; they shone on him as sparkling, as softly liquid as the glint of the pool under the waterfall where the moon found it out too. He drew her back, into a deeper shadow.

"Did — did Bob send any written message by you?" she asked.

"No." He didn't want to tell her now how badly hurt Bob was. And besides: "It would have been foolish to carry anything like that. Already Duke has gone through my roll; what if he had searched my pockets and found a letter to you from Bob?"

He could feel that she wanted to believe every single word he said; that she was trying to shut out all natural suspicion. Still he could not wonder when in the end she asked faintly:

"Who *are* you? And how did it happen that you and Bob met and grew to be friends so quickly?"

"If we only had time for me to tell you all this! And a place where we could talk!"

70

She had withdrawn her fingers from his arm, from under the warm pressure of his; he could see her hands so tightly clasped, raised as high as her throat. With her head back, her eyes raised to him, her attitude was one of prayer, and he knew that in her heart she did pray to a merciful God to at long last have mercy on her.

"If I only knew!" she said faintly. "Are you Bolt Haveril as you say you are, and a friend? Or are you the Juan Morada that Duke thinks you are, the man to whom he sent gold to pay him for finding and returning Bob here to the Valley, or holding him for Duke?"

"I am Bolt Haveril. I knew the only way I could get into the Valley and find a chance to help you was to have Duke take me for Morada."

"But you told Duke you weren't Don Diablo!"

"Of course. Duke has never seen Morada. If a man came up here and pretended to be Morada, saying he was Morada, Duke would smell a rat; that's the sort of suspicious devil he is. On the other hand when a man comes along with all the Morada earmarks on him, and pretends he's somebody else, well Duke is dead sure it's Morada and only wonders what he's up to. And next thing, Duke is going to want to get down to bedrock. I'd rather not be here for another chat with him! I stalled him off as best I could and for as long as I could — until Rick Mooney broke in on us with word that a lot of Morgan Outsiders had been rounded up and were to swing. Then — and that was what I had counted on — Duke had other things to think about."

"You knew that those men were to be lynched in Pocket Gully?" she demanded incredulously. "And that word would be brought here to Duke? How could you know that? How could you know that one of the Outsiders was going to escape and —"

"I've said already we haven't all night to talk in!" he muttered, beginning to grow impatient; most of his scant supply of patience, for that matter, had been exhausted when he crawled out through his cabin window to come to her. And now he sniffed danger all about him, and with it the utter defeat of his plan, the utter hopelessness then of ever helping her. "You have got to take a few things on faith until later. But I'll tell you this: Dan Westcott, a sheriff in Rincon County has been a friend of mine since I was a two-year-old; he was a friend of my dad's long before that. He is giving us a hand working with Dave Heffinger of Juarez County. To help us out they staged the roundup of the Outsiders; they made it possible for Rick Mooney to work himself free, knowing that he'd come here on the run. There are a hundred things you and I will want to ask and tell each other when we get a chance. Right now, Lady Morgan, you've got to make up your mind and do it quick. I'll try to get you out of the Valley to-night. Now." He bent his face over hers looking so fixedly up at him and said gently: "Don't be afraid of me. Throw in with me. And — well, from what Bob told me, I guess it's now or never."

For a lost instant she put her face in her hands. Then she stiffened abruptly.

"One more question!" she insisted. "If you are not Don Diablo — well, you can explain the horse El

Colorado and the gold — but how do you explain that tiny scar that shows when you smile?"

"I planned this thing with Bob four weeks ago," he told her. "I made a study of our Don Diablo and copied him. This confounded moustache and his are as alike as your two little fingers. Do you suppose I'd have overlooked the scar? It's hand carved for the occasion; an old Indian friend of mine did it with the point of a knife, rubbing some peppery stuff into it, making it as sore as a saddle boil, then getting this scar in ten days."

She shuddered. She looked at him, or tried to through the dark, more closely than ever.

"If you are telling me the truth —"

He shrugged. "You've got to decide that yourself. And you've got to make up your mind in a hurry."

"But I can't understand! If what you say is true, *why* did you come? You would have known that you were risking your life; that the chances were all against your ever going free of this Morgan trap! And why should you take such a chance? Just for the sake of a new friend? For the sake of that friend's sister whom you had never even seen?"

Despite his urgency he took his time about answering. He might have said to her, "Well, you see I'm the sort of hothead that's always doing mad things like this." He might have said, "Bob and I met up in a sort of fashion that brought us together close and fast; I guess either one of us would do a thing like this for the other."

There was another thing that he might have said: "This young chap they call Crazy Barnaby, he's a queer genius, isn't he? Crazy, I suppose, but a genius in more ways than one! I saw him quiet Stag; you should have seen him whispering secrets with Daybreak just now! And an artist, too, isn't he? He can make his own paints of berry juices and charcoal and mud and Heaven knows what; and he can paint a portrait that they'd hang up for the world to look at in a city art museum. Well, he painted a small picture of Lady Morgan, as big as your hand. And she gave it to Bob Morgan, and Bob carried it out with him — and when he told me his story and yours he showed me the picture! Right then hothead Bolt Haveril wondered if he was falling in love! He came up here to find out!"

Yes, he could have told her either of those things, both true. Yet he wondered whether she would believe either. Then a third explanation popped into his head; though there might be less of truth in it he was sure it would carry more conviction. At last he answered her question, speaking slowly:

"I've already said that Bob told me about everything up here. All Dark Valley belonged to your grandfather, then to your father, Thad Morgan. When he died, he left it to you and Bob together. It belongs to the two of you now. It's worth a thundering lot of money; some day it'll be worth ten times as much. That's why Duke has been keeping the two of you so close. When you're of age, which is in a few weeks now, he means to force a deed from you. And Bob fears, and so do you, that once Duke has had you sign away your rights to him, you'll be no longer of any use but a danger to him should you ever talk. So — well —"

"Well? Go on and say it. Duke would shoot the two of us down and go eat his dinner. He is like that. But still you haven't explained —"

"In a word," he returned, sounding quite cool about it, "there is the chance, isn't there, that Bob and I touched on the business angle? That I'm to have a half share in Dark Valley if I can get you safe away?"

"Oh!" Now she thought that she understood, now she was ready to be convinced. And what she had wanted so desperately was this conviction. Yet her "Oh!" was gasped out almost in the tone of one who had been slapped. Her voice was suddenly cold and aloof as she added: "I understand now. Yes, I believe you. I can see that it was a business deal, and you a business man ready to risk anything for the sake of a deal like this!"

"Anyhow, dammit," thought Bolt Haveril, "she believes me and now we can try to get going. Later maybe she'll let me tell her the truth."

"I'll go with you," said Lady in a small quiet voice. "If I am making any sort of mistake, if I come to find I can't trust you and that you are not what you say you are — even though you should turn out to be Don Diablo! — I could not be much worse off than I am here."

"You're still wearing the gun you buckled on for Stag? Any time I lift a little finger to you, why just blaze away!"

She ignored that. "How do you think," she asked, "that we can get out of the Valley? Duke took only about twenty men with him —"

He said, quite frank about it: "I don't know how we're going to do it, but we've got to, one way or another. We don't dare try to find a way up the south cliffs, the way Bob got out; he said you couldn't possibly make it and neither could I unless he were along to point out every foot of the climb. There are the three gates. They're all guarded, of course?"

"They always are, more or less. Hidden back in the laurels where you came in this morning is a little hut; I know that two men are watching there to-night. It will be the same at the other gates."

"Two men?" he muttered. "Well, for one thing, maybe they won't be expecting us. Anyhow we'd have a better chance of tackling two men to-night than forty to-morrow!"

He stopped there, stiff and rigid and still, and she wondered at him. He didn't seem to be looking at her; she couldn't be sure. His silence, however, was of the shortest; perhaps not over five seconds.

She heard him chuckle, and that amazed her. And when he spoke again she was still further puzzled by a queer if intangible change in his tone. He seemed like another man. He said:

"And so now, Miss Lady Morgan, you are ready for any desperate chance, are you?"

"I — I don't understand you!" she exclaimed.

No, she couldn't understand. But that was because she did not know the man who, already dangerously masquerading in the Valley, was trigger set and ready for any fresh bit of simulation. And most of all she had not seen what he saw, could not therefore have the vaguest inkling of the thoughts which during his silent few seconds had sped lightning fashion through his brain.

The moonlight that had brightened her eyes and had put a mirrory glimmer into the pool had this time chanced to glint on something not ten steps from them that shone like bright silver. Bolt Haveril caught the glint of it and knew it for what it was. There was someone standing there, listening to them, and the thing that gleamed in the moonlight was not silver but steel, the barrel of a pistol which was no doubt already cocked.

Bolt Haveril could give her no inkling of what he saw, but neither did he mean to give the watcher any inkling that he had been discovered. The thing to do was to throw the watcher off his guard for a moment — to throw sand in his eyes somehow. So Haveril from chuckling softly began laughing, for his spinning thoughts had clicked into position and he saw his one chance. It would be Sid there, wouldn't it? Sid, as evil a devil as any man he'd ever known. Sid who would see evil in another man as readily as he would see his own face in a looking glass. Sid who had overheard fragments — only fragments — of what had been said.

Laughing, Bolt Haveril began to make mock of the girl.

"So you're the silly little simpleton that Duke Morgan thinks you!" he jeered at her. "You'd believe all the wild tales any stranger came to tell you! Why, if I weren't Juan Morada — Don Diablo to you, my dear little maid! — do you think I'd be here at all? And you thought I'd lift you out of your cage! Well, maybe I will — after you've signed the papers Duke wants; maybe I will! Permit me, Señorita, to make you an enormous bow of admiration; the bow of Don Diablo of the border!"

While she stood rooted to the ground he did sweep off his hat and step back from her — drawing away so that he considerably shortened that already brief distance between him and the man spying on them.

"When I tell Duke about this," he laughed at her, "how he is going to laugh! And he is going to say, 'Juan Morada, you are a fine fellow; and there will be more gold pieces for you!'"

"Oh!" gasped the girl. "You — you —"

She whirled and fled, racing away among the trees. As she did so Bolt Haveril, still chuckling, made a seemingly careless half turn. Now he saw his man, almost within reach, and knew it was Sid; a mystified, uncertain, hesitant Sid who did not know which to believe of the broken tales his ears had told him.

He must have seen his Don Diablo shrug after the Mexican fashion, one which as much as says, "See, amigo! I lift my shoulder like this so that I spill down to the ground all cares and responsibilities." He must have thought Don Diablo about to stroll away, back toward his cabin. For Sid was taken utterly off guard when something struck him like a cannonball. In one incredibly swift movement Bolt Haveril hurled himself on Sid Morgan, toppling him backward, knocking him clear off his feet, sending him crashing down into the thicket with his assailant on top of him, a hard muscular hand gripping his gun wrist.

Sid opened his mouth for a yell that should bring help to him. But he had to do with a man who meant to give him no time for that. Already Bolt Haveril's gun was out. He swung it up and brought the barrel crashing down on young Morgan's head. Only the one blow was needed. Haveril didn't know whether or not he had killed the man. He didn't tarry to see. Sid Morgan lay as limp as a wet rag, and Bolt Haveril was off at a quiet run to overtake the fleeing Lady Morgan.

And as he ran he realized fully that if he ever did come up with that fleet-footed girl he was going to have the devil's own time explaining! She hadn't seen Sid; she hadn't turned to look back and so knew nothing of what had just occurred.

"Maybe I overplayed my hand, poking fun at her," he thought heavily. "She was mad clean through; Morgan-mad! It was hard enough making her believe me in the first place. Now what?"

CHAPTER
EIGHT

He could catch no glimpse of the girl who had vanished as completely in the dark under the pines as a drop of water in dry sand; nor could he hear any slightest sound of her flight. But he had noted this morning after Crazy Barnaby had rescued her from Stag how she sped straight to a certain moss covered cabin standing a little withdrawn from the others, and had judged it her own place. Doubtless now she would run as straight to it as to a mother's arms. So it was in that direction that he made what haste he could.

He judged aright. Coming to the edge of the clearing in front of Duke's house, between it and the river, he caught a glimpse of her at last, her hair streaming out as she ran, the moon making it look like a black, wind-tossed mane. Again instantly she vanished in the shadows under the trees upon the farther side of the open space.

He wanted to shout to her but did not dare; his voice would be sure to bring others than herself to attention, rushing out to see what was afoot. So he charged straight on across the clearing, reckless now of being seen. For he had not the slightest doubt that, once she was within the sturdy log walls toward which she raced, she'd slam and bar her heavy door, and he might plead all night without convincing her of anything save of that of which she was already so certain; that he was Don Diablo and the most despicable of men.

When he saw her again she was already at her door and he a score of paces away. Haveril, still racing toward her, did call out softly to her then, pleading with her for one instant more. He did not expect an answer; he knew she was all throbbing eagerness to get behind the safe barricade of her log walls and be done with him. But her door was as clumsy an affair as it was heavy; it did not open as readily as she could have wished then, but dragged on the floor. And in the little time that was required for her to get it open and slip in and start to close it again he had hurled himself against it, his weight matched against hers.

"I'm going to shoot!" she cried. "You yourself told me to shoot when I found out what you were! If you try to push the door open — if you dare try to come in —"

"No!" he cut in. "No. For God's sake, Lady, go slow now or we're both done for. I want to tell you —"

"You and your lies! And then to have you laugh at me like that for the little fool I was!"

"Will you be still? Will you listen? While we were talking —"

"I won't listen! Get away from my door and let me shut it or I'll shoot, and —"

"Sid Morgan was out there! Listening to us, hearing every word we said. I had to —"

"Liar!" she called him.

"All my lying was forced on me, all for Sid's sake. I could not let him know that all I had told you before was the truth. He stood within ten feet of us; he had a gun in his hand —"

"And now?" she asked cynically.

"I jumped him and hammered him down with my gun before he could gather his scattered wits and squeeze a trigger. He's lying out there dead to the world. Snakes are hard to kill though, and there's every chance that he won't be long in coming to and raising a rumpus that will stir up the whole valley."

"Have you told me a single thing that I can believe — except that you are Don Diablo!"

"I've told you — Sh!" He broke off short with his curt hushed command for silence. Then he said so softly that she could scarcely hear him through the thick wood of her door: "There's someone coming!"

"Sid?"

"Not so soon. Someone else coming up from the river."

"I told you there was a man guarding the bridge. I suppose he heard or saw us running —"

"Open your door!" All the while he had held it ajar, now at last he started shoving it back. "Let me in. Quick, I tell you!"

"No, I won't! You shan't come in! If you try — I'll shoot if you do!"

"Shoot and be damned!" grunted Bolt Haveril then, the last shred of his hard-held patience blown sky-high in the gust of his anger. He threw his weight against her door, flinging it open, driving her back. It was dark inside, yet a faint glow came through a window from the moon and he could see her and the gun in her hand, lifted almost shoulder high as she stood with her back to the wall levelling it at his chest.

Both of them now heard hurrying steps. Bolt Haveril closed the door and stood close to it.

"It's your chance, maybe your last chance, Lady Morgan," he told her, very grim and stern and short spoken, "to think straight and fast to some purpose. I came here to get you out of the valley. You can believe I'm the devil himself if that suits you, but I'd think you'd grab any help to go free. After this, Duke will never let you out of his sight until he gets what he wants out of you, and you know it. And when he's got it — then what?" He gave her a moment to answer that for herself; then he also answered it in short simple words which conveyed the brutal truth brutally: "He'll knock you on the head, and that's something else you know. Bob knows it too."

She rested her shoulders against the wall as for necessary support. He could see the heavy weapon in her hand waver; he thought grimly, "If it's cocked and her finger's on the trigger, I'm apt to get a hole shot through me any second."

Outside the steps came hurrying on. They stopped close outside before the closed door. A man's voice called:

"Lady! Are you in there?"

She didn't answer She didn't know what to say. She was desperate.

The voice called again, more sharply: "Lady! I know you're there. I saw you running. There was a man too. Who was it? Is he with you?"

Bolt whispered: "Don't be a fool! Your last chance to get away; ever to see Bob again —"

Lady moistened her dry lips, steadied herself, commanded her utterance and spoke back to the man outside.

"Yes, I'm in here. What do you want? Who are you?"

"I'm Blount; Morg Blount. I was down at the bridge. There was a man with you, wasn't there? Or chasing after you? Who was it?"

"Sid has been prowling about —"

"He's in there with you!"

"No! No, Sid isn't here. He's — he's somewhere else."

A heavy hand was laid on the latch of her door.

"I'm coming in," said Morgan Blount.

"You're not! If you dare —"

Bolt Haveril shook his head at her, then nodded emphatically. A board creaked as he took a step nearer her, ignoring her pistol, to whisper almost in her ear: "Let him come in! It's the only way now! *Let him in!*"

In her moment of confusion, of bewilderment, of a chaotic mental state in which thoughts seemed paralyzed, his curt command directed those thoughts for her, his will if for but the instant became her will.

"Come in, then," she said faintly to Morgan Blount.

He thrust the door open and stepped in. Bolt Haveril stood just behind the open door. Blount saw Lady in the pale glow from the window.

"What the devil?" he grunted. "Why haven't you got a light?"

He never got any answer to that. His back was to the man behind the door. Deliberately, striving calculatingly to measure the force of his blow, Bolt Haveril struck him down with his gun just as he had felled Sid. The fellow's bones seemed to turn to water and he melted down in his tracks without a groan.

A muffled exclamation of horror sprang from the girl's lips.

"You — you murderer! And coward — to hit a man like that!"

"Call me all the names you like," Haveril snapped back at her, "but keep your head screwed on right. First, I haven't killed him. Second, it was the only possible way I could handle him . . . And now — are you coming with me? The road's partly open."

"Coming with you!" She shuddered.

He yanked the door open.

"I've risked my life coming here to help you. If I'm here when Sid wakes up, or this fellow — if I'm here when Duke comes back in a very few hours, my life won't be worth a plugged nickel. So I'm going — if I can. And I'm going right now."

He wasn't going to do anything of the sort, not if it meant leaving her behind. But he was playing out his hand the best he could, as a man sometimes plays poker. Many a pot has been raked in on a pair of deuces or a six high. He started out.

"Wait! Tell me; tell me the truth: are you Don Diablo or not?"

He answered shortly, like a man tired of arguing with a silly girl: "What if I am or am not? Wouldn't you rather take your chance with Juan Morada? If he got you away, later you could buy him off, couldn't you? You and Bob with your rights to Dark Valley?"

"Did you lie to me about Sid, too?"

"Time is short. But if you'll hurry I'll show him to you, lying where I left him. You can keep a dozen steps behind me; at any time you like you can start blazing away with your cannon, mowing me down and waking up all the echoes and Morgans in the valley. It's an invitation. I'm on my way. Come if you like. Stay if you like. I'll tell Bob that I did my damnedest."

"Go ahead! I'll follow you as far as the waterfall."

They found Sid Morgan lying as Bolt Haveril had left him. Timidly, both drawn and repelled, Lady came close to look down at him, a white-faced, dark, formless inert thing lying there. She asked whisperingly, "Is he dead?" Bolt stooped and put his hand on Sid's heart. "He's alive; his heart is beating all right. Do you want to make sure? Put your hand down here and feel it."

She whipped back, standing straight again. She was thinking: "He is right; I've got to decide. And it *is* my last chance and my last hope! Is he Don Diablo? — Of course he is! He said, 'Don't be a fool,' and I'd be a fool to doubt it. There's the general description of him; there were the two sheriffs trying to arrest him, with him fighting them off. There's the horse, El Colorado, and there's the gold that Duke marked and sent to him. There are his words of a few minutes ago when he laughed at me, and looked and talked and bowed like a Mexican and said, 'I'm Don Diablo to you, my dear little maid!' And there is the scar."

"Well," he was demanding, staring down his nose at her, looking, she thought, exactly as a border bandit should look.

Before she spoke in reply she strove to think straight on to the end: If he were Don Diablo, then what? Why had he come? Not conceivably because of any interest in her as an individual but, as he had so frankly said even when maintaining that he was Bolt Haveril, because he wanted what Duke wanted — Dark Valley. If he were Don Diablo and carried her away, would her danger, an uncertain one with him, be greater than the definite peril here with Duke, who would never let her again out of his sight? With a choice between two dangers — two evils, if you like — while the choice was in some degree still hers — which?

"What makes you think it possible that we can get away?" she asked.

"Nothing's impossible until after you've tried it."

"How would you try?"

"We'd go straight to the North Gate —"

"Have you forgotten the two men there?"

"Have you forgotten that I told you I'd rather have it out with two men than with forty?"

"Your horses — the men at the gate would hear us coming —"

"Of course. I'd hoped somehow we could get away on horseback. No such luck to-night. On foot, if at all. *And now.*"

"On foot! If we did get out they'd be sure to overtake us and drag us back!"

"Shall we think up reasons for sticking here and letting our one chance slide by? Or shall we see what we can do about it?"

He too was thinking fast and to the point. She had impressed him at the very outset, when he had first glimpsed her there at the gate in the early morning, as one who was at once frightened and yet as nearly fearless as a girl could be. He knew that hers was a fine, high courage; so he ended jeeringly:

"If you're scared — if you're just a little coward after all — well, let me go and you stick here for Duke to knock on the head when he gets ready."

She flared out at him:

"Of course I'm scared! I'll bet you are, too But — but I'm not afraid! I'll go with you."

Her words didn't make sense, yet they did! She heard his deep breath of relief.

"Now," he said. "Before the moon gets any higher."

So they started without any definite plan at all, only knowing that they were forced to hurry — without in the least knowing where they would go if they did win out to freedom — without in the least knowing how they were ever to pass the double guard Duke Morgan had set. These were all matters for the future, to be considered when the time came. That that time was but a few minutes off made no difference. They could only push on and trust to the brighter stars of their destinies.

They went cautiously, keeping in the shadows. He led the way; she followed.

CHAPTER
NINE

They heard voices, the drowsy voices of men whose long, eventless vigil had evoked that sort of monotony which grows to be like a drug. The fugitives crept closer and closer under the laurels of the roadside. It was still quite dark here; the newly risen moon failed to finger through the thick foliage so blackly over-arching the place. Haveril extended a warning hand backward, brushing the girl who followed so closely now.

"Hoped to get them one at a time," he whispered. "Well, luck has been with us so far."

"God has been with us," she whispered in her secret heart, and the whispering grew to be a silent prayer: "Oh, be good to us now!"

"Keep back," he commanded in that same stealthily hushed tone. "If things should go wrong —"

"They mustn't! They can't! They won't!"

"But if they do, you can slip back and be no worse off than you were before. But don't get panicky; watch for a lucky chance. No matter what happens to me, maybe you can somehow make a break for it and get away alone."

"I wouldn't know where to go, what to do —"

"The Good Lord would take care of you," said Bolt Haveril. He even patted her arm. Then he began inching still closer to the two men at the padlocked gate.

He listened a moment to their desultory talk, a stop-and-go sort of jabber about nothing that amounted to anything to either of them or the man overhearing them. Then he shrugged mentally, said to himself, "Here goes!" and spoke out sharply:

"I've got you two boys covered! Stick your hands up like you were grabbing at the moon! *Look out!* If you get funny you're cold turkey before you can unleather a gun."

He could see them distinctly now and that was because he had crept within ten feet of them, one man leaning against a fence post, the other sprawling with his hunched-up shoulders against the gate. And he knew that they could not see him in the least clearly where he crouched under the laurels.

Up went four empty hands every bit as fast as their owners could lift them, for there was that in the hidden man's voice which commanded respect. Further, though they couldn't in the least understand how he had managed to come on them without Sid Morgan and Morg Blount giving the alarm, it remained that they felt dead sure that they had to do with a certain gentleman of the border who had made himself a reputation as a Don Devil that any man might respect.

Bolt Haveril stepped promptly out into the road and as promptly the girl followed him. He could hear her sudden release of breath and knew that she had been holding it in her stilled lungs. He grunted.

"Sure, this part of it was easy enough," he said, and might have been speaking to her or to himself. "But what's next? Well, a step at a time. Miss Morgan, will you pull these gents' guns out of their leathers? Just circle about; don't come between them and me. If either of them so much as wiggles his ears I'll kill the two of them."

She was all haste to obey, to do her part. Each man had a belt gun and a carbine; she gathered up the four and came back to Bolt.

"What are we going to do with them?" she asked breathlessly.

"With all this artillery?"

"With these two men! They'll spread the news —"

"Are they Morgans?" he demanded, all the while keeping his eyes on those four lifted hands. One man still stood, the other squatted at his feet.

"Yes. One is Curly Morgan. The other is his cousin, Duke Baylis."

"Snakes, both of them. Maybe we better kill them before they poison any more folks."

She shuddered. For the life of her she could not tell from that even, cold tone of his whether he meant that or not. He seemed merely dispassionately dallying with an idea.

"You — you can't do that!"

"We've got to do something with them." Until now neither of the two Morgan men had so much as opened his mouth to say a word; suddenly both started speaking up at once.

"Shut up!" snapped Haveril, and again there was that quality in his voice which commanded obedience.

There was just enough moonlight for him to see the whites of their eyes rolling anxiously. They looked at him, at Lady, at each other, all about them as though for some miracle to save them from destruction at the hands of a man known for hundreds of miles as a cold-blooded killer.

"I'm kind of uncertain in my own mind," said Haveril. "So I'm going to leave it to Curly and young Duke here. Tell me, boys; would you rather be dead or alive, right now?"

They spoke up quickly enough now, being permitted, but again he cut their words short.

"It's funny," he told them casually, "but I've a sort of reason for not wanting to finish you boys off unless you hanker for it. In that case, of course, I'd shove my own wishes aside and let you have it your own way. Will you boys do what I say and just like I say? And you might remember that the works of this old gun of mine are filed so darned hair-trigger that if one of you spoke out of turn and gave me a start the thing might go off by itself."

They were all eagerness to please him right down to the ground.

"Fine," said Bolt Haveril.

He ordered the recumbent men to their feet. He made them unlock the gate and go through, followed by himself and Lady, who was still burdened with their weapons. Then the gate was locked and the key handed to their captor.

"Go ahead now, boys, close side by side, and don't ask any questions. I'm reckoned a fair shot; the first man to open his mouth or to make any sort of slip, even a stumble, is apt to get an ear shot off. I think I can do that little thing and not hurt you much, but the light's tricky and if I should pop you through the head it'll all be unintentional on my part and you'll have to overlook it. Head straight for that dead tree, the one white as a bone on the hill yonder. Step!"

They stepped, Haveril keeping about three paces behind them. Lady, following him closely, asked:

"What'll I do with all these guns? Throw them away?"

"It would kind of be nice," Haveril told her, "if you'd drop back behind us thirty or forty feet; and then if one by one you'd sort of scatter all that hardware, lamming it piece by piece in the brush so that if these boys ever do come back this way they'll have some fun finding 'em. Think so?"

She did not answer but did as he said. By the time the three men had come to the dead pine, something like half a mile from the gate, she had caught up with them and was no longer burdened with the excess weapons.

"We're going fine," Bolt called to her. "Feels good to be outside again, huh?"

Once again he heard that deep intake of breath of hers. He could only guess, could never altogether know how already her heart was singing within her.

"Over the hill now, boys, and down the other side," he commanded his prisoners. "Another half mile, say, won't be far, will it?" He chuckled as he added, "What are you betting it wouldn't seem a long walk back though?"

They couldn't understand what he meant, nor could the girl; but they and she alike experienced a chill creeping of the flesh, since not one of them dared guess what he had in mind, not one but feared it was to be cold-blooded murder in some lonely, hidden canyon.

He did find the canyon, and he did drive them along down its steep flank and into its dimly lit bottom. Then he commanded them to sit down, unlace their boots and take them off. That done fumblingly by two thoroughly mystified men, he made them remove the heavy buckskin thongs from their boots, and they began to understand. He made them lie flat on their bellies with their hands behind them, wrists crossed. And then he did a thorough, workmanlike job of tying their hands where they had placed them, and lashing them to their belts.

Lady breathed easier. So, for that matter, did Curly Morgan and Duke Baylis. Once more he saw the whites of their eyes; that was when he made them wriggle over and sit up. He saw too, the workings of their faces in mute rage.

"One more favour, boys, and I won't be troubling you any more," he told them genially. "I'm not going to leave you so you'll starve to death or so the coyotes will come and eat you; no, I'm sort of kind-hearted and I wouldn't want to play a trick like that on you. What I'm doing now is hobble you; you'll be able to walk like a hobbled horse does; I'll fix it so maybe you can take steps five-six inches long. If you start walking as soon as we do, shucks, you ought to make it back to the locked gate in a couple of days, anyhow; maybe just one day if you're real spry. Only be sort of careful about stubbing a toe; I'm taking your boots along."

Curly started roaring out curses; Bolt Haveril whipped his gun over, sighting at Curly's ear, and Curly's mouth closed like a trap.

The hobbling task was soon accomplished, another workmanlike job. Then Haveril took up the four boots, nodded to an excited, elated, frightened, wondering girl, and led the way up the steep bank, out of the canyon. It was a hard climb. She could not help thinking of the two men, hands lashed behind them, legs hobbled and feet bare, labouring their way upward. It was cruel, *cruel*. But —

"It was the only thing I could think of off-hand," said Bolt. She nodded.

"Which way now?" was all that she said when they came again to the ridge above.

"It's pretty much guesswork with me," he admitted. "I'm a long way from my stamping ground and this is all new to me. What do you know of the lay of the land around here?"

She knew virtually nothing of it. Long and long ago when she was a very little girl and her father was alive, she had had her own pony and had ridden on many a brief expedition. But that all seemed part of another life. Of late years she had been a prisoner in the Valley, never once going outside.

"Hadn't you planned any place to head for, when you came up here first?" she asked him.

Yes, he had planned, but those earlier plans like so many others must go into the scrap heap. He was to meet Dan Westcott and Dave Heffinger; they were waiting for him now in Red Luck: but Red Luck was a good twenty miles away. He explained.

"You see, I thought we'd make it out of here on horseback. It didn't work out that way. Now, if we strike for Red Luck how far would we be before the Morgans would cut us off? It won't be many hours until things start popping down there in the Valley; Sid and Morg Blount are apt to come to any time. Likewise, Duke and his men ought to be back at daybreak and maybe sooner; you never can tell. No, Red Luck's out; they'll be sure to think of that."

"On horseback, with us on foot, they'll be sure to run us down wherever we go!"

"Don't think so," said Bolt and hurled a boot as far as he could into a thicket of buck brush. "Anyhow, let's not say it. Let's head into the rough country over yonder." He pointed to a savage looking bit of wilderness, black and ragged under the climbing moon; there were bald peaked mountains soaring among the white stars, their bases timber-clad; there were deep-cleft ravines and gorges; altogether it was as wild a country as the southwest knows. "Once we get in there, how're they going to smoke us out? And, holing up by day, travelling by night, we can get clean away long before they can poke into one out of a thousand of the hiding places we'll find. — Here goes another boot!"

From his tone she hazarded that a good-humoured grin was softening the muscles of that dark face of his which at times could be so implacably hard and stern. Could nothing on earth disturb this man?

"Hope the boys won't be sore at the way we've scattered their things hither, thither and yon," he said. Yes, he was chuckling. Away sailed another boot. "I'll be through sowing these to the wind pretty *pronto*," he went on. "Then we'll angle off a bit to the left and strike for — See that big star flaming out like a light welcoming us home? Let's steer for that. It isn't Venus, by any chance, is it?"

"I don't know," said Lady very briefly. And added, "Might be Mars!"

Whether Venus or Mars or some other heavenly body, they directed their course by it.

CHAPTER
TEN

"Now this is the life!" said Bolt Haveril cheerily. She noted, marvelling, that his face in the firelight looked young and eager and undaunted; in fact one would have said that he hadn't a care in this good old wide world of ours.

The girl sighed; right then that was the very best she could do. Had she striven to answer him she must have moaned from very weariness. When, almost at the outset he had said, "This is going to be tough going on both of us," he had prophesied well. He, like all south-western ranchers, was little used to walking; horses were made for men like him, men like him for horses. His high heels on these rocky uplands hampered him; he had sat down and managed with a knife and a stone to lessen their stature by a good half. Of the two, the girl got along better; she wore walking boots and was used to walking. On the other hand her strength was not his; they both grew unutterably weary before he called a halt in this spot, many long wilderness miles from Dark Valley.

He had chosen this spot cannily. He told her, "If by any chance they should hit out in this general direction looking for us, they will figure roughly about how far they think we'll walk before we have to make a stop. Then they'll figure on our picking a spot close to water. So we fool 'em on both counts. We've come farther than they'll think. And we'll have a good long drink at the next creek, then keep on going for another quarter mile, anyhow. You can stand it, can't you?"

"Yes!" She could scarcely speak even then for weariness, but she said, "Yes! I can stand anything but being taken back."

So they drank and rested and drank again and then clambered and crawled up here. The rocky mountainside was scarred and gashed with gorges; boulders that long ago had come crashing down from the crest were like grim grey mis-shapen giants standing wherever they had found foothold, in some crease or fold in the weather-worn slope, on some shelf-like level spot, at times one piled on another. Where his tiny fire now blazed was a brush-rimmed hollow the size of one of the smaller Morgan cabins, sheltered by a low cliff on one side, by several of those boulders on the other; and since they had not climbed above timber line, there were sturdy mountain cedars all about them.

"Do we dare have a fire?" she asked from where she lay spent and anxious, her whole body throbbing, her brain spinning with the rush and swirl of visions, making it like a den of fevered nightmares; she saw Sid lying unconscious, a dark smear on his forehead, and she saw Bolt Haveril as he stood when he jeered at her and named himself Don Diablo, and she heard the oncoming footsteps of Morg Blount, and saw Bolt with the two men at the gate, forcing them to his will; again she threw their weapons into patches of brush; Bolt hurled boots afar; they trudged on and on and on; and now she was lying here, half dead, and Bolt was making a fire, and she murmured dully, "Do we dare?"

"You bet we do," he said genially. And when the first blaze aided the moon in showing him where she rested at the base of a rock, he added: "You and I dare anything!" And then, gathering a few small dead sticks, he said, "If we can't have any nice hot supper, and are already remembering how fresh and cool that water was, and haven't any snug beds to crawl into, anyhow we're going to have our one luxury. What's more, this is going to be an Indian fire, about as big as your hat — which reminds me you haven't any hat."

He sat with his back against a young cedar, only half a dozen feet from her across the fire, and made and lighted a cigarette.

"Talk about luxuries! Man, but this tastes good," he told her. And then, as though ashamed of himself for partaking alone of the soothing weed, he muttered, "It's sort of too bad girls don't smoke, huh?"

"I've sometimes thought that, too," she admitted. And of course added the words so common of old, no longer thought of: "Men seem to get such comfort out of their tobacco."

He flipped the thing into the fire, having drawn only one mouthful of smoke from it. That was something she was never going to forget: he wasn't going to indulge in any relief not permitted her.

"Please go on and smoke," she said.

"Don't feel like it after all," said Bolt Haveril.

100

She began to laugh and he jerked his head up, startled; it was nervous laughter and he knew that her nerves were jumping, and it was right next door to wild weeping. The thought had struck her: "Listen to the sort of things we're saying! And he knows he may be dead before morning, for Duke will surely kill him if he comes up with us; and I know they may be dragging me back by the hair of the head — and I might as well be dead to-day."

He jumped up, no longer seeming tired.

"Look here," he said, "I'm going to fix up a sort of bunk for you and you'll be asleep in two shakes."

The big blade of his knife served him well in hacking off several armfuls of cedar tips. He brought them to her, put them down nearby where there was a little level spot covered with coarse dry grass, arranged them for her to lie on. She thanked him and crept onto the couch he thus constructed for her. How good it felt to her weary body! She closed her eyes; they flew wide open on the instant. She fixed them on the moon which had gone so far on its journey since this night's adventure had started. She felt that if she closed them she'd begin seeing all over again everything that had happened since she saw Sid Morgan creeping through the dark to spy on this man's cabin.

He could see her eyes, looking big and round, gleaming in his firelight. He knew how it was; sometimes you were just so damn tired, sleepy, too, that you couldn't go to sleep. He saw that her lips were slightly parted; she kept touching them with the tip of her tongue. She must be like one in a fever.

"See if you can keep awake until I come back," he said lightly. "Oh, I'm not going far. I want a bit of a look around before I call it a day."

Really he wasn't gone very long, but it seemed long to her before she heard the scrape and dragging thud of his boots returning. She started to her elbows. Maybe it wasn't he at all, but someone else!

Then she saw him coming up the steep slope.

"Went for a drink," he said. "Got to thinking about how cool and good that water was."

As he came close she saw that he was bare-headed. His hat was in his hands. He had dented the crown down, the high crown of a big southwestern hat. He had soaked his hat in the creek; then he had filled the cupped crown with water. He must have hurried back; little drops falling gleamed as bright and gay as diamonds; he had brought her two or three cupfuls.

She started to speak. He grinned down at her and said:

"No time for idle chatter! Want this all to leak out? Drink hearty, Lady Morgan."

She drank every last drop — she lay on her side among the fragrant cedar tips, her face hid in the crook of her arm — and the tears came — and she went to sleep.

When she awoke breakfast was almost ready! And was there ever a breakfast like it? Bolt Haveril was grinning down at her as she brushed the loose tresses of hair from her face and shook the sleep out of her eyes. It was, though she could not suspect such a thing, a grin specially made for her, one which he had created only as her eyes opened. Before that he had stood looking down at her with a sort of thoughtful tenderness — she looked so young asleep, a baby he called her, and so helpless.

"We're still alive and running free," were his first words to her instead of a mere good-morning. "Feels good to be alive and out in the open, huh?" She sat up and rubbed her eyes and he turned back to his newly kindled fire. "You can climb down into the canyon for your own drink this morning," he went on. "You'll want to wash your face, too." He chuckled at her as he turned to look back over his shoulder. "If anybody asks you, you tell 'em that Mr. Haveril says you've got a powerful dirty face."

She scrambled up at that and hurried down the long steep slope to the creek. When in a few minutes she returned her cheeks were clean and pink and fresh, her hair tidied with her fingers, her eyes just as when he had seen them for the first time down there at the gate to Dark Valley; they were softly bright, they were eager and they were unafraid. She said, determined to match his lightness of touch upon their situation:

"I hope breakfast isn't all done to a crisp waiting for me — and I hope you haven't eaten it all up already! And, most of all I want to ask you a question?"

"As a rule, no questions before breakfast. This time, shoot."

"I've asked whether you were Bolt Haveril, a well-mannered young rancher — from Texas. And I've asked if you were the wicked Don Diablo. And now I just want to know: Are you a magician!"

It was the breakfast that suggested this, the delectable aromas floating out in the air from it titillating responsive nostrils, making hunger a delight.

Handfuls of green grass and green leaves plucked down by the creek were the platters. The bed of glowing coals had been the stove. And the morsels, brown and tempting, were a big trout and — and something else. One couldn't quite be sure; one feeling half starved didn't know whether it were wise to ask or not!

"The creek's crawling with trout," he explained. "I chased this fellow into a shallow pool, headed him off and went after him the way a cat goes after a mouse. And this" — he pointed to that something that she wasn't sure about — "a young tree squirrel as fat as butter. I took a chance shooting him, but this far out and this early in the day, I don't think it was much of a chance. For seasoning, for salt and pepper, and all that, both are nicely sprinkled with wood ashes and some sort of weed that smelled good and that I wrapped 'em up in. Now if you'll pull up your chair —"

They picked the bones.

They went together down to the creek and washed and drank and rested.

All the while the new day was coming in through the dusky mountain passes, brightening all about them. A little day breeze rustled the leaves of the willows and alders and slim young aspens, and made cool laughing wrinkles and dimples in the pools.

"There are a hundred questions I want to ask you," said Bolt.

Of course. And there were as many that she wanted answered by him. But explanations had to wait.

She did say, "You did not bring your rifle away with you."

No; there had been no time. He had left that and other things he regretted — Daybreak and another horse for instance.

And she did ask: "And the money? The gold?"

No; he hadn't brought the gold. And now:

"We'd better start on again, right away. We'll climb up again to where we camped last night; I'll hide all signs in the brush; we'll keep straight on and up, over the mountain. By the time we get tired again we've got to find two things — water and a hide-out. All the rest of the day we can lie low and rest. At dark we can start on again."

She thought, "When we get tired again!" She was tired already from last night, stiff muscles aching. But after they had travelled a while the stiffness and most of the ache departed. They climbed laboriously to the mountain top; by that time the sun was well up. From this high spot they could look out far into the south; range after range lifted ragged, empurpled fronts into the sky; wide, thick-timbered expanses lay in between; as far as the eye could run there was no sign that any human being had ever gone that way before them; just the glorious expanse of unspoiled wilderness as God had made it when he found His work good.

"That's fine wild country," he said approvingly. "If we can hide away safely during the day, then if we can get along as fast as we did last night, there's not a chance in a thousand that our Dark Valley friends will ever come up with us. Now to set our point to steer for."

He stood surveying intently all that sweep of country extending below and before him. She stole a swift glance at him, then fell to studying him with an interest as keen and intent as that he bestowed upon timbered slopes and valleys and granite ridges. There was no good-humoured grin on his face, crinkling the eyes and making them both merry and friendly; nor was there the mockery there she had seen more than once, nor yet the flash of fire. But there was a brooding stillness, a dormant forcefulness which impressed her strongly. As she saw how piercingly he looked far out, as she marked the erectness of his carriage with a hint of something that was almost arrogance in his bearing that was certainly a steely sort of confidence, she thought of a young eagle high upon its rocky eyrie, calm yet stern, poised yet patient, soon to hurl itself outward in its triumphant flight.

Even yet she did not know who or what he was. She had never heard of any Bolt Haveril until now; she had heard much talk of Juan Morada whom men along the border called the Devil Don. They said that he was unthinkably cruel — wicked and vengeful and blood-lusty; they said of him, too, that he could kill a man and be quite gay, somehow gracefully gay about it. No doubt he could be very attentive, very courteous to a woman, very thoughtful in little flattering attentions; no doubt, too, he could laughingly put his sinewy brown hands on her slim white throat and choke her to death.

He turned swiftly, as though he felt her eyes upon him. They stood looking at each other fixedly. Slowly the colour deepened in her cheeks — and suddenly the familiar smile brightened his face.

"You'll have to figure it out for yourself, I guess, lady," he said. "But I'll make a suggestion. If it does work out that you're sure — well, surer than you are now, anyhow — that I'm Juan Morada, just you remember you're still carrying that belt gun you dug up for Stag! You'll get lots of chances when I'm not looking, like just now; shoot me in the back, between the shoulder blades, and run for it. You'd make out somehow and —"

"Don't!" she exclaimed, and turned her face away from him.

"Down yonder," he continued composedly, pointing, "is where we go. It's downhill now, and that'll rest us up. We'll head into that deep canyon, keep going down toward that open meadow, but off to the left a bit where the big timber is, and head on straight south to where you can see a V-gap in those far, blue mountains. That's where we hope to be to-morrow night. This morning we ought to have only six or eight miles to go before we hole-up for the day. See that little blue patch down yonder? A lake the size of a duck pond, that's what it is. Then, just beyond, that rocky, low-lying ridge?"

She just nodded and said nothing. She didn't see anything at all clearly; for some strange, silly reason everything was suddenly blurred.

"On that ridge," he went on, "there ought to be a hundred better hide-outs than we had last night. Suppose we start?"

It did rest her going downhill; and after an hour of that it was a further relief to be again on fairly level ground, skirting the meadows he had pointed out, keeping always to the timber. For the most part he kept ahead; she didn't know whether it was merely to lead the way or to give her every opportunity to shoot him in the back. She did know that a score of times she exclaimed within herself: "What a fool I've been! No wonder he makes fun of me. Of course he's Bolt Haveril and a friend of my brother's." And, she did not know how many times she thought of the red stallion and the marked gold and the scar and his way with Duke and that air of sheer diabolism which seemed so natural to him — and was afraid.

They found a racing crystal rivulet down in the canyon, and drank and rested a few minutes; and he found some berries in a bosky thicket and brought her a handful. They weren't too ripe but they were delicious; and they stained her red mouth and her fingers and made a smudge on a cheek exactly where a dimple was. He didn't know about the dimple then; it came out only when she smiled, and this morning she wasn't smiling.

On the low rocky ridge he had pointed out from the cliffs he found exactly what they were looking for. Half way up the ridge at the base of a broken-down cliff was a thick grove, perhaps an acre in extent, of cedars. There was a small stream of clear water at the base of the slope, making its singing way down to the lake, to be reached by an easy, five-minute walk from the camp site. Bolt named the spot among the cedars ideal for their purpose.

"And here," he said as Lady dropped down with a grateful sigh, "I'll leave you for a little while. I want to scout around; and we've got to do something about filling our larder. I won't go far; I'd hear you call, or anyhow I'd hear a pistol shot."

"I want to do my part —"

"Later, maybe, when we find something to do. Now why don't you stretch out and finish that sleep I spoiled for you so early this morning."

She was no longer sleepy. She watched him out of sight, then did stretch out and relax — and she was sound asleep when he came back about an hour later. She didn't look so tired now. She was breathing lightly and quietly, the cheeks on which her long lashes cast such dark shadows were faintly pink — there was almost a smile on her lips. Maybe her nightmares had exhausted themselves; maybe she was dreaming of freedom accomplished.

He watched her a long while, thinking how precious, how priceless she was, how immeasurably more charming than even that inspired, piquant painting Crazy Barnaby had made of her.

He hoped she would sleep and sleep, so that she would be wholly refreshed. He wished she would wake up now; he wanted to see those soft eyes of hers shake off the mistiness of sleep and meet his own, to be held a long moment by his in that sort of communion which is so much more direct, so much more eloquent, than mere words. He found it strangely pleasant to just sit there and look at her, yet found it oddly disquieting too. In sleep she withdrew; she ran away from him; she shut some sort of mystic gate and left him outside. That was why he wanted to see her eyes fly open. There wouldn't be that mystic barrier then.

He didn't note that he was thinking altogether in terms of desire. He wanted this and that and the other, and they all had to do with this little wild rose of a girl. He was growing impatient to know all about her — of how she spent all her days; what her thoughts and yearnings and young dreams had been; how much of joy she had known despite that apprehension and even stark terror which must have dwelt with her of late as inseparably as her own shadow.

"Looks like every day was going to be Friday for us for a while," said Bolt. "For one thing, as you've already seen, these brooks are made up of about half water, half trout. Then, if I go out gunning for game, every shot is asking to tell somebody, if there's anybody to hear, where we are. On top of that — well, a man never knows when he might need his extra ammunition."

Lady did smile at him then, altogether gaily, and he did see the dimple in the exact spot where the berry stain had been.

"It's been fun," she said. "And I want trout for supper and trout for breakfast tomorrow."

It was mid-afternoon, a lazy, blue, still, high-mountain mid-afternoon, and they had just licked their

110

fingers over the last morsel of their meal. For two hours he and she had pretty well forgotten that they were in flight for their lives. Down at the creek Bolt had found a place where the shallow water meandered through a patch of deep sand. He had scooped out a hole in the sand at the edge of the creek, had made a narrow canal leading water into it, had further outlined and fortified the mouth of this gateway so that the loose sand wouldn't wash back into it and fill it. Thus he had contrived a sort of pocket into which unwary trout were invited, a trap from which they'd find no escape.

He and she sat down on the grassy bank and watched the water clear; then watched the quick, hard-bodied fish go darting by, and waited for some curious one of them to investigate the little new swimming hole. Like quick-silvered gleams the trout flashed upstream or shot downstream; now and then one would hang in the clear current all but motionless, fin and tail stirring just enough to maintain that appearance of pause just at the opening into Bolt's pool.

"He's going in!" whispered Lady. "You watch!"

But he didn't go in.

"If one of them doesn't make up his mind pretty quick —"

"Tell me about Bob," she said, "where you saw him and how you happened to meet him and what happened and — and how badly hurt he is."

"Who're you talking to?" said Bolt.

"Why, to you, of course. Who else —"

"Who're you talking to?" he repeated.

"I don't understand —"

"Happens you want the story as told by Bolt Haveril or Juan Morada!"

"Oh. Tell me, please — Bolt."

"Fine. It happened like this."

"It was about a month ago, down in Texas. Bolt's ranch spread out close to the border, and right on the border was the little rough-and-ready, raring-to-go town of Cajob. There was a saloon keeper there named Shorty McKibben, a hard man, an ex-horse thief, a pretty tough citizen all round. Yet there was one thing to be said for Shorty that could not be said of a lot of better men: he knew the meaning of gratitude. Long ago Bolt Haveril had stood his friend in a pinch, when Shorty needed one as never before.

Bolt rode into town. Shorty promptly called him aside.

"Don Diablo's on his way here, Bolt. A couple of his men rode in a little while ago and have been looking the place over. That's the way they do now that Cajob ain't over healthy for Morada."

"Thanks, Shorty," Bolt had said.

"For things had come to that stage where men counted on Haveril and Morada shooting it out the first time they met. There had been trouble between them for upward of two years; recently and explosively that condition of affairs had come to a head."

"What sort of trouble?" asked Lady.

"Never mind," said Bolt. "That's another story, and I don't know that it ever needs to be told.

In Shorty's saloon Bolt had noticed a young fellow, a stranger scarcely more than a boy, slumped over a

112

corner table. At first he thought the boy looked not only despondent but hungry, too; worse than that, sick and hungry and pretty badly down in the mouth altogether.

"Ever hear of the Morgans, way up in the mountains?" asked Shorty. 'A place they call Dark Valley? Well, that kid's a Morgan, and it's on account of him, I reckon, that Juan Morada's coming to town.'

"Bolt looked again at the boy. He was unarmed and looked penniless; every now and then a shiver shook him like an ague. Like a shudder it was." Lady bit her lip, and the small hands at her sides clenched.

"I sort of got interested," Bolt went on. 'It was like this: One of Juan Morada's hunting pack, a half-breed that used to be a friend of Shorty's when Shorty was doing a good many things that weren't lawful, was getting scared. He figured that Morada's number was up; that before long they'd pull Morada down and he'd go down with him. He got to coming to Shorty and telling him things. He told him, and Shorty told me, that this young Bob Morgan had run away from the Valley, and that Duke Morgan for some reason would tip hell upside down to get him back. That Duke didn't know for sure the kid had come this way, but was watching all trails and figured this one a chance. That he had sent a fistful of money down to Juan Morada with a promise to double it twice over if Morada would nab the kid and hold him safe, and with nobody to talk to, until Duke could get him again.'

"Bolt had naturally asked what the kid was doing here. Shorty didn't know. He did know that young Morgan had come into town a couple of days before; he had looked sick and hungry then; he had been heard to ask for Con Hathaway, a ranger just then away on some secret business; he had had on him an old Colt revolver that must have been made before he was born; he had traded it off to an Indian for something to eat. Didn't even have a horse, it seemed."

" 'He was sort of feverish when I talked with him,' said Bolt. 'His eyes looked sort of wild. You could see he had had some tough going. I got him to say he'd come out to the ranch with me.'

"Bolt hired an extra horse at the stable. It was only about twenty miles out to his place, first across a narrow barren stretch, then into the hills. They were well along in the hills when Juan Morada overtook them. Morada had three of his men with him."

" 'Bob and I rode on our spurs, you bet! But we saw the best we could do was pick the spot where we'd fight it out. It was in a narrow pass. We got down and stood behind our horses. Well, it was quite a fight. Anyhow Bob and I got out of it alive. He got hit once in the shoulder; not bad and it wouldn't have bothered him like it did except that he wasn't in good shape to stand it. I got grazed, but not bad either.'

"And as far as Bolt Haveril was personally concerned it was worth it! He got Daybreak that day, and the other two horses that he had led on to Dark Valley; he got Morada's marked gold. And best of all he carried Juan Morada along with him, Juan Morada done up just the way Bolt admired him most! For the bandit had three bullets in him, was unconscious and lay like a sack of wheat over the saddle of a led horse.

114

"You see," chuckled Bolt, "he'd been keeping pretty clear of American soil of late. When he woke up he was in a good tight little American jail, and the sheriff was guarding him like the apple of his eye — and if by now Mr. Devil Don Morada hasn't swung high, he knows he won't have to wait much longer."

"And Bob?" the girl asked anxiously.

"He's still down at my place. He's getting good care, doctor and everything."

"Oh, God bless you, Bolt Haveril!"

Bolt looked at her then.

"He has," he said. And looked away. "Darn that old son of a gun of a trout! Look at him turn up his nose at the nice little swimming hole I made him!"

They talked a while longer. Then Bolt stood up and said, "I'm going to see if I can't herd our dinner into my trap."

They took off their boots and went into the stream, he far below and she high above the trap, and started driving fish! Before they were done they had made a game of it; Bolt slipped on a slippery smooth stone and came by a good ducking, and it was the first time he had ever heard her laugh. He came up grinning.

"It's worth getting wet, to hear a girl laugh like that!"

And then he had his turn and laughed at her when she, wildly excited by a big lightning-swift trout trying to shoot by her, clutched at the silver streak and came down on hands and knees in six inches of cold water. As he whooped gleefully she made a face at him — then started to laugh with him — then went racing through the water making the spray fly as she cried exultantly: "He's in! He's in your trap! We've got him!"

"We'll rest and sleep if we can until moonrise," said Bolt. They had dined and he was smoking and they were surrendering to the lull and peace of the vast embracing wilderness; too, they were both feeling an uplift of their spirits; hope was grown into confidence.

"I'm too happy to sleep," said Lady. "It's all I can do just to sit still and rest."

"Remember we want to travel all night, if we can stick it out."

Towards dusk she did doze. From dozing she slept soundly. Bolt, near by, lay on his back and watched the first star come out and he, too, dozed. But it was always with one ear open, instructed by his last conscious thought to stand sentinel. Any slightest sound brought his eyes open.

It was quite dark and the moon was not far from rising when a distant sound disturbed him. He listened a moment drowsily, catalogued it, closed his eyes again —

Then there was the girl at his side, stooping over him, shaking him by the arm, whispering excitedly: "Did you hear it? Oh, Bolt, did you hear it?"

He listened again.

"Nothing for us to worry about," he told her as he got up. "It's only a timber wolf howling at the rising moon. But, anyway, it's about time —"

She clutched his arm tighter than ever.

"It's not a timber wolf! Listen again! It's Stag!"

CHAPTER
ELEVEN

All this time Bolt Haveril had done what he could to keep from leaving behind them any signs of their passing: He had covered their camp fires, buried the few scraps, bones mostly, left from their meals, disposed of the cedar tips that had gone into the making of the girl's couches, had even just now obliterated all trace of his fish trap and brushed out their tracks in the sand. But never once had he thought of Stag.

"You're sure?" he asked.

She shuddered. Stag was Sid's dog. Since Stag was a puppy, and that was now nearly four years ago, Sid had done all that he could to make the dog hate Lady. He had invented a hundred cunning, spiteful tricks to bring that about, never tiring of his sport. And now did she know Stag's howling bark when she heard it? All her old terrors came rushing back, engulfing her.

He stood listening intently, his head cocked aside, his lean body rigid. The sounds died away and there was a silence. The girl started to speak, but fell silent at his almost savage "Sh!" Presently the dog's queer howling bark came again.

"It's hard telling how far off they are —"

"Oh, hurry, hurry! Let's hurry!"

"Sure. We'll hurry along, but we won't be in too big a hurry doing it. We can't outrun that dog and we can't outrun men on horseback. Wait a shake."

She knew that he wasn't listening now; he was done with that. But he remained very still so long a time that she found it hard not to scream at him to hurry away, to run with her somewhere, anywhere — faster and faster —

"That gun you're wearing," he said abruptly. "You know how to use it, I suppose!"

"Yes!"

"Are you a good shot? And could you have a steady nerve —"

"Yes!"

"Anyhow, if a man came say within thirty-forty feet of you, could you hit him?"

"Yes! And I would if —"

"I think I've got it figured out," he said, and was brisk of a sudden. "Maybe we can fool 'em yet. Leave things as they are here; no time and no use now trying to hide our camp sign. Come back down to the creek." Then they did hurry. "Here's where we go wading again," said Bolt. "With our boots on, down stream."

They waded down the middle of the creek for a couple of hundred yards, and though thus they were not distancing but actually going toward the wolf dog, the girl made no demur; when Bolt took matters firmly in hand as now she was all eagerness to do as he said and ask reasons later. At last Haveril, leading the way, stopped.

118

"This is the way we came this morning; here's where we first came to the creek," he said. "We'll give Stag some fresher tracks to work on when he gets this far! See that rocky out-cropping on the hillside over there? The moon's just reaching it. Now you make a bee line for it; when you get there walk on rocks all you can; take a little jump off to right or left once in a while; then make a circle around by the base of the hill there, a good wide loop and come back to this spot. Got the idea?"

"And you?"

"I'm doing another circle on this side of the creek, just like yours. When Stag gets here he's going to have his choice, and whichever he takes is going to bring him back where he started! Got it? Look out you don't take a fall but — Well, you wanted to run, didn't you? Let's run!"

She sped away. Once she looked back and saw Bolt Haveril, a lean dark figure in the moonlight, running as she ran. It seemed such a crazy thing to do, such a mad thing if any third person should look at them and see them running in circles. But she sped on. She came to the rocky land and raced nimbly across it; she sprang from one rock to another; several times she did stumble, but she did not once fall. She swerved off to the right, now and again broke her trail by leaping to right and left, and at last, panting and flushed and with her heart thumping, came back to the creek.

They arrived at almost the same instant. There was enough moonlight for her to see — Yes, just as she might have expected, he was grinning at her, and he said with his rumbling chuckle:

"Great games we invent, huh? We ought to grow to be bully playmates, give us time!"

"Now what?"

"Into the creek again and keep on downstream. Stag will be led here first of all; when he gets through chasing his tail around in rings, he'll find our other tracks and go on upstream. Let's scamper."

As they went along with the creek its flow grew gentler, it widened and grew shallow with a sandy bottom, with fewer and fewer rocks to stumble over. Thus, splashing along as fast as they could, they made almost as good time as they would have made on dry land. Only once again did they hear the clamour of the dog; it still sounded far away. The moonlight grew brighter; presently they saw the little round lake glinting like a pool of quicksilver. They kept steadily on, at times with water rushing about their boot tops, most of the time only a few inches over their insteps; and so, with the stream leading the way and growing lazier as they grew swifter, they came to the lake.

"We keep in the water a little longer," he said. "It's easy going if we walk close to the shore where it's shallow. We bear off to the south-east here; that's not getting us any closer Stag, anyhow. There's a rocky shoulder of the mountain that comes down to the lake half a mile farther on; I noticed it this morning. We'll start getting our feet dry there."

Again she couldn't help saying:

"Oh, let's hurry, Bolt! We've lost so much time already."

"Sure, we'll hurry. What do you think we're doing now?" he asked good-naturedly. "But, as to losing time, shucks! We weren't more than ten-fifteen minutes at it, and I'll bet a man it holds Stag up a good couple of hours."

When they came to the spot he had selected, where the lake's wavelets washed softly against a rocky promontory, they exercised the greatest care to leave no sign of their passage from water to land. Bolt crawled directly up to the flat-topped boulder which, water-washed through the ages, was marked with a high-water line plain to be seen even in the moonlight. He reached down, gave the girl his hand and drew her up to his side. Then, stepping from one rock to another, they began toiling up the blunt-nosed ridge.

"But we're going so slowly now!"

"Yes. You're right. Well, we've done our best to play hide-and-seek the right way. So now we strike out again. We'll still steer for that gap we saw in the mountains this morning; but we'll hunt out all the roughest country we can find. We'll leave less scent for Stag to nose out for one thing; for another, men on horseback can't do a whole lot better among the rocks than we can." He turned and looked at her a moment. "Terribly tired?"

"I was never so rested in my life!" she cried. "I'm just plain scared."

He took off his hat. Maybe it was only to mop a streaming brow, but the gesture rather fittingly accompanied his words:

"Lady Morgan, I'm darned glad that I met up with you!"

"So am I, Bolt Haveril! And I'm grateful, and I'll always —"

"Better pour the water out of your boots before we start —"

"No! I —"

He sat down on a rock and started getting his own boots off.

"We're going to raise us some blisters *pronto*, if we don't look out," he went on. "Then where'd we be?"

They went up that long rocky slope which was only a spur of the lofty mountain beyond; they kept on going, up and up, stopping frequently to rest because they had to; listening always for a wolf-dog's baying, because they had to do that, too. They didn't hear Stag again, and Lady began to feel easier because of it. Bolt said, "Maybe he's lost our track somewhere." But he was thinking, "I'll bet they've gagged him; muzzled him somehow so he's got to keep still. They can tell they're getting close." And, futile as he knew the speculation to be, he couldn't help wondering how many men spurred along at Stag's heels? "They'll have rifles, too. That's not so good. Well, if they do overhaul us it's up to me to pick the spot. Right up at close range a rifle hasn't got anything on a six-gun."

At last on the mountain top they came in to a place, seeming weird under the moon, of fantastically riven spires and slabs and turrets of ghostly-grey granite. They were breathing heavily from the long, steep climb; neither spoke when they stopped. They stood there looking about them, looking far off and down to the south across the vast sweep of the rugged, moonlit

122

wilderness. They would rest here a moment, then go on down the southern slope, selecting one of the several rocky ridges which were like enormous bony fingers with shadow-filled, deep cleft ravines between them.

Lady, her whole body throbbing, her shoulders drooping, was leaning against a boulder. Bolt was just lifting his arm to point; the gesture was never completed. The next thing Lady knew he had caught her by the arm and dragged her bodily behind the boulder; already his gun was in his hand; he whispered into her ear:

"Still! Maybe he hasn't seen us yet. There's a man standing on a big flat-topped rock not fifty feet from us."

She wanted to turn and run, run anywhere down the mountain side, run and run until she dropped dead rather than be taken. But that was only the first wild impulse; a moment later she and he were peering out together at the figure Bolt Haveril had glimpsed.

The man standing there was as still as the rocks about him; they could see his outline only, nothing of his face.

"Is it Sid?" queried Bolt. "About his size and build —"

The figure turned just then, and very lightly and with a queer supple grace, leaped down from his rock. As he did so they heard the soft musical jingle of little bells.

"It's Barnaby!" she gasped. "Only dear Barnaby! Oh, thank God, thank God! We're safe yet, Bolt!"

"Wait a minute! Maybe he's not alone. The others —"

"You don't know Barnaby!" she cried softly but so very, very gladly. "Barnaby is always alone!"

"And Stag?"

"I — I had forgotten Stag! Of course Barnaby and Stag are always going off together ... Barnaby and Stag love each other as much as Stag and I hate each other. But I'm never afraid of Stag when Barnaby is near."

"Just the same," Bolt cautioned her, "we'd better go mighty slow right now and keep our eyes open and be ready for 'most anything."

Barnaby, erect and slim and walking lightly on moccasined feet, was coming straight toward them. At every quick, lithe step, the little bells attached to his staff jingled musically. At every second they expected to see Stag come leaping out of the shadows to join him. But Barnaby came on alone.

Lady, moving out from behind the boulder despite Bolt's attempt to stay her, called softly:

"Barnaby! Oh, dear Barnaby!"

Barnaby came straight on. He brushed the long black hair back from his brow; they could see his eyes, large and dark and brilliant, shining, thought Bolt, like some nocturnal animal's; flying squirrels had eyes like that, large, lambent, luminous.

"You are tired, Miss Lady," said Barnaby, in a voice as sweet and gentle as a girl's, as soothing as a crooning young mother's. "You are frightened, too. You ran away!" He shook his head, and the long black hair came tumbling back all about his lean, eager face, and he tossed it back with a swift, oddly birdlike jerk of his head. "You should have told Barnaby first. He would have told you to wait. The time is not yet. But never mind. You brought nothing to eat and drink. So I brought you these."

He unslung a pouch from his belt and gave it into her hands. Then he untied something else from his belt — a leather-jacketed flask.

"Parched corn; it's good for a journey," he said gravely. "With plenty of water in the brooks. And a flask of sour red wine, a sip when you are tired."

"And you came just to bring me this, Barnaby?"

"Why, of course," smiled Barnaby.

She patted Barnaby's lean dark hand and he looked infinitely pleased. Then she thought to ask anxiously:

"But, Stag, Barnaby? We heard him barking. I don't see him. Where is he?"

"Yes, I heard him, too, Miss Lady. He was far off then, but Stag can run fast! A fine dog, Stag —"

"You mean Stag didn't come along with you?" demanded Bolt. Barnaby shook his head. "Then how did you find us?"

Barnaby laughed in a delighted sort of way at that. He looked at Lady as much as to say: "He doesn't understand, does he? He doesn't know!" To Bolt he said gaily: "Barnaby can find anybody, anything. Near by or far away, in the day or in the dark. Barnaby is not like other men; he knows things they don't know; he hears voices they don't hear; he does things they can't do." He laughed again softly. "That's why they call Barnaby crazy," he confided.

Instantly the alarm and apprehension which had just now lifted dark wings to take flight came speeding back.

"But Stag!" cried Lady once more. "Oh, then Barnaby, he is bringing the others after us!"

Barnaby nodded. "He is smart," he said pridefully. "Oh, Stag is smart. Yes, he will bring them after you." The thought in nowise appeared to disturb him. "You won't have to walk all the way back," he said. "They will have horses, you know."

"But Barnaby! Barnaby! They mustn't find us! I won't go back! They — they would —"

"Oh!" said Barnaby brightly. "I know now! You are hiding from them."

"Yes, yes! That's it, Barnaby. Do you remember how you and I would play hide-and-seek?"

"But I always found you!" laughed the boy. "Nobody can hide where Barnaby cannot find them. I always hear whispering voices. The whispering voices lead me straight, straight." Abruptly he turned, cocking his head to peer up into Bolt Haveril's stony face. "You are Juan Morada," he said. "They call you Don Diablo, don't they? They say you are a wicked man, a killer and even worse than that. They are fools! Barnaby knows. You are a good, kind man, Juan Morada."

"Why don't we hear Stag any more, Barnaby?" asked Bolt.

"Because they have made him be still! Oh, Stag loves to bark and howl like that, especially when he is running with his nose to a scent, especially on a night with a moon! Sometimes we run together and then I howl too, like Stag, and he likes it. Yes, they have made him keep still. I can do that, just talking to him. But they tied a string around his nose. They don't want him to talk. They want to creep up on you —"

"How far away is he, Barnaby? How long before they can come up with us?"

"An hour yet, Juan Morada. Even maybe two hours, for, though Stag can run fast, faster even than Barnaby, the men on horses have to go slower climbing the mountain where it's all rocks. Yes, maybe two hours."

"Let's hurry on!" cried Lady.

"Right," said Bolt, and Barnaby exclaimed:

"And we'll hide? We can fool all of them but Stag! Yes, let's hurry. There are fine places to hide in these good old mountains." He patted the rock against which they stood, and it was like patting an old, understanding friend.

Bolt Haveril pointed out the V-gap in the mountainous ridge next ahead.

"That is where we are going," he said.

Barnaby, with a softly merry jingle of bells, started off like a running deer.

"Follow me," he invited them. "I will show you the best way."

They followed him and Bolt said, curious about this strange being:

"Tell me about him. Just who and what is Barnaby?"

"I think that no one quite knows," she told him. "He came to us, down in Dark Valley, about three years ago."

Even those few who had known the boy on the Outside before he came to Dark Valley could have told little more of him than Lady knew. An old miner who had read Dickens had christened him Barnaby, and surely he was as strange and wild and weird as Barnaby Rudge, lacking only his raven. He harkened to voices in the wind, in the murmuring treetops, in the babble of creeks, in the patter of rain and boom of thunderstorms — and in the deep, throbbing silences. He said that when he was in the far-out lonely places God came down and talked with him. It was inevitable that men like the Morgans should call him Crazy Barnaby after that!

He was gone for days at a time, wandering alone in the wildernesses. He said sometimes that a sparrow had been caught by one wing in the tangle of a distant brushy thicket, and that he must hurry to set the bird free. He said sometimes that a deer had broken its slim foreleg and would perish unless he sped to its succour. He said that the little mountain-meadow rabbits and the lean timber wolves and the striped chipmunks and the eagles were his brothers.

And always with Crazy Barnaby went his packet of food and his flask, for he would go as swiftly to the aid of a woodchopper caught under a falling tree or a prospector whose tunnel had caved in on him, as to the wild things; and also there went always with him his tinkling jingle of little bells. He said that those bells, swinging from his staff, talked for him, saying the things he could almost think of but could never quite get the words to express.

Now leading the way, playing at the game of hide-and-seek, skipping and frolicking tirelessly before them, he would spring from one big rock to another, he would even at times leap up and catch the branches of a tree and climb and swing out on the far side, catching another branch if it were close enough, otherwise dropping lightly to the ground again, calling back gleefully to them, "That will tease good old Stag! That will make him growl and grumble and hunt all the harder! And then, when he finds the track again — Oh, he will! Stag is smart! — he'll laugh and come running after us!"

A scrambling half hour brought them all the way down the mountainside. They crossed a long green valley, winding its narrow way in and out between the bases of the mountains; they forded a small river, stopping to drink; they waded downstream a half mile; they began climbing again, Bolt's V-gap straight ahead and above, bluish-black under the stars, filled with shadows cast by the moon. It was just then that Barnaby, who had vanished ahead among the trees, called back to them gleefully:

"Listen, Lady! Listen, Don Diablo! It's Stag! Do you hear him? Good old Stag! And he's closer now, too!"

Lady started running. Bolt overtook her, took her by the arm, steadied her.

"Listen to me a minute," he commanded, and she turned to look up into his face, detecting a new note in his voice. "I think I've got this thing worked out. We'll fool 'em yet. Will you do exactly what I tell you to do?"

She didn't hesitate a second.

"Of course I will! Haven't I done so all the time? But for you where would I be now? Anything, Bolt!"

"Fine! For the present we keep climbing, only you don't have to run. We're going to have plenty of time. Taking it easy we can be up at the Gap in another twenty minutes. There we'll rest a minute; there I'll explain."

Barnaby called them as they started on:

"Stag is smart! He got the string off his snout so he could bark again. I understood what he said. I would have called back to him only I remembered we were playing hide!"

"Don't you dare call to him, Barnaby!" cried Lady.

Barnaby laughed and promised and went on again.

CHAPTER
TWELVE

They stopped in a grassy, gently sloping clearing in the timber within ten minutes' walk of the V-cleft in the cliffs. Bolt and Lady sat down on the grass; Barnaby was already half way up a big solitary pine, saying that from up there he could look all over the world and that he would be sure to catch a glimpse of their pursuers.

"Here's what I've been thinking," said Bolt. "The one high card Duke Morgan's crowd holds against us is Stag. They'd never track us now if it wasn't for Stag, would they?"

"I don't see how they could! I'm sure we could get away. But how can we do anything? I thought of something myself; I hope that isn't what you're thinking! That we could send Barnaby back; he could make Stag do anything he wanted. But — Duke would kill him!"

"No, I wasn't thinking that," said Bolt. "There's another way to rule Stag out, but Barnaby mustn't know. Now all this time the dog has been following the two of us together, hasn't he? If your and my trails parted for a little while — *then what?*"

"Bolt! What do you mean! Stag doesn't even know you and — Oh, Sid has taught him that I'm his quarry!

You saw him down there in the Valley! If Stag was hot on the trail of any game in the world and saw me — he'd take after me! Sid for years has done everything he could — he even tortured the poor little puppy whenever I came near it; he made it feel that I was to blame."

"I guess you've answered me. That's what I was thinking. If up here you went one way and I went another way — Well, Stag wouldn't hesitate a minute, would he? He'd be off after you like a shot!"

She drew away from him, staring at him, feeling terror grip her again, once more experiencing that goad of doubt; "Is this Bolt Haveril, Bob's friend? Or is it Juan Morada?" Just now he had prepared her, asking, "Will you do exactly what I tell you to do?" And she had been swift to answer, "Anything!"

Suddenly she stiffened. She got her courage in hand; he saw the flash of her eyes. Her chin was up, her voice cool and steady, when she said:

"Yes, I understand. They are almost on us. You will go one way, I'll go another. Stag will follow me!"

"If you were about six years younger and nine pounds lighter and I had a minute or two on my hands to spend having a good time," Bolt grunted at her, "I'd sure take you across my knee, young lady, and give you what Paddy gave the drum. Suppose you don't fly off the handle?"

"I'm sorry," she said, and was on the instant contrite.

"Here's what we do," said Bolt. First he had felt her hand on his arm; next he had patted it; now he was beginning to get his boots off. "We change boots just

132

this side the gap. You can get mine on easy enough." He wasn't too sober to grin fleetingly at her, and to admonish, "Look out you don't get lost in 'em. If you do lose your way, no use trying to climb out; the soles are pretty well worn out, and you can dig your way through. — Then you hand me your boots; if I can't get my feet in 'em, I can mash 'em down and tie 'em on the bottoms of my number twelves."

"*Bolt!* And you will fool Stag into following you —"

"Not far. It's going to be easy. I never thought I'd have to kill anybody's dog, but you can take it from me it won't hurt me much to polish off this pet wolf of Sid's. You will turn off to the left before we get to the Gap, and will keep on around the mountain, then due south again as long as you can keep going. Before you go very far you'll hear a shot. That will mean that Stag is out of it. Before morning, or anyhow to-morrow night, I'll overtake you. Doesn't sound hard, does it?"

"You talk as though Stag was all alone against us! Don't you know that Duke and Sid, if he is well enough, and maybe a dozen men will be right after Stag?"

"If you'll tend to your part of this game," he said quietly, "I'll tend to mine."

"But *how?*"

"I'll go straight on into the pass; among those cliffs there'll be a place where it narrows and where the banks will be high on each side. I'll find a place like that in ten or fifteen minutes; sure to. I'll pass it twenty steps, then double back and make a jump to the top of a rock. I'll find a place up above where I can hide,

133

where I can look down into the cut. Mr. Stag will lead the rest. I'll put a bullet through him where it will do the most good — and then I'll take to my heels and run like the devil! By the time the crowd spills out of their saddles and comes up where my shot came from — and they'll come walking sort of easy, ready to dodge bullets! — I'll be a mile away. Didn't I tell you it would be so easy it won't hardly be any fun?"

The way he told it, it did sound easy! Just the simplest thing in the world! But deep down in her heart she saw through this man as one could see to the bottom of a clear pool. He was cool and laughing, funning with her; and she knew that it was because they had reached a desperate crisis and its desperation bit into him. And she knew that he, drawing the chase after him, would somehow hold them as long as he could, hold them to give her her slim chance, hold them though he died playing out this amusing game of his.

"Bolt," she said with a little catch in her voice, "I won't! And — and you are the finest, the most wond —"

"Off with the boots," said Bolt. "You promised to do as I told you! Off with 'em, dammit!"

"I — I won't, dammit!" cried Lady, near tears.

"Fine!" said Bolt. "Have it your way then. What'll we do?"

"We'll keep going on. As fast and far as we can. Together!"

"Sure. And when they come up with us?"

"We'll fight it out with them!"

"Sounds good. Hm! let's see. They'll be careful not to hurt you, won't they? Duke needs you alive for a

134

while, huh? They'll cluster round with rifles; they won't have to come too close, either. There'll be several of them; they'll have plenty to eat with them, too; they would, wouldn't they? They can take their time; no hurry. Sooner or later they'll starve us out. They'll come gather you in and take you home. They'll knock me on the head, and serve me right! — Yes," he drawled sarcastically, "I reckon you've got it figured out the best way."

By the time Barnaby came down from his tree everything was arranged. The report that Barnaby brought sped them along. Their pursuers would be here in less than an hour, Barnaby judged. And he had seen, or thought that he had seen, and that was the same thing with Barnaby, several riders on the mountain they had left so recently.

To him they explained only a part of their plan, Bolt making it appear that they meant just to have a bit more fun with Stag, puzzling him.

They said nothing of the change of boots and of Bolt's plot against Stag; that Barnaby should not notice they sent him hurrying on ahead again. When he was within a hundred feet of the pass he was to turn to the side, and keep on slowly until Lady came up with him. Then the two were to strike straight south; Barnaby knew how to do that, steering by the stars, as did Bolt and most other Southwestern riders.

Then came the moment for Bolt and Lady to part. They stood very silent a moment; Bolt had pulled his hat off and the moon brightened both their faces.

"Good luck, Lady," said Bolt. "You're a girl in a million, and —"

"Oh, Bolt, be careful! I — there is so much I wish I could say to you! But — Bolt, be careful, won't you?"

He smiled at her and gave her hand a good hard squeeze.

"Didn't you just hear me say that you're a girl in a million? I'd just as leave make it ten or twenty million! Don't you reckon I'm going to play mighty safe and make mighty sure I see you again? Soon, too, Lady!"

She lifted his hand and pressed it against her cheek. Then she went as swiftly as she could — but she did have trouble with those boots of his, lifting them the way he had told her, stepping with as long strides as she could, walking this way and that to keep on rocky ground.

And Bolt went on his way into the pass, and for his part took infinite pains to leave a track that Stag could not possibly miss, dragging Lady's little boots almost like a man skating, rubbing them in soft dirt wherever he could find it, wiping the soles back and forth on the dry grass. Thus his progress was slow; thus he could keep watching Lady's slim graceful form as she followed on after Crazy Barnaby. Then she vanished among the boulders and Bolt entered the mouth of the narrow and narrowing pass.

Walking with her boots tied on that way under his feet was like walking on stilts, but he was in no slightest haste now. To go slowly, to take it easy, was to rest his body and to get his nerves as steady as they needed to be. He went on a hundred yards, another hundred, climbing gradually and all the while eyeing the steepening banks on either hand. The farther he led the chase this way, the more time would Lady have to make her clean get-away. Then his job would be to hold Duke's crowd as long as he could. "And then, if they leave me alive, to run barefooted like a scared rabbit!"

At last he came to a spot which suited him perfectly; he felt that he could not have designed it better or more fittingly placed the moon. Here some ancient cataclysm had split the mountain crest so that there resulted a rift, sand floored, not more than fifteen feet wide, between two cliff-like banks rising sharply a score of feet; and right here the moon shone directly down into the bottom of the gap, making it as bright as a summer dawn. Bolt kept steadily on another dozen paces, dragging Lady's boots scufflingly; he turned then, retraced that short distance and stood studying both banks, making his final selection. He chose the one on his left for its more jagged crest, for a sort of leaning spire up there, for the blot of shadow it threw. There was the spot for him to lie while he drew a fine bead on the wolf-dog.

Standing in the middle of the pass he gathered his forces and made a leap to the side which brought him, with bruised shins, to the top of a boulder which long ago had rolled down from above. There he removed the troublesome boots, tied them together, slung them about his neck, and started clawing his way up. He found crevices affording hand and toe hold, and so came swiftly to the top.

He thought that he could count upon a half hour, perhaps an hour, for his own devices, and so first of all, like a wise general who in planning battle has an eye to the terrain in his rear, scouted around for the way he would go when he left this place.

"I'll sure be wanting to travel fast," he grunted.

For ten minutes he reconnoitred; he knew just which way he should run, what irregularities he could count on for shelter, the canyon he would follow all the way down into the next valley, the spot there where he would swerve off to the right — he'd make a wide, wide arc, miles long before he sought to rejoin Lady Morgan.

Then he returned to his vantage point above the gap, lay on his belly in the leaning pinnacle's shadow and watched and listened and waited for Stag.

For a long while he lay without stirring, finding the respite grateful, glad for every minute which gave Lady just that greater chance of success. Nothing stirred; there was no sound. The stillness, the silence, were so profound that they began to seem infinite, inviolable, twin eternities that nothing could ever disturb. But all things mundane come to an end, even patient waiting grows impatient, and at last it was with a sense of relief that he heard the long-expected sounds.

First there was the clang of a shod hoof against a rock, then the scuffling of horses, coming up the slope, then a deep angry voice speaking a word or two. That was Duke Morgan. Bolt couldn't catch a word of what he said, but gathered the impression that Duke was cautioning those who rode close behind him; no doubt he'd be saying, "We've just about run 'em to earth; better watch out for bullets."

And then Bolt saw Stag bursting out of the timber and into the clearing below the gap, and made out that the dog, in a frenzy of pursuit on a hot trail, was held in restraint by a long rope — and that it was Duke Morgan, following Stag into the open, who held Stag checked.

Following Duke into view came one horseman after another until Bolt had counted seven of them. He thought that Budge was one; that Tilford and Camden and Rance were others; surely one was Sid.

Bolt slid his gun out of its holster. They were still too far away for any accurate shooting; the target he was cherishing a bullet for, the wildly excited Stag, was to be glimpsed only fitfully among the rocks and bushes.

Again Bolt thought "Hang it, I hate to kill a dog. I'd rather shoot Sid Morgan who made Stag like that." But a man had to do a lot of distasteful jobs in his time. And at least he'd make sure that Stag never knew what hit him. He'd wait until the dog was in that patch of moonlight in the sandy floor of the pass almost directly below and send a bullet crashing into the brain.

The dog, leading the man-pack, came straining on, rising on hind legs and pawing at the air when the taut rope maddened him, darting forward again, nose to the ground, and thus came to the spot where Bolt and Lady had separated. For just an instant Bolt tautened throughout his body. Then Duke gave the dog a little more slack and Stag shot straight on, past Lady's point

139

of departure, straight on toward the gap, following the track that Bolt had made for him in Lady's boots.

Bolt's stiffened body relaxed. There had always been the off-chance that the dog would blunder. Now the hand was as good as played out. One cool, straight shot, the end of Stag and —

But something had gone wrong! Stag came to a sudden stop and sniffed; sniffed the ground, raised his head and sniffed the air. He began running in small but widening circles. He turned back while Duke, stopping his horse and letting the rope out to its greatest length, commanded him softly, urging him, "Good dog! Good dog! Hunt 'em out, Stag!"

For a moment or two Stag seemed to lose his head entirely, to go stark mad. He dashed one way and another, he stopped abruptly and squatted on his powerful haunches and pointed his nose straight to the moon; he started fighting the muzzle they had put on him as though he was bound to get the thing off though he tore his hide off along with it.

Sid, spurring to his father's side, lifting his voice so that Bolt could hear every word, urged:

"Give him rope, Duke! Give him more rope! He's on the hottest scent he's hit yet; it's red-hot! Give him a chance."

"Shut up; keep still!" snapped Duke. "I've given him all the rope there is. What's the matter with the fool dog?"

Stag was working again, nosing the ground in those ever widening circles of his, and Duke had to rein

140

backward and whirl his horse to keep from getting entangled.

And Bolt Haveril forgot to breathe.

For Stag had found what he sought, what he wanted most on earth! He shot out along the track he had picked up like something fired out of a gun; a big rock stood in his way, and he went over it in one long, lean grey streak and such was the impetus his big body gathered, such the unexpected jerk on Duke's arm, that the end of the rope was whipped out of his hand — and Stag was off at full speed.

And of a sudden Bolt Haveril, horror in his veins, understood everything. He knew now why Stag had hesitated and fumbled and had gone briefly mad with indecision. Where he went now was not where Lady had gone in Bolt's boots; it was no longer that he sought either Bolt or Lady. He had picked up Crazy Barnaby's tracks. For hours the dog had been tireless in striving to run down the thing he hated most, the thing his master had trained him into hating. And now if he had hesitated a moment it was because he had come to a forking of the ways where the object of his hatred had gone one way and the one human being he truly loved had gone the other.

He followed Barnaby — and by now Barnaby and Lady were fleeing side by side.

Duke let out a roar and spurred after the vanishing dog, and close behind Duke rode Sid and the others. Almost before Bolt quite knew what it was all about the whole posse was out of sight. And to make everything as bad it could be, the slope of the mountain where

Stag led the way was comparatively open, comparatively free from rough, rocky going. The horsemen would be able to keep up with Stag, at the very least to keep him in view.

And somehow, in his frenzy of a moment ago perhaps, Stag had freed himself of the thong clamping his jaws together, enforcing silence. There was silence no more, but as the dog sped along he filled the night with a new sort of clamour, a glad, happy barking.

Bolt sprang up and started running, not a full flight as he had so confidently planned, but running around to the other side of the mountain top, hoping against hope that somehow he could come between Duke and Sid and the rest, and Lady and Barnaby.

He saw the riders shoot down the long slope, riding recklessly. He heard Stag's joyous barking again, more glad and eager than before. He even caught a glimpse of the great greyish body running so swiftly, so surely, swimming through the air over log and boulder, going straight to his quarry.

It was less than an hour later that Bolt Haveril, lying flat in a pool of black shadows, saw a small cavalcade riding at a brisk trot down in the meadow, curving about the base of the mountain, heading back toward Dark Valley. He saw Duke riding at their head, massive in the saddle, his big-bodied figure standing out boldly in the moonlight. He saw just behind Duke a slight, bowed figure, a figure of utter dejection and hopelessness. The others came close behind.

142

Barnaby he did not see, nor did he see Stag. They had all forgotten Stag now; none of them ever wasted a second thought on Crazy Barnaby. They were content, even, to go back without troubling to quest further for Bolt Haveril.

Well, they had all that they wanted. They had Lady Morgan and, their rifles flashing in the moonlight, were guarding her well. And it did a thoroughly wretched Bolt Haveril not the slightest good to ask now why he had not thought that Stag might follow Barnaby — that he had not taken the final precaution to have Barnaby go one way, Lady another.

It was a tormented man who watched them pass swiftly out of sight.

CHAPTER
THIRTEEN

"Something's sure gone wrong," remarked Sheriff Dan Westcott gloomily, swirling the red liquor in his glass and forgetting to down it, an unprecedented oversight on old Dan's part.

"If you listen to me tell it, everything's gone wrong," said Sheriff Dave Heffinger. He was scarcely less gloomy than Sheriff Westcott; his face was puckered like a man's who has just tested something sour; his eyes were troubled. He added, altogether unnecessarily, since old Dan was the last man in the world to have forgotten; "It's been three days now, and never a cheep out'n your young friend from down Texas way. Likely the Morgans have tucked him under a couple of feet of ground and forgot to put any marker up."

Sheriff Westcott's gnarled old hand, leathery and with blue veins that stood out prominently, grew into a clenched fist around his glass.

"Don't believe it!" he said testily. "Ain't heard of any dead Morgans lately, have you? If they got him, he'd of got him a few of them! But, happens you prove to be right, Dave, and they have killed that boy —"

He broke off, suddenly remembered his whisky, gulped it with almost incredible swiftness and dexterity, and brought the empty glass down emphatically on the table.

"The valley of them damn Morgans is in both our counties, Dave," he said angrily, "and it's a disgrace to the two of us and a blot on our pedigrees. Seems like we've waited long enough. Let's go clean up on 'em. We could get a hundred men to ride with us."

"I'd kind of like that sort of ride," admitted Dave Heffinger, "even if it was the last ride I ever took. Only — Shucks, Dan."

They were again in Red Luck, off by themselves in a corner of Red Luck's drink emporium which was the heart and centre of the community, a big barn-like room with its long bar and its tables and a section of bare floor for dancing; the place where men naturally forgathered, where news came dribbling in and got itself reinforced and expanded and was off again in a hundred directions; the place for business deals and card games and brawls and killings. If you were looking for anyone, friend or enemy, the Barrel House was your place.

It was late afternoon; it would soon be night, the third night since they had waited here for Bolt Haveril. In their reasoning minds they had given him up, both of them; but Dan Westcott in his tough old heart hung on bulldog fashion to some skimpy hope that Bolt would turn up yet.

"Nope," said Heffinger. "He'd of sent you some word, wouldn't he?"

"If he could," muttered Dan. "But you can never tell; we don't know what happened."

"Well, we know what happened up this way — over to Pocket Gully, and I wish now it hadn't. We saw to it, like your young friend wanted, that a lot of the Morgan sympathizers was rounded up and the fear of the Lord and sudden death put into their yeller hides. And, like your uppity young Texan wanted, we just did that for the looks of it, to pull the Morgans out'n their nest. If we'd of hung them sons of sin instead of letting 'em get loose again —"

"Anyhow they don't know we turned 'em loose," Dan reminded him, salvaging all the slight comfort he could. "They think they done it themselves. And, one good thing, I'll bet some of them is running yet!"

"Nary," snorted Heffinger. "Duke Morgan and his fellers came a swarming out like a herd of young cowboys heading to town for Sat-day night; and inside ten hours he got word spread all over the country he was backing them loafers up with everything he had in the Valley. One or two of 'em went back along with him; the rest maybe will make themselves sort of scarce for a few days. But we've still got 'em with us, Dan'l."

"Someday —" said Dan.

"Sure, someday. I wonder when?"

"I'm about ready now." He began twirling his glass again. "I'm about ready to raid my end of Dark Valley, Dave, if you're ready to kick in on this end. We'd meet together like the upper and the nether stone, grinding the corn fine."

"Sounds good," Heffinger had to concede. But also he had to shake his head. "You know as well's I know, seeing we've talked about it a thousand times, that

146

there's nothing we can pin on this Morgan outfit legal and by due process of law." He had to sigh over vanished days. "I can remember, before the country got all gummed up with law-books, how you and me could sort of make the laws ourselves, or anyhow interpret 'em, and that was just as good and less trouble. If we rode in hell-for-leather and yanked every last Morgan out by the scruff of the neck, then what? They'd go to court and there wouldn't be any witnesses again 'em and we couldn't prove they wasn't a flock of angels, and they'd go laughing home and all we'd have done was maybe get ourselves shot full of holes."

Dan glared at him. "What do you have to tell me all that for? Don't I know it?"

"What's eating you anyhow to-day, Dan'l?" demanded Heffinger and stared at him curiously.

"I'm worried about young Haveril."

"You better be. By the way, Dan, how does Rincon County get along without its sheriff? You've been up here three days now."

"Hell take Rincon County," growled old Dan. And Heffinger said "Sure," and ordered two more whiskies.

At this early hour an atmosphere of listlessness hung over the Barrel House. Though the third bartender had just come on duty, there was as yet little to do, there being not half a dozen men in the big room, the entertainers not due to put in their lively appearances for some hours. But it was almost first-drink time, and presently men began drifting in.

Old Doc Bitters — his name was Bitner, by the way, but most folks had forgotten that — grey and imperialled and paunchy under the wide black hat he wore at a piratical angle, led the procession as usual. The rum and bitters, uncalled for, slid down the bar to him, and he captured it with a practised hand. Sol Baumer from the General Store was a close second. Anyone in Red Luck could have told you that he had glanced at the store clock which he kept punctually fifteen minutes fast with an eye toward hastening the daily first-drink time, and turned over the slack afternoon business to his boy, and would come to anchor next bottle to Doc Bitters, and that the two would spend the hour in mild and contemptuous argument over the merits and demerits of their special beverages. Sol Baumer shuddered at bitters and made Old Doc shudder with the reckless way he splashed water into his whisky.

These constituted the vanguard of Red Luck reporting for duty. In their wake slowly the place began to fill and hum with voices and chink coolly and pleasantly with bottles and glasses, and grow fragrantly blue with the sort of thing they smoked in their pipes and cigarettes. Judge Dalton, going "Hem, hem, hem," all the way from the swing door as he got his throat clear, was as usual always a safe third and had been known to place, and even infrequently to nose Old Doc out of first place. Thereafter came the stragglers, the younger men, a careless generation who took less seriously the responsibility of a good Red Luck citizen.

"Didn't know it was that late," said Dan.

Heffinger made a move as though to get up. "Come along over to my place, Dan'l, and have supper. I got a damn good cook now; he can make a mulligan that's worth going to El Paso for. Remember that dago sheepherder that went crazy —"

"*Went* crazy? Them fellers are born —"

"And I had to keep him in the hoosegow a while until he sort of come to? Well, I've got him out on parole now, and if I'd of knowed he could cook like he does I'd of —"

"Squat!" said Old Dan in an undertone which though hushed was emphatic. "There's company coming!"

Heffinger sank back into his chair and looked curiously to see whose entrance could have snared Dan's interest like that.

The double swing doors had snapped back, wide open, under the impact of ponderous shoulders, and Duke Morgan and "Preacher" Tom Colby came in abreast with a compact, swaggering squad of Morgans at their heels. Altogether there were ten of them, and they entered like the vanguard of a conquering army. Dan Westcott knew about half their number, at least by sight; Dave Heffinger knew the last man of them. Had Bolt Haveril been there all would have been familiar to him.

There was Duke's nephew, Budge Morgan; there were Duke's four sons, the brothers Tilford, Rance and Camden, and their half brother, Sid. There were Curly Morgan and Duke Baylis, the two guards Bolt had encountered at North Gate and had sent on their way bound and bootless. There was Morgan Blount, the man Bolt had put to sleep in Lady's cabin with the end of a six-gun.

"There's blood on the moon," grumbled Dave Heffinger, "and me, I'd be just as glad if I wasn't here."

"Me, too, Dave," said Dan. And added: "I thought when the Morgans wanted to get good and drunk they did it at home in the Valley. They're sure loaded to the muzzles right now."

"Yes," agreed Heffinger. "They're drunker'n lords already. As a usual thing, like you say, they keep a clear eye and a steady hand when they ride Outside. Something must of stirred old Duke up. He's not only drunk but he's mad and ugly and walking down the middle of the road."

"Who's the big fat man alongside him? No Morgan, is he?"

"Tom Colby," Heffinger explained. "Calls himself a preacher just to defy the Good Lord Himself, seeing he figures he's already defied the Morgans. Preacher Tom Colby that the devil could use to run his shop for him while he's off up here somewhere prospecting around."

By now Duke Morgan and Tom Colby, the two biggest-bodied men in the saloon, were forcing their way, still side by side, to the bar.

"Make room, make room, dammit!" roared Duke, and shoved a man out of his way. It was clear enough that he hadn't singled out any particular individual for his rough usage, it just chanced that the man he sent reeling and almost falling was a nondescript, slack-jawed newcomer to Red Luck who knew nothing of the Morgans and their ways and who, severely

150

jostled, had no desire to know them any better. He caught his balance, indulged in a bit of stifled cursing and retreated hastily to the far end of the long room.

Duke and Tom Colby got their elbows on the bar, the rest of the Morgans lined up alongside, and Duke's bellowing voice demanded the best in the house and plenty of it and damn quick if the barkeep didn't want his bar pulled up by the roots and scattered from hell to breakfast.

"And," roared Duke, pulling off his hat and flapping it down on the bar and then drunkenly getting it awry on the back of his head, "every man here that's a friend of Duke Morgan's steps up to the bar and has a drink. Any others can go to hell."

To Dave Heffinger, out of the corner of his mouth Dan Westcott remarked, "With a darn sight less advertising than this, I've seen right lively parties get under way." He brooded a moment in silence, horny thumb and forefinger tugging at a pouting lower lip while his shrewd old eyes were everywhere at once, taking in the expression of men's faces. But most of the men here wore their expressions at such a time as over a poker table. So Dan said to the Juarez County sheriff, "You know these fellers up here better'n I do, Dave; what's likely to happen?"

"Trouble, Dan, and plenty of it," sighed Heffinger, "but not right here and right now, maybe. You see, there's ten of them Morgans, every man of 'em packing a gun, every man anyhow half drunk and ready to start shooting at the drop of the hat. The other fellers here haven't got any particular personal quarrel with them,

151

and I guess they got sense enough to step soft out o'
the way and get home all in one piece. Let's see how
many stacks up to drink with Duke."

The first to stir after Duke's sonorous thunder rolled
away were the town's three patriarchs, old Doc Bitters,
the Judge and Sol Baumer. Without a word among
themselves or to anyone else these three took up their
glasses, quitted the bar and came over to a table near
that occupied by the two sheriffs in the corner.

Duke Morgan looked after them, at first with a frown
settling on his beetling brows like a storm cloud; then
he brought his hammerlike fist smashing down on the
bar and put his head back and burst into his
deep-throated laughter. Tom Colby stared after the
three old men, then pulled down the corners of his
wide mouth, rolled up his little piggish eyes in a way of
comic sanctimoniousness, while his mellifluous voice
carried on from where Duke's subsiding laughter left
off.

"The Lord gleaneth the harvest," he proclaimed. "He
picketh out the lumps of dirt from the bag of sound
beans; he winnoweth the sheep from the goats. Them
that is worthy shall be called to drink free whisky at the
right hand of Duke Morgan and the Right Reverend
Tom Colby. The rest, like Duke says, are hell-bound.
Let 'em slide, brethren, let 'em slide."

Other men for the most part ignored Duke's
invitation, going on quietly about their own drinking.
Six or eight men did line up at the bar; bar-flies they
were for the most part, bums and loafers, who would
drink with any man who paid the score. Duke looked

152

them over and promptly turned his broad back on them. Thus again he confronted Tom Colby.

"Tom," he said thickly, "you're drunk."

"You're drunker'n me, Duke," said Tom Colby. "For every drink you've downed, I've took one as big and sometimes bigger. There's no man living that can drink Tom Colby drunk."

"You're a liar, Tom," said Duke. "I can prove it." He yanked his gun out of his holster. "See that picture on the wall?" It was a faded likeness of America's first president against a background of red, white and blue. Other men, even those who did not appear to be listening, must have heard; as by magic a generously broad lane opened up through them the entire length of the room. "The left eye's the target, Tom, and the man that comes closest is sober."

Tom Colby shoved his hand down.

"No," he said. "No, Duke. That wouldn't prove nothing but that you're a better shot than me. So you are, drunk or sober. A better shot, Duke, but not a better drinker. There's no man living that —"

"You're a drunk fool, Tom!" shouted Duke.

Tom Colby winked slyly at any who would look at him.

"No man's a fool that's drunk," he chuckled. "He's a wise man! 'Look not on the wine when it is red,' says the good Book. That's wisdom for you too, Duke. Here's what the wise man, the man strong in the sight of the Lord, doth! Just watch, Duke!"

He pressed his enormous belly against the bar, reached for the bottle, filled his glass, tossed it off, filled it again, tossed that off, filled it again — and then stood looking at what his own hand had set before him as though he didn't know what it was or how it came there.

As he had done, so did Duke. With two swift drinks taken he was going Tom Colby one better, raising the third to his loose mouth when the soberest of his four sons, Rance, put a restraining hand on his arm.

"Look here, Duke," said Rance, "we'd better —"

Duke shot the contents of his glass into Rance's face. The young fellow staggered back, pawed at his eyes, got some of the fiery liquor out of them and gave voice to a roar of rage worthy of Duke himself.

"Damn you, Duke!" he yelled.

Duke, drunk or sober, was quicker and stronger and more brutal than most. His fist lashed out with all his weighty bulk behind it and Rance, taking the blow on the point of the chin, was unconscious before his head thudded on the bare floor. The wonder of the thing was that his neck was not broken.

No one said anything. There was not even a murmur to run through the crowd. The first to stir were Camden and Tilford Morgan. They lifted Rance from the floor and carried him out through the swing doors, into the open air. Nor were there changing expressions to be read on most faces. One, however, grinned and kept grinning; that was Sid's.

Then Tom Colby laughed.

"You can't get away with it like that, Duke, throwing your drink away," he said jocosely. "Already you're one drink behind me."

154

Duke refilled his glass, gulped it and filled it again. He turned then, caught both elbows on the bar behind him and sent his eyes roving up and down the room.

"I invited any of you boys that wanted to have a drink," he said slowly and heavily yet with no very great thickness of enunciation; even when drunk the man's forceful will was not to be altogether drowned. "Some of you took me up and some didn't. Those that did, I count Morgan friends. Now I'm going to tell you what it amounts to to have Duke Morgan for a friend. It might be a good idea if you listen good!"

"The other day some fellers tied rags over their faces, being scared of the Morgans, and went out and rounded up some other fellers for being Morgan's friends. They took those other fellers, all tied up hand and foot, over to Pocket Gully. They was going to round up another few Morgan friends and in the morning have them a fine hanging party!"

"Now, here's what happened: One of the fellers they was going to hang got loose, and he high-tailed to Dark Valley with the word. And when they heard that word the Morgans come out to take a hand. Because it ain't the habit with the Dark Valley Morgans to let their friends get hung. And it ain't going to be any Morgan habit!"

"Well, here's what happened: Them fellers that had hid their faces behind their rag masks found out that one man had got loose and had come high-tailing to me with the news. And they knew damn well what the answer would be, that the Morgans would pour out of

155

Dark Valley and into Pocket Gully to square the deal. That's what they knew so damn well that —"

"Well, here's what happened: Them fellers with the rags over their faces never lifted a hand against a single one of the fellers they swore they would hang! They fixed it so that all those fellers could get loose, that's what they did! They didn't have the guts to hang 'em, and they was scared of folks laughing at 'em if they didn't, and so they just fixed it so they could get loose themselves — and then it was them that did the high-tailing, and nary a man of 'em has opened his mouth about it since. Scared? Was they scared, them fellers that for a little while got too big for their britches and then wished they hadn't?"

He paused a moment, then slapped his leg and shouted: "Boys, was it funny? Was it the funniest damn thing you ever heard of?" And he roared with laughter.

Tom Colby laughed with him and smote him friendlywise on the beefy shoulder, and then all the Morgans still in the room laughed, and loudest and longest of all did Sid laugh. A few of Duke's invited guests along the bar cackled with him.

When the laughter subsided Duke Morgan wiped his eyes on the hairy back of a brawny forearm and said the rest of his say.

"I'm naming no names because those fellers all had masks on and so I can't be sure yet. But I've got me a hunch and it's a damn good hunch because news does leak out and I get to hear it, and here's the way it looks to me: There are two old fools not so far away right now that they can't hear me say it, and if they got as much sense as even a fool or a jackass has got, maybe they'll listen good." He craned his neck to look over into the corner where the two sheriffs sat; his eyes were clear enough to make out that over in the corner now were not two old fools only, but five. To make pointed that he ignored Doc Bitters and the Judge and Sol Baumer, he particularised sufficiently to indicate Dan Westcott and Dave Heffinger.

"I know I ain't seeing double," he said and sounded vastly good-humoured, "because if I was I'd just see four and I can see five old billy goats in here. I'm talking about two of 'em that maybe got it in their heads they can run the law in two counties when they lock their horns together like now. I give 'em fair warning like I do to all such as took it on themselves to hawg-tie some friends of mine over in Pocket Gully. They better remember that the Morgans were here in Red Luck and in Dark Valley long before a bunch of egg-sucking yeller pups yelled for the law to come in and stiffen their backbones for 'em. And the Morgans is here yet, to stay. Them two billy goats is warned."

When he stopped there was a silence, and every man in the room looked to see how Dan Westcott and Dave Heffinger took it.

Dan and Dave, old-timers at their trade, men who knew every bit as much lawlessness as of law, who had seen tall blusterers and cold killers come and go, had given no indication that they so much as heard a word Duke Morgan spoke. They too had sat silent, but not looking at him, neither of their old faces, finely

157

carved by time and weather and the strenuous lives they had lived, showing the least change.

It seemed that they would take no notice whatever of Duke, so long did the silence continue.

Then Dan Westcott spoke. He spoke across the table to Dave Heffinger and did not raise his voice above the quiet conversational tone, yet spoke with a clearness which carried his words to every attentive ear.

"Dave," he said, "I reckon somebody must have left a door open. Seems like there's a lot of wind blowing in here."

CHAPTER
FOURTEEN

It was their turn now for those others to laugh who had kept silent while Duke Morgan guffawed at his own wit. They had waited for something to release the pressure that had been storing up within them and their hearty volley of "Oh, ho, ho's!" if it didn't make the rafters ring must have set them quivering.

Duke's face turned crimson. His first natural, involuntary gesture was toward the gun at his hip. But drunk though he was he had not lost the use of that canny, cold mechanism which kept ticking away in his brain even when his blood was hot. The volume of suddenly released laughter told him something, and he listened and stiffened his big body as though to command it to steadiness, and to re-acquire that co-ordination of forces and faculties which was in danger of being disrupted.

That laughter told him how many of the men nearly filling the room now — for they had started crowding in pretty steadily as soon as Red Luck realized that the Morgans had come to town — were with him, how many against. Save for those few nondescripts who had crowded along the bar at his bidding to mop up free liquor, an obviously undependable crew, there were none here favouring the Morgan camp. If a Morgan started anything now the Morgans would have to finish it and — Well, the odds weren't right.

Here was a new experience for Duke Morgan; no man had ever laughed him down before. But then he usually looked the ground over before he took a step; he did not go out on the end of a limb. Too much strong drink to-night, too much swagger on the ride up from the Valley, too much heady triumph arising from the fact that the anti-Morgan faction that had thought itself bold enough to try to make an example of Morgan Outsiders had lost its nerve, had gotten cold feet, had in haste freed the men it had rounded up so courageously.

But there was a sort of rough, primitive dignity in Duke Morgan, that sort of dignity which is so impressive in an old lion, even though caged. He held himself in check as he would hold a rebellious horse; he kept his mouth clamped shut and his head up; he drew a long, whistling breath through his distended nostrils and slowly the crimson tide receded from his face.

"I guess you're right, Westcott," he said after a man could have counted a measured ten. "I guess I spoke out of turn. I guess I talked too much. I guess maybe I am drunk after all." He swept his arm backward, sending a couple of bottles and several glasses flying. He put some money on the bar without looking at it, gold pieces. "That's for drinks for any of my friends that's still thirsty," he said. Then he jerked his hat forward and for a moment stood there, his big thumbs hooked into his belt. He started to say something else by way of putting the rose petal on the full cup but repressed himself and turned toward the door.

"Just the same," shouted Budge, "what Duke said goes as she lays, and don't forget it. The Morgans are damn well fed up and —"

"Shut up, Budge," said Duke. "They heard it once. Let's go."

He shouldered his way out through the swing doors, Tom Colby following him with a quart bottle in his hand, Budge and the others bringing up the rear. Outside they came upon Tilford and Camden standing over Rance whom they had propped up against the wall; they had doused him with cold water and he was now blinking and looking about him stupidly. There was not much light where he was, as the moon was not yet risen, but a wan, diffused glow from above and below the half-doors showed him to his father.

Duke stooped over him, put a hand on the slack shoulder, giving it a not unkindly shake, and said:

"You're all right, Kid. Get up. We're riding."

"Sure," muttered Rance, and got to his feet. Duke helped him, put an arm loosely about him and took a step toward the hitching rail where the horses were. There he stopped and stared, and the rest stared with him as soon as they saw where he was looking. But they had turned their heads a second too late to see what Duke had seen.

They saw Crazy Barnaby with Stag at his heels.

Duke had seen Bolt Haveril pass in through the swing doors.

At least he had seen a man in rags, his feet wrapped in rags, going into the Barrel House. The man had not appeared to notice the Morgans. But he had heard Duke's voice, and just as the doors were snapping shut he had looked back.

"It's Juan Morada!" roared Duke.

Tom Colby began to laugh.

"I told you you was drunk, Duke," he jibed. "That's just Crazy Barnaby. The feller with him maybe looks sort of like Don Diablo, only it happens it's just a dawg and his name is Stag. Stag, short for stagger, and you're drunk."

He thrust his face into Duke's and Duke sent him reeling as he leaped to the door.

Inside, the lane which had opened up between Duke and the men in the far corner, had not yet closed in when Bolt entered. Dan Westcott, with a hard old eye still on the door, saw him and came to his feet with what amounted to a whoop of joy unbounded. Such was his old time affection for the young fellow, such his relief in seeing him alive, that he forgot all about the part Bolt was playing up here in the Red Luck country. That he did not shout out his name in greeting was just a bit of good luck, just because this was a moment when affectionate profanity would have its due.

"You son-of-a-gun!" he shouted gleefully, by way of warming up and culling richer epithets as he went on. "You —"

But his confrère Dave Heffinger, having only a sort of academic interest in young Haveril, though never a shrewder man than Dan, was just now a man steering

162

by cold reason instead of allowing himself to sail along on any emotional tide. Promptly he kicked Dan in the shin. He said sharply under his breath:

"It's that damn bandit Morada, ain't it? We're bound to arrest —" In a harsh whisper he said, "Here come the Morgans!"

Dan caught on, as they still say around Red Luck, like a house afire.

"Morada! Got you!" he yelled, and, his old gun with its worn walnut grip already in his hand, he made a bee line toward the door, and where he went there went also Dave Heffinger, likewise seemingly determined to have this desperado dead to rights, though he and Dan had to cut him down where he stood. "Get your hands up, Don Diablo!" added old Dan, and put in the warning he meant Bolt to grasp: "Make a mistake right now and you're a dead turkey."

By now the Morgans had crowded through the door and back into the room. Bolt saw them out of the corner of his eye. But he understood Dan's play and it was Dan he answered, paying no attention to the men at the door, appearing not to have seen them.

"If you're talking to me, Grandad," he said, leisurely about it and unconcerned, "haven't you maybe got your brains addled with too much Red Luck licker? Me, I'm a stranger up here. Morada and Diablo, who are they? Me, I'm Bolt Haveril, from Texas."

"Like hell you are!" yipped Dan still bearing down on him, then coming to anchor with their noses not four feet apart. "Don't I know John Morada when I see

163

him? If you ain't him, well then, you're his twin and will do just as well."

"You're Westcott, ain't you?" demanded Bolt, still easygoing. "Sheriff down in Rincon County?"

Duke Morgan, only a few steps behind Bolt, shouted:

"Damn you, Morada. It's me that's got you! You — !" Curly and Baylis and Morg Blount and Sid were all clamouring, every man of them with a personal grudge. But Westcott and Heffinger were every whit as eager and as swift, and again Dan was shouting them down.

"Keep your hands off my prisoner!" he warned them. "I been hunting this man for a solid week; he's wanted for murder down Texas way; he's a desperado name of Juan Morada and —"

Bolt with a single step had got his back to the bar. He thought, "There's apt to be wholesale murder here in a minute, and I'm dragging old Dan into it." He spoke to Dan now, but his eye was watchful on Duke and on the small, tight group of men behind him.

"No Rincon sheriff can arrest me up here in Juarez County," he said. "Keep out of this, Westcott."

Here was Dave Heffinger's cue and he snapped it up promptly.

"Me, I'm sheriff up here," he said, brisk and business-like. "Morada, you're under arrest; bat an eye and I'll blow your head off. You, Morgan, hands off. If you got any quarrel with this man —"

"Boys," said Duke to his followers, and sounded cold sober, "this man Morada is my bacon. And I want him alive, or anyhow only half dead when we drag him out, as I got some questions to ask him. If anybody else starts in, let 'em have it!"

As quick as a flash Dan Westcott called out:

"All the rest of you fellers here is deputized right now deppity sheriffs! Burn the Morgans down, the whole bloody pack, if a man pulls a gun!"

Somebody called out, one of the Morgan nondescripts it was, "How's the Rincon sheriff deppitizing men in Red Luck?"

Again Dave Heffinger was ready for his cue.

"Boys," he announced, almost quoting Westcott word for word, "I'm deputizing every man of you. Fill your hands for the good of Red Luck and start dropping Morgans as fast as they start anything." Then he stepped up to Bolt and clapped a hand on his shoulder. "You're under arrest, Morada," he said.

"Me?" said Bolt. "But I tell you —"

"Never mind telling me anything until I ask you something," snapped Heffinger. "Come along."

"Listen," said Bolt. "Listen, sheriff. If you want to run somebody in, grab that feller." He jerked his head around toward Duke Morgan. "He's a damn horse thief that we ought to hang to the first tree. I'll come along later; it's just a mistake anyhow; but Duke Morgan there stole my horse, a big red stallion. It's tied out there to the rack now."

"Why, you — !" began Duke.

"That horse would clinch the proof this is Morada," cried old Dan. "Everybody knows that horse; a big red stud they call El Colorado —"

165

"Shucks," said Bolt. "He's my horse now and his name's Daybreak."

All this talk had slowed down action which otherwise would no doubt have been of the violently explosive order. There was now a compact semi-circle forming about Bolt and the two sheriffs and Morgan's party, Red Luck citizens who little by little had warmed to the occasion. And in nearly every hand was a gun, in nearly every pair of eyes a look that boded no good to Duke Morgan.

Again Duke paid respect to the high card. He knew he could never drag his Don Diablo out of here alive, and he wanted him alive long enough to come to some understanding of a riddle which was mightily perplexing and troubling him. He knew too that if he came to grips with those two old billy goats, backed up as they were by a roomful of anti-Morgan men, there was little expectation of any Morgan riding home all in one piece that night. So again he showed that he could accept the cards as they fell and could hold a check rein on the hardest man to handle he had ever dealt with, namely Duke Morgan.

"Let's go," he commanded, and turned back toward the door. But over the thick bulk of his shoulder he said to Bolt, "I haven't finished with you, Morada."

"Right you are," returned Bolt coolly. He looked Morgan in the eye a moment, then added with quiet gravity: "I want my horse back. And I want a word or two with you yet. I'm not going to jail in this man's town, Duke, and you can tie to that. I'll be dropping in on you down in the Valley before long."

166

Duke stared at him, looked more mystified than ever, and went out without replying. Sid, most reluctant of all to abandon the chase, was muttering to Duke as they went out:

"He's making a monkey out of you, Duke. I don't believe he's Morada at all. I told you what I heard him telling Lady —"

"Shut up!" roared Duke. "You heard him tell her he was and he wasn't, didn't you?"

As the doors closed the second time on the Morgans' departure, the two sheriffs closed in on their prisoner. Westcott slid the gun out of Bolt's holster and jammed it in his own belt. Heffinger, coming up to Bolt's other side, said to the quiet roomful of men:

"Thanks, boys," and added with a grin, "Consider yourselves all un-deppitized and fired. Me and Dan can take care of the rest." He paused a moment, thought it over soberly, then added: "I won't say I won't be taking you on again soon. Duke Morgan's kind of overplaying his hand of late. If it happens we need some help later on, well I'll see that you boys get a chance to get in on it."

Then he and Dan escorted Mr. Bolt Haveril from Texas out through the back door, down a dark alley, and toward an old adobe house on the edge of the town, the bachelor abode of Juarez County's sheriff.

"Wait a shake," said Bolt. He was between the two, his arms were tucked through theirs, one couldn't have said for certain whether here went two officers of the law hanging on tight to their desperado or whether they were three friends triumphantly arm-in-arm. "I almost forgot Barnaby."

"Crazy Barnaby?" said Heffinger. "Was he with you? I saw him come in right behind you; him and a big dog."

"He mustn't slip away," said Bolt. "It's important."

"I'll go back and get him," offered Heffinger. "You two go ahead to the house. But we won't want Barnaby with us, will we? While we sort of talk things over?"

"No. But I want him later. He's hungry; we're both half starved. Maybe —"

"Sure," said Heffinger. "I'll get one of the boys to stake him to supper and keep an eye on him."

So he turned back to the Barrel House, and Bolt and Dan, still arm-in-arm, went on to Heffinger's house.

"Kind of good to see you again, kid," said Dan. "Even if you do look like you'd been to a masquerade party and had maybe met a mountain lion on the way."

Bolt gave Dan's sinewy old arm a squeeze.

"It is sort of kind of good," he admitted, and added, "I hope Heffinger's got something to eat over at his place —"

"He was just bragging of his cook and inviting me to supper. What about the girl, Bolt?"

"They got her back, Dan. I'll tell you when Heffinger's back with us. And after we make him prove what his cook can do."

"Hmf! So they got her away from you, huh? Well, I told you, Kid —"

"I haven't finished yet," said Bolt.

168

CHAPTER
FIFTEEN

"Dave," said Dan Westcott when the three drew their chairs up to the table, "I don't rec'lec' that you and this young limb of Satan has ever been introduced proper. Sheriff Heffinger, shake with Bolton Haveril, known of late as Don Devil Morada."

"Glad to know you, Haveril," said Dave, and the two shook, as commanded. "I was afraid that maybe Duke Morgan would exterminate you before I got a chance to see you, and I didn't want that to happen — being as you owe me for a new hat."

He had sent his cook, Frenchy, out of the house, giving him a couple of dollars and watching him scurry off to the Barrel House. Then the doors had been locked, shades pulled down and the three had their chance to talk over their supper.

"Didn't I tell you Bolt was the best shot in seven states?" chuckled old Dan. "Me, I taught him how, that's why. Huh, Bolt?"

"And how to ride and rope and most everything else, Dan," said Bolt and reached for his coffee cup. "Man, but this is good! And talking about hats — what about footgear? Wonder if I can ever coax these feet of mine back into a pair of boots? And I could do with a shirt, too, and —"

"Funny to come home without any boots on," murmured Dan. "A feller would say offhand, just looking at you, that something had scared you so bad you jumped clean out'n 'em, and had been running ever since. Let's have it, Bolt."

"Give the man a chance to eat, can't you?" said Heffinger; " 'Tain't every day a man gets a show to eat Frenchy's cooking."

When the tale was told Dan Westcott sat head down rolling a meditative cigarette, his lips puckered, and Dave Heffinger sat like his *alter ego* stuffing tobacco tight into the black, cracked bowl of an ancient pipe. Neither man looked up for a long while, neither had any comment to make or question to ask. The full data of a present problem were before them; each liked to do his own bit of thinking before he spoke.

At last Dave Heffinger lighted his pipe and stood up.

"I'll step over to the store and bring back some boots for you to try, Haveril," he said then. "And a shirt. Anything else?"

"Get yourself a new hat," grinned Bolt. "I haven't any money with me so you better charge it to Juarez County."

"The boots, too?" grunted Dave.

Dan unpocketed a money pouch. "Here you are, Dave," he said. "I'll take it out'n the Kid's hide later."

"And get the biggest boots in the store," Bolt added. "These feet of mine are swollen seven sizes. And some arnica, if you haven't got any, and socks. Then some day when you come down my way I'll barbecue a beef for you and put flowers in your hair and give you the ranch."

Dave Heffinger stepped along, taking time on his errand, time to smoke his pipe and think. But when he returned and dumped his bundles down on a chair there was no light of inspiration in his eyes.

"We're right where we started," he said bluntly, "and them damn Morgans is still laughing. And let me tell you boys something: It ain't healthy for a sheriff's business to get laughed at too loud and too long. If we can't handle that outfit pretty *pronto* I'd better quit and make room for some young feller with more enthusiasm than brains. He'd *do* something about it."

"We ain't licked yet," growled Dan Westcott.

"Then I don't want ever to get licked! What do you call it? And what are we going to do about it?"

"I've had a few words with Bolt," said Westcott.

"Me, I said we could dig up some good enough reason to raid the Valley and drive the whole caboodle of them Morgans clean out'n the State. Bolt he says, 'No.' He swears they'd kill the girl rather than —"

"Oh, damn the girl!" snapped Heffinger. "She's got to take her chance. And she's another Morgan anyhow, and —"

"Slam on the brakes, Dave!" Westcott let his eyes slash sidewise at Haveril. "Seems as though our young friend here is already dead in love with her!"

Bolt stared at him, wondering what on earth had put that into the old fellow's head; surely he himself hadn't said a word of such a thing! But as both men probed at him with those shrewd old eyes of theirs he felt his face getting hot until even his ears burned. Dan stabbed him with a horny thumb and giggled at him; Dave said, "Hmf!"

"Suppose you two old turkey buzzards cut out the comedy and get this straight," said Bolt tartly. "Here's why you can't raid the Valley: It belonged to Thad Morgan and he was the father of the girl and young Bob, who's trying to come through alive, down at my place, after being shot up by Morada and his gang. Thad Morgan's will left Dark Valley to Lady and Bob, share and share alike. They're both minors. So Duke planned to keep them sewed up tight until they were old enough to sign their ownership over to him. How he would have made them do what he wanted — well, you boys know as well as I do. Let Duke get anybody shut away in Dark Valley and he'll find the way to get what he wanted."

"Yes, but —" was as far as Heffinger got when Bolt hurried on.

"Hold it a shake, Dave. Bob got away. Duke figured he might streak south, figured he had to get safe away; and that's why he sicked Morada on him, knowing enough of Morada by a reputation that smells to high heaven to know that he'd do anything for a fistful of gold. *Bueno.* But now we've got Duke rattled: He figures me for Morada, and even of that he isn't dead sure, for it's a cinch Sid told him all he overheard me saying to Lady Morgan. Next, Duke don't know whether young Bob Morgan is dead or alive. It's to get the right slant on these things that he's so anxious to get me back where he can talk to me like a couple of Dutch uncles. Got all that?"

"Now this, why you can't raid him. I tell you he'd never bat an eye at killing the girl; he'd do away with her and simply make sure we never found any sort of trace of her, and that would be dead easy for him to wangle down there in that wild valley. With her out of the way, then with somebody making sure that Bob was tucked under, you can bet that he'd see that the property was scooped into his hands. The title would go from these kids to the nearest of kin, some Morgan or other. It would mean a mess for him to straighten out, not anything like as simple as getting deeds from Bob and Lady, but better a damned sight for Duke than letting the thing he loves most on earth, the only thing that he does love, that Valley, slip clean out of his claws. Got all that? *Bueno, amigos,* then you've got all there is, and you see why you can't scare up a hundred shooting rampaging Morgan-haters and turn 'em loose to grub the Morgans out."

They listened attentively, nodded grudgingly and waited for him to add something. For his part he got up, opened Dave's bundles and began trying to get a pair of boots on tortured feet.

"You got something in mind, damn you," said Dan testily. "Fire ahead and me'n Dave'll listen some more."

"I'm going back into the Valley, and I'm going alone," said Bolt. "I tell you Morgan's rattled already. I'm going to have a little pow-wow with him. And if I can't get that girl out this time — Well, you boys can raise your army and fly your skull and crossbones and march."

"I told Dan in the first place," said Heffinger bluntly, "that you had bit off more'n you could chew; that no one man could get away with a job like that one you picked out. And to go try it again — Hell, man, you might as well save time and trouble, hiring somebody to cut your throat. I'll bet Frenchy'd do it for two bits."

"No," said Bolt. "If Duke caught me when I wasn't looking for him, you might be right. But if I go looking for him it's different. Anyhow, I've got to do it. To-night. You boys can scare me up a horse, can't you? Two horses."

Dan said a thoughtful, unpersuaded, "Hmmm," drawing it out like the hum of a drowsy old bee. "After what you've told us," he commented, "I've a notion you wouldn't get any farther than the North Gate; pretty sure not to, Bolt, if them two fellers you played tricks on the other night happen to be there. Curly and Baylis; I saw how friendly they looked at you just now. If they don't take you apart this trip —"

"I wouldn't go in at the gate," said Bolt. "There's another way in that even the Morgans don't know about."

"There is, huh?" exclaimed Dave. "It's hard believing — Say! The way young Bob Morgan made his getaway?"

"No. Bob didn't know about it either. He climbed the cliffs at the south end. You see he'd got to be dead certain that if he stuck in the Valley he wouldn't be living a couple of months from now. It was either get out somehow or wait for the time for Duke to cut him down — him and Lady, too. So he took all the chances there were, as a man would to escape certain death. He told me, even so, he wouldn't tackle it again, no matter what. He barely made it; a bit of rotten cliff broke off under his feet; a sort of fingernail hold saved him. And he says now, with that chunk of cliff slipping, a squirrel could hardly make it. No, Dave, there's another way, and none of the Morgans know where it is. They do know that there is such a pass, and they'd give a lot to know where it is. That's all."

"Then how in thunder," muttered Westcott, "do you expect —"

But Dave Heffinger glimpsed the truth.

"Crazy Barnaby!" he exclaimed. "Crazy Barnaby!"

"Barnaby, yes. That's why I've asked you to keep him here a while. You see he dropped in on the Morgans about three years ago and they didn't know how the devil he popped up under their feet with nobody seeing him coming into the valley. Duke would have beat it out of him but it didn't take him two shakes to see that Barnaby wasn't like other folks; you could beat him to death, cut him to ribbons, do anything all hell could think up, and Barnaby would just go on laughing or singing or listening to voices."

"Crazy folks is different," conceded Dan.

"Crazy? Gosh, I wish I knew, Dan! Maybe it's just that he's so darn much smarter than the rest of us that we call him that. I've spent the last three days and nights with him; with him and the dog Stag. They're a funny pair, Barnaby and Stag. I got to — hang it, they're all right, those two."

"Crazy Barnaby has always come and went as he pleased," said Heffinger, thinking back. "Folks has tried to pump him, to ask all sorts of fool questions about what goes on in the Valley; me, I've even had a whack or two at him myself." He shook his head. "No good. That's why the Morgans would let him do as he pleased, I guess; they knew him. Start questioning him and he begins to hear voices; he darts off like a streak, his bells a-ringing, saying something is caught in a trap somewhere or a timber wolf is sick and can't fed its babies, or something."

"I think," said Bolt, "that the Morgans let him go free because they were always hoping they could find out which way he went. They'd sneak along after him and to Barnaby it was a game, hide-and-seek, you know, and every time he'd outfox 'em."

"And he's going to tell you? You mean to say he wouldn't tell anybody else, not young Bob, not Lady, who you say he's crazy about, and he's going to tell you?"

"Yes. It's funny; just a streak of luck. Nothing but luck it was that gave me the right idea how to wangle this out of him. He calls it his Secret; he sort of holds to it like something he was hugging tight in both arms. He would always laugh at the puzzled way the Morgans would look at him whenever he popped up in the Valley and they didn't know how in thunder be had done it. A game, that's what it was to Barnaby, *sabe?* Just a game. He wouldn't tell Lady even; he'd just laugh like a kid and start capering around whenever she'd ask him. And when she tried to show him how terribly in earnest she was, how scared to stay there, he'd just say: 'Nothing will ever hurt you, Lady. Duke won't. He can't. God won't let him.'"

"I don't know as even God could find His way into that damn sink-hole," growled Dan.

"You see," Bolt went on, "when Duke and the rest of 'em overhauled Lady and Barnaby and me, with Stag leading 'em on, Barnaby was having the time of his life. He wouldn't believe anybody was in any sort of danger; it was just his favourite game of hide-and-seek. And when he and Stag and I were alone after that, he was forever playing his game with Stag, trying to get me in on it, too. All of a sudden I got my hunch; I said, 'Barnaby let's you and me and Stag have some fun with the Morgans. They caught us this time; let's slip in on them in the Valley and surprise 'em and have some fun.' And Barnaby hasn't thought of much since. He won't tell me where his Secret is, but he'll show me. So now, if you two boys will scare up the horses, we'll get started." He made a wry face. "Gosh, it'll be good to fork a saddle again! I'm never going to walk another step in my life I don't have to. I'd rather ride from here to Alaska than walk a mile."

Westcott got his head down again over the long-drawn-out construction of a cigarette which those expert fingers could have rolled in a flash. Heffinger, sucking at a pipe that had gone cold, was every whit as thoughtful. He started to speak, looked over at Dan and shrugged. Dan and Bolt were old friends; it was up to

177

them. To Heffinger, as he had already said, Bolt's return to the Valley, especially right now with Duke in the murderous mood riding him, smacked of suicide. Well it was the sort of thing a feller like young Haveril would do, a young feller with his brains all gummed up with a girl.

Dan finally got his cigarette made; he kept rolling it until it was as smooth as a pencil.

"I've knowed fellers that could do it with one hand," he said looking placidly reminiscent. He glanced up. "Maybe you can, huh, Bolt?"

"Seems like you taught me that, too, Dan," Bolt grinned back at him.

"Hmmm," said Dan.

"Who's ready for another drink?" asked Dave.

"Let's see," mused Dan aloud. "You want a horse, huh, Bolt? It's a good twenty mile to the Valley. Hmmm. You'd ruther ride back and forth twixt this and Alaska twenty times than walk over to the Morgans'. Well, maybe me'n Dave can scare you up a pony; one for Barnaby, too. But horses costs something in this man's country, Kid. And you've about run out of credit, buying shoes and such, seems like."

"What are you driving at now?" Bolt had to wonder.

"I mean we'll make a trade. We'll do as you say provided you do as we say, which is a fair deal and not robbing anybody. You and Barnaby ride on ahead. Me and Dave and maybe some of the boys follow. You find the way to get into the Valley without the Morgans knowing you're there until you're there. And us fellers tails you in."

178

"No go, Dan. The set-up hasn't changed any; it's the same old thing of the Morgans being ready at any moment to do away with Lady. If you old fellers came storming into the Valley she wouldn't last five minutes. You can see that with both eyes shut. For more reasons than one, Duke won't ever let her go if he can help it."

"Well, there's this," said Dan. "Suppose you go alone, suppose your luck turns out no better'n last time. Maybe even a mite worse. Suppose you get kilt, Bolt. Then what happens to the cute girlie with the big baby-blue eyes?"

"They're grey, and —" Bolt got that far on the side track, then came back to the main question. "Yes, there's something in that, Dan. For some other time, maybe, you boys ought to know Barnaby's trail. All right; you and Dave come along. When we get pretty near there you can pretend to turn off somewhere else; I know darned well that Barnaby wouldn't stand for it if the three of us asked him his secret. You two can fall back and follow us. There'll be a moon pretty soon. Let's ride."

"Fine," said Heffinger. "I'll get us some horses —"

"Only," Bolt cut in, "you two have to promise me not to horn in on this play until I've shot my wad. That's understood, ain't it?"

"Hell, yes," said Dave and went his way. From the door he called back, "I'll bring Barnaby with me here. You two gents help yourselves to things."

They expected him to be gone fifteen or twenty minutes perhaps. When he had not returned in half an hour they thought nothing of it. When an hour had passed they began to wonder. Then Dave Heffinger came in and closed the door softly and just stood there with his back to it, looking at them. His face was as hard and stern as a face carved from granite. His eyes were about as pleasant as two polished stones.

"Dan," he said, his voice brittle with suppressed anger, "get your hat on. We're raiding the Morgans, and to hell with anything Haveril here has to say against it. We're closing in on 'em like you said, from both sides like the upper and the lower grindstone. We're stomping 'em into the face of the earth. I've sent word out for every damn man that can ride and shoot, and that wants to put in a lively night's work, to come along."

"Dammit, no!" shouted Bolt.

"Shut up, Kid," said old Dan mildly. "Can't you see something's preying on Dave's mind?" To Dave he said just as mildly: "Sounds kind of nice, Dave. Let's have the rest of it."

"Know Ed Daly, Dan? Rancher over at Rincon Alto?"

Dan wrinkled his forehead. "Can't say's I do, Dave — hold on a shake! Rincon Alto ranch? Say, that's the outfit —"

"Sure," said Dave heavily. "That's him, Ed Daly. His ranch got raided last spring. Dark o' the moon it was, and nobody could ever say who the raiders was. Anyhow they burned Ed out and they scattered his stock through the mountains; they got a bullet through Ed's right arm and — well, he had two fine, big,

180

half-grown sons, Dan — a couple young tigers that tore into the raiders like mad — and both got killed. Yep, that's who Ed Daly was."

"Was?" Dan demanded sharply.

"Likewise," continued Dave, and Bolt saw how the weathered, leathery cheeks had turned faintly pink, and how up on the cheek bones the pink was slowly turning into red blotches, "Ed Daly was one of our crowd that took a hand in the Pocket Gully fiasco the other night. Yep, he's been ag'in the Morgans most all his life. Well, they got him. Just now, and that don't happen to be all there is to it. They — they — Damn!" said Dave, and stalked to his jug on the table.

They waited in silence for him to drink and to take his time about it. He cleared his throat and blew his nose.

Bolt stiffened under the baleful gleam directed at him from Heffinger's wintry eyes.

"You and that damn Morgan girl of yours!" said Dave, firing up into bright anger. "As though she was the only girl in the world! Ed Daly was as fine a man as ever did his damndest to keep skunks chased out'n his hen yard. Well, he had a girl, too. That's Molly Daly that I've knowed since the day she was born. Only sixteen, little Molly, pretty as a doll, with great big blue eyes looking wondering at the world, as good and sweet a little thing — Well, she's gone."

"Good Lord," gasped Bolt. "You don't mean —"

"The Morgans has got her. Young Rance Morgan seen her once and kept looking at her. He never got a chance; Ed Daly saw to that. Well, Ed like I say, was in on the Pocket Gully play. He figgered that when his handkerchief slipped, one of the Morgan Outsiders saw his face. He remembered what they'd done to him once; he heard they was out hell-riding again; he got worried about Molly. He was on his way just now, bringing her to town, meaning to send her out to her aunt's, over in Bigby City. Well, he runs into the Morgans only a few miles out of town. Happened just after they left here. Rance wanted her. Duke had just slapped Rance down; you saw that. To show the kid there was no hard feeling, and Duke being drunk at the time, he says, 'Hell, Kid, you can have her.' So they shot Ed Daly down and took the girl along to the Valley."

"How'd you get to know all this?" demanded Westcott. "Daly still alive?"

"Nope. Dead when he got here, dead before the Morgans rode on. They wasn't taking any chances, same as usual. That is, they thought they wasn't. But for once they overlooked something. You see, Ed Daly was bringing Molly's trunk along with her, and so he was using a wagon — and in the bed of the wagon was one of his men that had took sick, and so Ed was bringing him in to the doctor. He was laying there with a blanket over him and he kept laying still; he heard all that happened. About that time Bud Clark and Sam Harper was jogging into town. They heard the shots. They brought Daly's sick man in. He's at the Barrel House now."

"I reckon after this," said Dan, "we won't have much trouble making up a party to ride with us, will we, Dave?"

182

"All hell couldn't hold 'em back now! There'll be a hundred men —"

"Listen to me, you two!" cried Bolt. "Damn it, listen!"

They looked at him, then at each other, and Dave sat down.

There was no denying a man who looked at them as Bolt did.

CHAPTER
SIXTEEN

Bolt Haveril was still talking in such desperate dead earnestness that he held his two listeners silent despite their restlessness, when there came to the three the sounds of the hurried approach of many men. The oncoming steps were like muffled drum beats accompanying a raucous chorus of voices; the voices were not unduly lifted but sullen, ominous, fateful. The steps came on, louder; the voices fell away. When a man struck with hard angry knuckles on the door and called, "Heffinger, come out here. We want you," there was no other sound.

Dave Heffinger's frowning eyes cleared and his head came up with a jerk.

"Well, I've heard you out, Haveril," he said in a curt undertone. "Now you better step in the next room; you're supposed to be my prisoner, remember."

Bolt went into the kitchen, leaving the door open. Heffinger opened the front door and stepped out on the porch. Dan Westcott sat where he was.

"Well, boys?" said Heffinger.

The man who had rapped and called spoke for the others. Dave knew him well, a young rancher named Steve Kendal. Ed Daly's nearest neighbour, was Steve, and of late men had been joshing him about Molly Daly. A keen, clean-cut fellow in his early twenties, yet Steve had been accounted a man since he was fifteen when he was out on his own, forcing others to accept him at his own valuation as an individual who had put boyish things behind him. Quick with the joy of life, Steve had always been; full of the devil, as men put it. To-night that long face of his and the large, generous mouth didn't seem properly to belong to Steve Kendal but to a man far older, one little given to humorous, good-natured ways. Heffinger, with all his experience with hardened humanity at its worst, had never seen a man who looked more like a killer.

"Ed Daly's dead, you know," said Steve. "The Morgans murdered him."

"I know," said Heffinger.

"They got Molly," said Steve. He spoke quite calmly and steadily, his voice low-toned and distinct; just the same Dave had seen his Adam's apple rise and fall before he spoke of Molly.

"I know," said Heffinger.

"Doing anything about it, Dave?"

Heffinger nodded. "Yes, Steve."

"What? And when?" asked Steve.

Heffinger didn't hurry in answering. First of all he wasn't used to consulting with others about what he meant to do, or how or when. Beyond that he was still thinking of all that young Haveril had said; there might be sense in some of it. Third, the Morgans had already got safe away with the girl; no use rushing off after them half-cocked, making a mess of things.

But also Heffinger had to take Steve Kendal into consideration; those cold, steady yet haunted eyes of his would take a good deal of forgetting. And there were the men, a score or so of them, behind Steve; and a lot of other men at the Barrel House, their numbers swelling steadily, men who he knew were growing more and more violent with every word said, every drink swigged down. For Ed Daly was as popular a man as ever spurred into Red Luck for a Saturday evening. And as for little Molly — Dammit, it was all Dave Heffinger could do to hold himself back from flying off the handle himself!

"We're going to bring little Molly back, Steve," he said. He put his hand on Steve's shoulder as he said that and gave it a quick, hard squeeze. He hadn't meant to; just couldn't help it. "And we're going to mop up the Morgans. To-night."

"We'll wait for you over to the Barrel House, Dave," said Kendal. "Quite a few of the boys will be wanting to ride along."

"Hold on a shake, Steve." Heffinger's eyes passed beyond him to the men on the porch and in the yard, a quiet, determined lot. "You boys do something for me, will you? Get back to the Barrel House as fast as you can; I want a couple of words with Steve here, then we'll be over. You fellers make as sure as you can that nobody ducks out that might be carrying word over to the Morgans; no use telling 'em we're coming. Me 'n Steve won't keep you waiting."

"There's nothing to talk about, Dave," said Steve. "Time's gone by for that."

"You might be sort of glad later if you did what I want," Heffinger told him and turned back into the house. Steve hesitated only a second, then followed. The others, one or two calling out, "All right, Dave; only, like Steve says, time's gone by for talking," moved off.

In the house, Dave closed the door and Bolt came in from the kitchen. Steve Kendal looked at him sharply, then at Heffinger for an explanation.

"He ain't Juan Morada at all, Steve," said Dave. "You two fellers can shake, Bolt Haveril from down Texas way, Steve Kendal from White Horse Valley, the other side Rincon Alto." They shook gravely, and Dave said: "Squat. It's this feller Haveril you got to listen to a minute, Steve, before we tear the lid off'n hell. First, I'll tell you about him."

He made his story short. Steve sat listening to him, looking now and then at Haveril.

"Well?" was all that he had to say at the end.

"It's like this," said Heffinger. "All along the Morgans had done pretty much all the devilment they wanted to, and yet they've kept clear of the law. We all knowed it was them raided Ed Daly last spring; but you'll remember Ed himself was one of the first to speak up and say that after all we didn't know it. We thought it, we was pretty damn sure, we said it must of been, but there wasn't a man of us could swear to it. It *could* have been somebody else; it could have been that wild bunch over beyond the Ridge that's been raising hell in the mining country of late. And Ed Daly himself said so, and he said he was damned if he was going to be a party to a lot of men getting killed and a lot of bad blood stirred up, unless he was sure."

"Ed Daly's dead now," said Steve stonily. "The Morgans killed him. And this time we're sure."

"But the Morgans don't know we're sure! As far as they know they didn't leave any witnesses. They didn't know Ben Shuckton was lying there in the wagon, taking it all in. They think, like other things they've done, the best we can do is guess about it."

"Well?" said Steve again, a hint more sharply now as it began to seem to him that Dave Heffinger, despite his promises on the porch, was about to hedge and temporize.

Heffinger turned to Haveril.

"Tell him your slant, Bolt," he said, and began filling his pipe.

Bolt thought that Steve Kendal looked hard hit. Must have been a mighty good friend of Ed Daly's, he thought. He didn't realize at first that it was little Molly that Steve was thinking about.

"It's like this," said Bolt. "Ed Daly's dead and we can't help that. It's his daughter we've got to think about —"

And then he understood as he saw the cording of Steve's lean jaws, and the sort of look that came into his eyes. He went on swiftly then, already sure he could count on having Steve Kendal's voice added to his own in an insistence upon carrying out Bolt's plan.

"There are two girls in the valley that we've got to think about. One of them is Lady Morgan; Dave has told you about her and how she nearly got clear and they got her back. She knows and I know that Duke Morgan would kill her before he let her go. Then there's Molly Daly. With the Morgans thinking they carried her off with no one seeing, what's the first thing Duke Morgan would do? He'd knock her in the head like another man would brush a mosquito off the back of his neck; he'd bury her so deep you'd never find a trace of her; he could even dynamite the side of a cliff to bury her under a hundred thousand tons of rock and dirt — and he'd swear and every man in the Valley would swear with him that they hadn't even laid eyes on her or Ed Daly either. He'd have to do that, wouldn't he, Steve? Wouldn't he know that if it was ever found out for sure that he had Molly Daly he'd be lucky to just get torn apart fast instead of having it happen slow?"

They all watched Steve as he sat staring down at the floor, turning all this over in his mind.

"Yes, you're right," he said at last. "I guess I wasn't thinking clear." He began taking Bolt's measure as he had not done before. "You've thought out something else. What is it?"

"I am going down into the Valley alone. Right away. I can get in without anyone knowing. I'm making another try at getting Lady Morgan away, and —"

"Alone? I'm going with you."

Bolt shook his head. "No can do, Steve. It won't work." He explained about Barnaby. "He wouldn't stand for it. Besides —"

"He'll have to stand for it! Or I can sneak along behind you two, and find my way in where you go."

"And when you get there?"

"I'm thinking clear too now," said Steve.

"I'll find Duke Morgan. I am going to kill him. Him and Rance Morgan —"

"Maybe!" cut in Bolt curtly. "You can be mighty sure they'll kill you!"

"Maybe," said Steve. "But there won't be any killing until I tell them that Ben Shuckton was in the wagon and heard and saw, and that now all Red Luck knows — and that if a hair of Molly Daly's head is touched every damn Morgan of 'em will be a dead Morgan in twenty-four hours."

"But look here, Steve —"

"You look here, Haveril! I've heard you out; I know what you're thinking about — you're just thinking about that Morgan girl. Well, get it into your head that there's another girl that's worth a million —"

"Easy, Steve!" said Heffinger sharply.

Steve swallowed a couple of times. "Sure, Dave." He tried to smile but couldn't make much of a go of it; still it showed his intent. He was quiet-spoken again as he resumed: "You see how it is, Haveril. I think quite a lot of Molly. And she — well, we was just waiting until she was a little older and — those damned Morgans! To have one of them even look at her —"

"I know," said Bolt. "I know, Steve."

He got up and limped up and down the room. He began to feel as though he knew Molly. A sweet little sixteen-year-old kid. To-night she had seen those drunk devils murder her father; she had been carried off by them, held maybe in Rance's arms or Duke's, their hot,

190

whisky-laden breaths burning her throat, stifling her. And by now? So he had to say, "I know, Steve," and limp up and down trying to think straight. The thought came to him that there were times when a man could do a lot better job of straight shooting than straight thinking. And it would be a lot more fun too.

When he spoke at last it was to the two hardbitten old sheriffs who like a couple of sphinxes had waited in all patience upon the younger men.

"Steve and I, more than any others outside Dark Valley, are most tied up in this thing. Let Steve come with me. He'll make it. I can fix it with Barnaby, or somehow I'll leave trail for Steve to follow me pretty close. When we get inside — well, we'll do what we can. If we just make a mess of it the way I did before, then you boys can cut loose and do your damnedest."

Then Dan Westcott spoke up for the first time in a long while. He was as brisk as a cricket.

"Dave, suppose we give these young wildcats their heads? They can't do any harm beyond getting their hides nailed to Duke's barn door, and that's where many a hide may be sunning soon. Your'n and mine along with the rest if the Good Lord's about ready to call us home. Meantime you and me'll get right busy."

"Let's have the rest of it, Dan," said Heffinger.

"You know all the boys up here better'n what I do. Suppose you scare up as big a party that's dependable as you can. Suppose then we split that party three ways. Get 'em started right off, one gang to the North Gate, one to Middle Gate, one to South Gate."

191

After that they sat in brief council, to arrange details and make sure that everything was understood.

Then Bolt and Steve went for their horses and to join Barnaby, and Dan Westcott and Dave Heffinger stepped along to the Barrel House.

CHAPTER
SEVENTEEN

Lady Morgan, again in the gloom of Dark Valley, mocked and jeered at and cursed, had been sunk so deep into despondency that it was like going down deep into the caverns of a jet black sea with the sun and moon and stars and all hope shut away. She thought that she had known despair before. Never had she dreamed of such despair as this. For Bolt Haveril had come and she had tasted not only freedom but an undreamed companionship; it was like birds in springtime singing in her heart. And now all that was as something that had never really been, something which had visited her in a day-dream under a blue summer sky.

She had tried to run when they had closed in upon her and Barnaby; it had been Sid, a laughing devil, who had captured her. She had tried to shoot him then, but it was no use; she was spent and Sid struck her arm down and dragged her weapon from her nerveless fingers and laughed at her until she screamed and put her fingers in her ears and then threw herself face down upon the ground and broke into wild weeping. Then Duke, sitting straight on the big red stallion, had ridden up and sat there laughing at her along with Sid. And then they had brought her back to Dark Valley. Duke had ridden ahead, singing in that lusty, deep voice of his.

Now, back again in Dark Valley, a new strange loneliness joined hands to utter hopelessness to crush her down into those profound depths which she had plumbed. Nearly all her life she had been much alone, but being alone is not what constitutes that bleak feeling which is so like an exile's nostalgia, which makes the world empty and meaningless and so infinitely sad. The most poignant loneliness is that of a wanderer among crowds that are utterly alien. Such was Lady Morgan's now.

When her father had died he had left behind him Lady's mother, a frail mountain flower of a woman who never got quite used to the ruggedness of the wild Morgans and who grew pathetically eager to withdraw from life after he was gone. Within two years of his death she had gone seeking him beyond the grave, and at the end had been quite happy, since she knew she was going soon, since she was not afraid of the great adventure and was very, very much afraid of Duke Morgan.

Thad Morgan, the finest of the lot, full-blooded like them and dominant and resentful of any sort of authority exercised upon him, who was authority unto himself and to others, had never known quite what sort his cousin Duke was; for, while Thad was alive, Duke was merely his right-hand man, as Budge was now Duke's. And Duke, though even then no doubt he had his ambitions and meant some day to be master of the

Valley, was also shrewd and could be patient, and knew that his Cousin Thad was already slowly dying from the results of an old accident, and so bided his time.

Thad would have willed everything to his wife. She shrank from owning anything, anything at all. The children would always take care of her.

So Thad Morgan died without realizing the position he was putting his beloved one in; rather than that he would have pistolled Duke from his deathbed. And his wife followed on as soon as she could, and Duke stepped into Thad Morgan's shoes and was dictator in the Valley from the outset, simply because he was Duke Morgan, the strong man after Thad.

He ignored the boy and girl, Bob and Lady, beyond making sure that they remained there and that nothing happened to them, neither sickness, a thing from which the Valley was remarkably free, nor accident of any sort. For Duke meant them to grow up to their majorities, to become undisputed legal owners of the Valley — and then to deed it over to him. For had they died before coming of age the whole Morgan outfit would have put in its various claims, and Duke would have seen any man or woman of them all dismembered rather than have the Valley parcelled.

So Bob and Lady, largely left alone, yet had the best of care as far as such a thing can be with no dash of love to go with it. As small children they played much together. Then Bob, coming along to man's estate, became more and more a Morgan every day, and likely enough in the end would have gone the way of the rest. Lady, little lonely Lady, became fearful. And then one

195

day, perhaps just in time to save Bob from the trail he was getting his feet into, they came to glimpse the dark thing in Duke's heart. Duke was drunk that day; his tongue was loose; Bob chanced to anger him in some small thing; Lady ran to Bob, putting her arms about him, lifting that defiant little chin of hers — and Duke with an unguarded angry word had given them a hint. What the hell did they think he was coddling them for? When they were old enough to sign a paper — He stopped there, glaring about him to see who heard. He went grumbling away and perhaps didn't remember that he had said anything at all; certainly he hadn't said the whole thing.

Fear got them then, and after it despair, though no such despair as gripped her to-day, for always over its blackness were the stars of hope. They had tried to run away, but Duke grew ever more watchful. Then Barnaby, a mysterious being, arrived mysteriously, none knew how. Duke bullied him and threatened him and beat him; Duke came near killing him; for some ten days Barnaby lay near death and in a strange exaltation of madness, yet not the slightest hint of his secret could Duke get out of him. Had Barnaby been like other men the truth could have been tortured out of him, especially since there could have been no clear reason for refusing to divulge it. But Duke promptly gave over that method, having seen its futility; instead every man, woman and child in the valley became a spy upon the youth's movements, confident that some day one of them would track him to his hidden exit. It was when Barnaby discovered this fact that the whole thing became a game to him; he came and went gleefully, at unexpected times. These furtive comings and goings drove Duke into many a towering rage and gave Barnaby a fresh zest and caused him to hug his secret knowledge all the tighter.

And though Barnaby adored Lady, much as he adored the stars and the wind through the trees and the vast still dark nights and his shy wilderness friends, he would tell even her no more than the others. Though she begged, though she strove so desperately to make him understand the danger she was in here and that it was in his power to save her from it, he would smilingly shake his towsled shock of long black hair and laugh at her fears and tell her:

"They can't hurt you, Lady. Even Duke can't. You see, God won't let him."

But Lady had never given up hope entirely. Some day Barnaby, for the bright, unselfish love he bore her, would share his precious secret with her. Now, in the Valley again, she felt that somehow she would *make* him tell her, for this brooding, sinister silence crushed her, and the voice of any Morgan stabbed her, and she was at the end of enduring it all. But Barnaby had not come back. One could never tell about him; he might be away a day, a night or many days and nights together. And one never knew where his wild steps led him, into what wilderness distances he carried the silvery tinklings of his bells.

Lady would have been glad now to go to him, if only for a touch of human companionship. It seemed to her that there was not a soul in the Valley with whom she

197

could be at peace. Duke's older sons, Tilford and Cam and Rance, had treated her with a certain rough courtesy. That was because the three of them hated Sid as sincerely as he hated them, and she came to understand that their attitude toward her was nothing but a slap in the face for Sid.

There was no woman in the Valley to whom she had ever been able to go for sympathetic understanding. A hard lot were the Morgan women; hard to begin with or made so by the Morgan men. They died early or they grew to be Morgans.

Yet to one of these women did Lady turn at last. And it seemed strange even to her that she should search out the Mexican woman Teresa, Duke's wife, Sid's mother. It was strange, yet there was a reason. Teresa, when she had been little, lovely, fifteen-year-old Teresita of the border, had been carried off by Duke, held prisoner here all these years. A prisoner like Lady. And Lady could understand how her wild southern heart must have suffered and yearned and all but broken; and she could understand too, Teresa's smouldering hate of Duke that a thousand years or a thousand lives would be all too short to soften. Lady, in her loneliness and her despair, went to the Mexican woman's little cabin.

It was a stone's throw from Duke's monster house, and Teresa had lived there alone for years, ever since Duke had goaded her into madness and she had tried to kill him with a butcher knife, and he had picked her up bodily and had hurled her out through the kitchen door. She had fallen among stones and had lain still for so long that he thought and perhaps hoped he had made an end of her. But after a while she had crawled away. Something had happened to her back; she never stood straight after that, never was strong again, always walked crookedly with a dragging limp.

"I'm through with you," he had roared after her. "Keep out of my sight. If you ever so much as speak to me I'll break your neck. I'd go get me another woman, just to plague you, you she-devil, but I'm through with women as long as I live. They are, the whole lot of them, a lot of —"

Teresa was Teresita then, very young, very pretty; Sid was only a year old. But she had never again spoken to Duke, had never come intentionally into his presence; he pretty much forgot all about her as the years rolled by. But her young hate of him was kept green. She would stand before her looking-glass, watch her beauty wither, think of fiestas and dances and flowers and all the gaiety of the time when she was thirteen and fourteen and fifteen — the time before Duke had come.

She knew that he would never let her go. It was not wise for the Morgans to let anyone go Outside and talk. She had Sid. She strove year after year, from his earliest babyhood, to make him hate his father. Duke, however, showed a queer, rough fondness for his youngest born; he made Sid proud of him; Sid thought that the finest men in the world were Duke Morgan and Sid Morgan. And still Teresa, with her deathless hate, worked on the growing boy and on the young man.

"Some day," she told herself stubbornly, "Duke will do something, say something, to make Sid hate him as I do."

Lady's horror of Duke matched Teresa's hate; alike, they were his prisoners. So Lady went to Teresa's cabin, going after dark, making sure that Sid was not there. It was the first time in her life that she had ever passed through the Mexican woman's door.

Teresa, with a great black shawl, as old as she was, drawn over her shoulders and framing her dark face, her crooked little body rocking regularly back and forth in front of her fireplace with its dying red glow of a few greying embers, turned her head quickly at the sound of an unfamiliar tread. Lady thought that she looked like a witch; like a little dried-up witch a thousand years old. She looked older than anyone else in the Valley, though she should be a young woman in her middle thirties. And she looked as wicked as a witch with those glittering night-black eyes of hers, with the lines and wrinkles about them, with a slit of a mouth as venomous as a snake's.

Lady saw all this, but with new eyes. Always she had been afraid of Teresa, terrified by her; now she was not afraid. Suddenly, and for the first time, she thought: "Poor thing! What I have suffered for a short time she has suffered all her life. When she was only fifteen — that's so much younger than I am! — Duke brought her here —"

"Do you mind very much if I come in?" she asked, and sounded hesitant though she was determined she would come in.

Teresa's wicked black eyes narrowed and narrowed, making her afraid again — and yet somehow she was not afraid, for she kept thinking: "Poor thing! Once she was young, too, younger even than I am. And Duke made her like this — the Morgans made her like this. It isn't her fault — she used to be young and pretty and happy, and she would dance and sing and laugh all day — and now she is crooked and lame and old and wicked — and it is not her fault!"

"Go away," said Teresa, and her voice that used to be so soft and melodious was as sharp as a knife; as sharp as the butcher knife with which she had wanted to kill Duke. "I don't like you."

"Let me come in, please," said Lady. "Let me come in and sit by you and talk with you."

"What do you want?"

"I am so lonely. I am so frightened. I am so unhappy. And I know you have been like that for so, so long. Won't you let me come in?"

The woman who was so young in years, so old in everything else, a hag and a witch and a bitter, ugly old woman, showed the pale gleam of white beautiful teeth in a sneer.

"You're a little fool," she said, "and a coward. If I was young again and pretty — young and pretty like you, like I used to be — know what I'd do?"

"What?" asked Lady faintly.

"I'd go drown myself in the river! I'd climb up a high place and jump off. I'd cut my throat. With a butcher knife. I'd cut my throat."

Lady shuddered and the woman began to laugh. Suddenly stern again she demanded:

"And you wonder why I don't do that now? Well, it's too late. I haven't anything to lose, I haven't anything to save that way. I'd keep myself like I was, like you are; I'd do it by being dead. Then Duke Morgan couldn't do the things he has done to me. Oh, in another way he is going to do them to you!"

Lady closed the door and leaned against it, feeling a need of its support. Teresa put a thin, bony hand out from under her shawl and beckoned. So Lady came close to her, standing by the fireplace.

"You got away, didn't you?" Teresa said, and whether she was mocking or not Lady could not decide. "You were away all one night and all one day and much of the next night. Outside!" And then Lady knew she was not mocking her. "Far from here, far! Where you couldn't even see a Morgan or hear one! What was that like, Lady Morgan? Was it like having died and being in heaven?"

"Would you like me to tell you all about it?"

"Tell me!" said Teresa fiercely. "Pull up a chair. Tell me!"

They sat by the fire together, and the ruddy embers grew grey under the film of ashes, and the faint light grew fainter so that their two faces looked grey like the dying coals, and they could hardly see each other, but Lady could see Teresa's eyes catching and reflecting all the wan light there was; and Lady talked while Teresa listened and rocked more and more gently. The creaking of her chair died away too before the end.

A last tiny flame blossomed from the coal falling apart. Lady saw a subdued flash of light on Teresa's cheek. Strange, that from those harsh, embittered eyes tears could still come!

"And you came back! After you had felt the free wind blow in your face, after you had tasted and smelled what it was like to be Outside, you let them bring you back! You had a pistol, too! Why didn't you kill with it? Why didn't you kill yourself, anyhow? — Tell me about this man Juan Morada! He comes from the border; he comes from where my home was! I would maybe have known him if I had stayed there; he must know people I knew; they must know him. Tell me about him."

"He is not Juan Morada at all! They call Juan Morada another name, Don Diablo, because of his terrible, cruel wickedness. This man is good and kind and not at all like that."

Teresa started rocking again, ever so slowly and softly; the chair did not creak now except once in a while and then only like a hushed and hesitant protest.

"Sid told me what he heard by the waterfall. He heard this man say he was not Juan Morada but an American *ranchero*. Then he heard him laugh and call you a fool, and say that he was Juan Morada. Even Duke does not know now, after Sid has told him; and I don't know. Maybe you don't know either!"

"But I do! He is not Juan Morada, he is not that kind of man at all! He is fine, splendid! He —"

"*Ay de mi!*" sighed Teresa, not at all the evil woman Lady had always known. It was quite dark now and in the darkness it was easy to think of her, building her up around that tender, sighing utterance, as the young Teresita, romantic to her finger tips, to the tips of her little dancing toes. It was a sigh for all the romance and love she had missed. Who knew what young *caballero* had tuned his guitar under her barred window of the long and long ago?

They talked for a long time after that. Teresa lighted her lamp and they sat in its dim light, growing at last to know each other. But Lady came to understand that there could never be any such bond between them as grows out of a sincere liking. For in broken, embittered Teresa's heart there was no room for love, nor even for the milder emotion of affection. There was no room any longer for anything but hate. It was a fearful thing to glimpse such hatred as the Mexican woman's, a hatred for Duke Morgan which had rankled and festered throughout the greater part of her life so that it was rank poison.

Lady had risen to go when they heard the hammering of hoofs and the loud voices of roystering men, and knew that the Morgans were again home. Lady listened to Duke's large laughter and knew that he was drunk, and shivered. She heard Tom Colby singing a hymn which he had clumsily and profanely parodied. Then came another sound that went through her like a knife. It was Molly Daly's shriek.

She gripped Teresa's thin arm.

"Whose voice is that?" she asked whisperingly. "Who is that screaming like that? It doesn't sound like anyone in the Valley —"

"I screamed like that the night they brought me here," said Teresa indifferently. "It didn't do me any good. It won't do her any good."

She grew vehement and cried out angrily: "Why doesn't the little fool kill herself? Why doesn't she drown herself in the river, or jump off a high place, or cut her throat? You'll see, she's young yet and pretty; oh, the Morgans like their girls young and pretty! I was like that once, do you understand? If I had died then I would never have changed —"

She began to laugh in a strange choking, smothered fashion. Lady shivered afresh; she began to think that the woman, after her long years of brooding, had gone quite mad.

CHAPTER
EIGHTEEN

"The council room," the big main room in Duke's house had been called since the first Morgans came here, and Jeff Morgan, a freebooting old land pirate, much like Duke, had built the place. On occasions when a clan gathering was decreed — sometimes to make wild holiday, some other times to plan deviltry — men gathered here. There was a long heavy table down the middle of the room, flanked by rude benches that would easily seat forty men. Fifty had sat down to it more than once. It was into this room to-night that the Morgans came trooping, bringing their captive.

Poor little terrified Molly screamed again as soon as she looked about her in the big room and saw the many men standing and looking at her. She was scarcely more than a child; it had never dawned on her that men could be beasts. The men whom she knew, those of her own family and of her father's broad-acred ranch, the few far neighbours, had all been brothers and fathers to little Molly, tender with her, fond of her, spoiling her, finding their many opportunities in their rough ways to lay Sir Walter Raleigh cloaks before her eager feet. And now she saw Duke, drunk and ugly and spraddling, red-eyed with liquor and viciousness, and heard his deep rumbling thunder of sinister laughter; she saw Sid leering; she saw the others, and all their faces seemed to her the faces of devils.

Rance came hurriedly to her, Rance who was perhaps the most nearly decent of the whole outfit and who in some queer, distorted, Morgan way did love her. He said awkwardly: "Aw, Molly. Don't cry, Molly. They — I won't hurt you. You just —"

"Let me go, let me go, let me go!" she screamed at him, and since he stood in her way she began beating at him with her small clenched fists.

She was small and dainty and sweet; no wonder Rance had wanted her ever since he first saw her — last spring, it was, just before they raided Ed Daly's ranch and shot him and killed her two brothers. She was like a mountain flower, like a wild rose. Her hair was reddish gold and curly, her eyes a tender, shining blue, her mouth soft and lovely and still with something artlessly babyish about it, and she was shaped, from head to foot, like a small pink and white and golden goddess. At her last dance, blossoming out all of a sudden, she had been the most popular girl on the floor, quite the belle of the ball. And not a man of all who danced with her but was conscious of her unsullied freshness and purity, and made the rude deference he paid her somehow fine and gallant.

"You can't go; you can't go now, Molly," muttered Rance, and sounded sorry that she couldn't. Maybe suddenly he was truly sorry, as even men like the Morgans could be for a deed done. He was as drunk as the rest, but it may be that the look in her widened, terrified blue eyes and on her tragic white face sobered him. He spoke to her as gently as he knew how. He might have been thinking, when altogether too late to mend matters, of how Ed Daly had looked when they shot him, of how Molly had seen that and had put her arms about him, trying to hold him back to her, trying to have him save her from them.

"It was a fool thing to do, a damn fool thing," muttered Rance, and began pawing at a sweat-wet forehead.

"What's that?" roared Duke.

"The Morgans were drunk to-night, Duke," said Rance heavily. "They did a damn fool thing. The Morgans have got as much sense as most men, maybe more sense than most men. But when they're drunk, they're just drunks. It was a damn fool thing to do."

Sid Morgan began jeering at him.

"If you don't want her, I'll take her, Rance," he gibed. "She suits me fine. She'd like me, too. I'll bet if you gave her her choice —"

"You keep out of this, Sid," said Rance, "or I'll break your neck. You keep out of this or I'll kill you."

"Look at her!" jeered Sid. "She's scared, but it's more than being scared with her. It's you; you make her sick. She'd come to me, I bet. I'll bet I get her, too." He moved swiftly and caught her by the arm, dragging her halfway into his embrace. "Say, Molly —"

Rance pounced on him, struck his arm down and gave him a shove that sent him reeling. Sid came charging back and Rance knocked him down. There was blood dribbling from Sid's mouth as he got up. Molly, with her white face in her hands, cringed back against the wall, shutting them out as best she could.

Sid started to drag his gun out of his holster but a roar from Duke stopped him.

"Take the white-faced little fool if you want her," he bellowed at Rance. "Get her out of here. What in hell does a man want a woman for anyhow? Sooner or later she'll stick a knife in you. Get her out. Damn it, get her out!"

"Softly, softly, Brother," put in Tom Colby, his voice gurgling with laughter made oily for the occasion. "When a man taketh a woman let him do so in holy matrimony, amen." He pulled his hat off and pretended a vast and quite hideous solemnity. "The moment asks for the ministrations of the Reverend Thomas Colby. Behold the blushing bride! Behold the handsome groom! You see in them two individuals and far apart. Hocus pocus! and in a trice you shall behold a miracle in which the Reverend Thomas Colby will make these two into one. Yea verily, Brethren, man and wife they shall be, for surely, surely no breath of scandal must ever enter this chaste and sanctified Valley. And by God," he proclaimed as he brought his big open palm down on the table top with a sound like a gunshot, "when Tom Colby marries 'em they'll know they're married. They —" and in boisterous vulgarity he launched into a drunken oration of such profanity and blasphemy that it made even those who knew him best wonder at the man.

He began then a burlesque of marriage. Rance looked puzzled, others began laughing and Rance reached out, caught Molly's hand and grinned.

"We're getting married, Molly," he mumbled into the bright red-gold of her hair that had tumbled all about her face, hiding her ears. "Drunk as he is, Tom Colby can do a right smart job of marrying folks. You and me, Molly, we'll be Mr. and Mrs. Rance Morgan in a minute."

Molly was past screaming, just as she was past any sort of hope. She heard Rance's voice as across a great wind-blown distance; she no longer attended to what anyone was saying, not even the jocose Tom Colby. She looked dazed as though from a stunning blow, her eyes dull. Perhaps she was about to faint. Rance put an arm about her, holding her up, and she did not appear to notice him at all.

It was then that Lady Morgan burst upon them. The door had been left open and she came running into the room, brushing by the men who were in her way, going straight to Molly Daly. She had heard enough, seen enough to make her grasp what had happened already and what was about to happen; in the shock of it, the horror of it and the spurt of anger that flared up within her, her own troubles were forgotten; forgotten along with them was any fear of the Morgan men.

She caught a wilting Molly into her arms, clasping her tight, fending Rance's arm off. Her eyes were flaming, her face hot with the flush of indignant blood. The two girls were like those of the old fairy tale, Snow White and Rose Red.

"Duke," cried Lady, tense and vibrant, defiant and unafraid, "you are drunk, but you are never so drunk that you don't know what you are doing. You have done something to-night that is maybe going to make an end of the Morgans in Dark Valley. You'd better look out, Duke Morgan! God is going to make an end of you —"

"Shut up, you hell cat!" roared Duke.

"I won't shut up! I don't have to! I tell you —"

"I'll break your damn little neck!"

"Do you think I'd care? Do you think I'd be sorry to be dead? But this little girl — this little baby thing —" She gathered Molly closer in her arms, mothering her. "You come with me," she began whispering. "They won't hurt you. I won't let anyone come near you."

A sob broke from Molly and, no longer inert but frantic, she threw her arms about Lady Morgan, clutching her tight. Lady turned back toward the door and all the men in the room, with curious and various expressions, watched the two girls withdrawing. Heads began turning toward Rance, to see what he had to say. This was supposed to be Rance's bride; if he let her go this way why should they do other than shrug, laugh, thereafter, and make ribald sport of him.

Duke was frowning and shaking his head; he too stared at Rance.

"Rance, you're a fool," he said, blunt and contemptuous. "Let a woman have her head the first night, she'll wear the britches long's you live. You're a fool to want her in the first place, a fool to start what we started outside when we put a rope over this little white heifer's horns, the biggest fool of all now. Make up your mind."

Duke's attitude, the contempt of laughter from the other men, now the renewed jeering of Sid, made up

Rance's mind for him. His face darkened and all the kindness he had manifested toward the girl vanished from it; he sprang after the two girls, got in front of them and blocked the door, and commanded angrily:

"Lady, you keep out of this. Let that girl go."

"I won't!" cried Lady passionately. "Don't you dare, Rance Morgan —"

Rance tried to drag the girls apart but they clung all the tighter and fat Tom Colby clapped his thigh and laughed louder than all the rest in high delight. Rance doubled up his fist as though to strike Lady in the face; at a sharp warning from Duke he stood raging and irresolute.

"Keep your hands off Lady Morgan," Duke said. "Do what you please with your little white moo-calf, but I won't have Lady harmed."

No; of course not. Duke had always protected Lady; he always meant to until he brought her safely to her majority and closed his transaction with her. They all knew that, even Rance, raging.

So again Rance strove to pry the two girls apart and found the task not as simple as it might have been, considering his strength, which was greater than that of Lady and Molly combined. There was also to be considered the desperation with which they clung together. In a flash Molly's wilting resignation was gone; when Rance did jerk one of her hands loose she slipped it out of his and struck him in the face. Louder than ever did laughter swell up in the room.

"I wasn't meaning to hurt you," Rance said thickly as again he got Molly's hand in his, holding it so tight now that she cried out with the pain of a wrenched arm. "I wasn't meaning to hurt you, but now —"

He was closer than he had ever been in his life to having a bullet through his heart just then, but that was something he could have no inkling of. A moment before both Duke and Tom Colby had stood very close to death, knowing no more of it then than did Rance now. For they weren't even thinking that there might be someone outside, looking in on them. And they had never so much as heard of a young rancher named Steve Kendal.

But both Steve and Bolt Haveril, arrived only as the party of Morgans returned to their Valley, had been on time to see them bring their captive into this room. And Bolt Haveril made it his affair to keep his head cool when Steve's grew hot. He had shoved Steve's gun arm down, saying in a warning whisper:

"Damn it, Steve, you promised — and she's got a chance yet if we do our part. Hold it, Steve!"

Steve held it. His promise would not have restrained him then, even though he was not a man to break his word lightly, but he knew that Bolt was right. They did have a chance, slim as it was, to get Molly away alive and unharmed; no chance at all if prematurely they abandoned themselves to haste and hot blood.

"All right, Bolt," Steve whispered back. "I'll keep my shirt on. But before this is all over, if I don't get Duke Morgan and that rotten-hearted Tom Colby and Rance —"

"Sh!" Bolt cautioned. "Just remember if you start slinging lead now — Well, you might as well make a clean job of it and be sure you drop Molly dead the first shot! Got me, Steve?"

"I got you, Bolt."

Rance at last and after a scuffle had his way. He got between the two girls, sending Lady plunging and almost falling, pulling Molly into his arms.

"Go ahead, Tom," he called out savagely. "Marry us."

"Amen, Brother," shouted Tom Colby mirthfully. "And I'll be first to kiss the bride. Hear ye, hear ye, hear ye! I, the Reverend Thomas Colby, by that divine authority —"

"A wedding, is it?" said a cool, well-remembered voice from the door. "Fine! As a friend of the family, I guess I'm invited? Huh, Duke?"

They stared at him, every last man of them — yes, and Lady Morgan, too, and even Molly — as they might have regarded an apparition that had popped up through the floor; as they might have stared had Ed Daly, recently dead, dropped in to say, "I guess I'm invited, huh?" For they had to ask themselves, in the first place, what insane impulse brought Bolt Haveril — or Juan Morada — here. And second they must wonder how he appeared all without warning? The bell over the gate had not rung; no Morgan had come to announce his arrival. It was simply that he was standing there in the doorway, looking in on them coolly and even a thought impudently.

"I'm damned!" muttered Duke Morgan.

"I'm not going to start a row by contradicting you, Duke," Bolt grinned back at him. "You ought to know best."

Then he let his eyes, which told absolutely nothing of his thought or emotion, wander over the room. They rested lightly and seemingly unconcerned on Molly's white face; they travelled on until they came to Lady. Then Bolt remembered his hat and removed it with something of a flourish.

"Howdy, Lady Morgan," he greeted her.

"Bolt! Oh, Bolt! You came back!"

He meant to mystify Duke Morgan, to spar for time until he and Steve Kendal found some crack in the walls of the Morgan defences; and it might be that he would have to mystify her as well. He did not think so; by now she should know him pretty well. He said, ignoring the others and addressing her lightly, his mood seeming utterly care-free and light:

"Bolt? Sure. *Seguro que si!* Bolt Haveril."

From her he turned to Duke Morgan, clapping on his hat again, saying coolly:

"You haven't forgotten me, have you, Duke? Your old friend, Bolt Haveril —"

"Of all the nerve!" said Duke, muttering and mumbling. "Bolt Haveril, are you?"

And Bolt finished lightly:

"From Texas."

215

CHAPTER
NINETEEN

"Watch him, boys!" shouted Duke. "Get between him and the door, and get the door shut, too. There's something damn funny here."

It was Budge Morgan who got the door shut and stood with his bulky shoulders against it; like Duke and all the rest he looked puzzled. More than the others he was plainly apprehensive. He said explosively:

"You're damn right it's funny, Duke! How'd he get here? Which way did he come? What gate, Duke? And how does it happen no bell's rung and nobody has come along ahead of him to tell us he was on the way?" He glowered all about him, stirring uneasily; he used those same familiar words Dave Heffinger had spoken earlier in the evening. "There's blood on the moon, Duke!"

"It'll be Morada's blood then!" roared Duke. He pulled himself up short. "How'd you get here?" he demanded. "And what the hell are you up to, anyhow?"

"You and I might have some unfinished business, Duke," said Bolt in an offhand sort of way. "When I slipped out on you the other night I left some things here. There are three horses of mine and my roll and a fistful of money —"

216

"He's dripping wet," put in Budge. "He's had a ducking or —"

Bolt had foreseen the necessity of a ready explanation. It was promptly forthcoming.

"It seems a habit with you boys to have a watchman on the bridge. Well, I didn't cross the bridge, and I'll bet your watchman didn't even hear me splash in the river." He looked humorously at Duke. "Do you know, Duke old boy, I'm afraid you grow lax here in the Valley. Some day you're apt to come up out of your doze and find the place all overcrowded with Outsiders!"

Duke stood silent a long while, drilling into him with eyes which through sheer force of will he made grow clearer with every breath he drew; he shook his head to get it clear, as a dog, coming out of the water, shakes itself. He pulled his hat off and dropped it to the table; he ran his fingers through his hair, upending it so that it stood every way in bristly tufts, scrubbing at his scalp, muttering and shaking his head again. Then, still with his lips tight locked, he stood looking stormily at Bolt Haveril. No one in the room spoke; all looked at Duke. At last he spoke.

"Morada," he said quietly and very, very deliberately, "you've got me guessing. You've had me that a-way since you first came here. I was going to straighten things out with you; then the Pocket Gully affair popped up and I had to put you out of mind until I settled that. When I got back you was gone. You and Lady. And now you're back."

Bolt made no reply when Duke paused. Instead he glanced about the room; he didn't dare let his eyes traffic too long with Lady's nor tell her too much. She just had to know, to know deep down in her heart, why he was here, and that, no matter what happened, she'd have to trust him. In the flicker of a glance he hoped to flash that expectation over to her; he was sure she understood, too. For her eyes were bright again; her head was up; the look she sped back to him was one of joyous gratitude. She was at Molly's side again; she put her lips down to the bright ruddy gold of Molly's hair and began whispering:

"Oh, Molly! We're saved! He is the finest, bravest, most splendid man on earth and — But Molly, careful! We don't know what he is going to do; we must be ready for anything."

"What's Lady whispering to Molly about?" said Sid sharply. "Look out, Duke; there's something fishy —"

"From now on you keep still or get out of here, Sid," said Duke. "The same goes for the whole damn crowd. I'm doing this."

He pulled out a bench, sat down and got his elbows on the table. Again he took his time, silent for a spell, staring at Bolt Haveril, shaking his head now and then, shaking the drunkenness out of it, making it the crafty thinking machine that had served him so well so many a time. What he said next puzzled all those who heard it, all save Bolt Haveril who understood. What he demanded of Bolt was:

"Where's Crazy Barnaby?"

"Why ask me?" countered Bolt. Might as well make Duke come straight across with it.

"Crazy Barnaby was with you and Lady out in the woods," said Duke. "When we brought her back, you and Barnaby kept going. Both of you was in Red Luck to-night."

"That's so," said Bolt.

For the first time Duke grinned broadly. He thumped the table as he said:

"You're a slick guy, Morada, but me, I can be slick too! For about three years I been trying to find out how Barnaby slips in and out of the Valley, no one ever catching him either going or coming. Well, somehow or another you got it out of him. He brought you in his secret way, huh?"

Bolt deemed it advisable to match grin with grin.

"Think so, Duke?" he retorted.

"Now," said Duke, "here's something funny: Barnaby, being crazy, you couldn't handle him like other men. You could cut off his ears, burn his feet or tie him between two horses and pull him apart, and he'd never speak up. With you it would be different! You know Barnaby's trail now — and I'm going to know it too, inside the hour!"

Bolt saw Lady out of the corner of his restless eyes. At the first clear implication of what Duke had thought out, that now Bolt knew Barnaby's secret, a new swift hope leaped up within her. As she followed Duke's thoughts through to the end, her heart sank. She knew what Duke could do to a man to make him talk.

Bolt was twitching his shoulders as though in frank distaste of the sort of things Duke threatened.

"Duke," he said, "I didn't come back here to-night to get pulled apart. Me, I like to go on living and fooling around just as much as the other feller. I'm here because I wanted to come, and I'm here with both eyes open. What do you say we cut out talk like that? Haven't we got a thing or two to come to terms on before we start knocking each other over?"

Duke started playing a devil's tattoo on the table top with big brutal blunt fingers.

"Maybe," he said. "Maybe. Speak up, Morada."

This time Bolt overlooked the "Morada." He continued deliberately:

"You sent a handful of gold down to the border, to buy you a job of work done. Who did you think you was buying, Duke? Some feller that thinks a silver dollar is as big as the moon and a gold twenty all the money there is in the world? If you've looked around since I walked out on you the other night maybe you've found what I did with the fistful of gold you earmarked and sent down to the Rio Grande to buy Juan Estrada Talvez y Morada! I left the stuff where it lay! *Caramba contigo!* What the hell! Do you want to make me laugh, Señor Duke Morgan?"

He was doing a rather good bit of play-acting and knew it. Mildly he surprised himself, but that was only because he overlooked something. In nature, in moments when men get down into primitive situations, where it is not a question of some absurd convention, of some minor stake to be played for, but of a man's life and the life of one dear to him, the man of these later times is the man of primitive times. And the closer we turn back to the origins, the more convincing actors do we find on the mundane scene. Thus a dove, protecting its nestlings, gives the most startlingly convincing imitation of a wounded, broken-winged, flutteringly helpless thing — and it leads danger far from its hidden nest. A man, like a raccoon, or a tarantula when he sees a tarantula hawk and plays dead, or like any other of his natural brothers, can under stress play his part.

He even set Lady wondering.

"A high-priced killer, huh?" growled Duke. "And a dirty Mex double-crosser on top of it." His restless hands grew still; he demanded curtly: "You'll tell me now, damn you: What about Bob? Bob Morgan?"

"A high-priced killer? *Bueno*. But no one has been killed, Señor. No one." He paused, then added significantly: "Not yet."

"You haven't even told me what happened to him! You haven't told me where he is or if you ever saw or heard of him! You haven't —"

"It might be a good idea, Duke," Bolt cut in sharply, "for you and me to get off by ourselves and have a talk." He glanced expressionlessly toward Lady Morgan. "The three of us, maybe; Lady, too," he added.

Duke laughed at him.

"These boys stick with us and listen to every damn word," he said emphatically. "Just what you've got up your sleeve I don't know. But I do know there are ten of us Morgans here and there's just one of you, and every

Morgan will have a hand mighty close to his gun, and if you try any monkey business you'll go down with anyhow ten bullets in your gizzard. No secrets here to-night, Mr. Juan what-the-hell Morada."

"Juan Estrada de Talvez y Morada is the name you're trying to think of, Duke. Me, I'm Bolt Haveril. From Texas, you know."

Baylis and Curly, the two who had been hobbled and deprived of their boots, from looking at each other and at Bolt, turned hungering eyes on Duke.

"Dammit, Duke," burst violently from Baylis, "what's all the palaver for? We've got this feller dead to rights, and when it comes to dealing with snakes it don't make any difference how you weed 'em out; it's just do it quick and dig 'em under."

Duke answered him patiently.

"Get back inside your shirt, Kid," he said. "Just because you've got blisters on your feet and a stubbed toe is no reason we should get all het up. You leave this to me." Baylis ceased erupting; a patient Duke was a deadly Duke and Baylis knew it. Of Bolt he inquired, "What happened to Bob?"

"He's alive," said Bolt. "He's where I can put my finger on him."

"What happened to Shirt-tail Kennedy?" asked Duke.

Bolt cocked up his brows inquiringly. It was as good as to ask, "Who the devil is Shirt-tail Kennedy?"

"He's the man I sent down to visit with you," said Duke, still ominously patient, giving the impression of a vastly tolerant man. "He's an Outsider, but he's a

222

Morgan man just the same. He rode down to see you. He carried word from me. And he did see you."

"Who told you?" asked Bolt softly.

"The gold money told me. Them gold pieces I'd put my mark on. He handed them to you, and he spoke his piece and — what happened to him?"

"So that was Shirt-tail Kennedy? No wonder he didn't run around telling folks what his name was!"

"Never mind all that, Morada! I'm going slow with you, I'm walking soft with you, I'm giving you every show, but if you make a mistake and get to thinking that —"

Bolt's interruption, curt and crisp and with a fillup of challenge in it, cut Duke's words off.

"You better go slow and walk soft, Duke," he rapped out. "If you don't already know it I'll tell you something: You're out on the end of a limb right now, and the limb's cracking off and if it falls and lets you down, that's the end of you and of the whole crowd of Dark Valley Morgans."

"Yes?" said Duke more softly than Bolt had ever dreamed the man could speak. "Yes?"

"Yes."

"You might tell me about it," said Duke. "There's times when I'm a damn good listener; this is one o' them."

"You ought to have somebody write it all down on a piece of paper, Duke," said Bolt dryly. "There's so many things you might miss one or two of 'em. First one is this: There's a way to get in and out of the Valley that you don't know about. Me, I know."

Duke nodded heavily. "Sure, you know. I said that already. But if you think, Devil Morada, that you're going to be turned free to tell all the things you know —"

"Thought you said you were a good listener? Who's telling this little good-night story, you or me?"

"Go 'head," said Duke. "I spoke out o' turn."

"If I know Barnaby's trail," said Bolt, "maybe some other folks know it too. I don't say yes and I don't say no; but you might get busy asking yourself what might be. It might be that all Red Luck knows it by now. Huh, Duke?"

"Go 'head," said Duke.

"That's number one," Bolt went on. "And it's kind of bad, Duke; bad for you. It's like a man locking himself up in a dark room and then finding out that there's a trap-door somewhere that other fellers can creep through to jump him, and he don't know where the trap-door is. Kind of bad, Duke."

The others who were listening as intently as Duke Morgan himself — his four sons and Budge and Baylis and Curly, Morg Blount too and even Tom Colby — showed in their eyes and in their tense faces that they agreed. It was kind of bad!

Duke didn't show anything, didn't turn a hair or bat an eye. He just waited.

"I've been thinking," Bolt continued, and seemed thoughtful and judicial, willing to be fair, rather frankly interested in making sure of things, "that maybe you're not the big gun men say you are, Duke. Maybe you're just a pair of deuces or a bob-tailed flush. You've made one or two pretty bad mistakes of late, Duke Morgan. And me, well I don't care much for chipping in with any *hombre* that can't play the cards right when they drop into his hand."

"I'm a damn good listener, Kid," said Duke, his big body stirring restlessly, the anger bright and hot in his eyes, "but I'm damned if I'm going to listen to this sort of stuff all night."

"Sure," said Bolt. "Sure. Maybe some: times I talk too much. Well, here's number two: You did a damn fool thing sending Shirt-tail down to talk to Morada all alone. You don't know what luck he had; you don't know what happened to him; you don't know as much about what went on down there as a jumping bean knows about three card monte. You ought to 've gone yourself, or you ought to have sent three-four men, Morgans all of 'em."

"Thanks for telling me," said Duke. "Anything else?"

"There's number three," said Bolt imperturbably, though he did not fail to, mark the still outward signs of a wrath that gave Duke Morgan a sort of cold reptilian deadliness. "To-night, Duke," he said coolly, "you did the biggest damn fool thing of your life. What kind of a man are you, anyhow, for a stranger to tie to?"

"To-night?" said a quiet, stony Duke. "Put a name to it, Morada."

Bolt frowned.

"Me, I'm Bolt Haveril," he said crisply. "From Texas, you know. But we'll let that go. To put a name to it is dead easy. You went a long way out on the limb when you killed Ed Daly and stole his girl."

"Who says I killed Daly?" asked Duke, never more soft spoken. "Maybe somebody killed him. Maybe folks, guessing wild, will say the Morgans did it. But they'll never know, Morada." He grinned broadly. "You're not figuring, are you, that you'll pop out and tell 'em? Tell 'em that you found the girl here?"

"I don't need to tell 'em," said Bolt. "They know already."

"You mean they guess, don't you? There was Molly and her old man. He's not talking any, I promise you. Neither is she. Nor you, either, Señor!"

Bolt shook his head; sadly, you might have said. Commiseratingly.

"You didn't poke into the wagon, did you, Duke? You didn't ask yourself why Ed Daly and Molly, folks that fork their horses mostly to go anywhere, went to all the trouble and slowed themselves down by taking a wagon?"

Duke did blink then. "What are you driving at, Morada?" he snapped. "Daly was taking his girl to town to send her away, and there was a trunk and some packages and that's why the wagon."

Bolt shook his head as though Duke wearied him. He said:

"You might have taken time to poke around in that wagon bed, Duke. You ought to."

"I asked you once already what you're driving at. Put a name to it, Morada!"

"All right, I'll tell you. — No, maybe better not."

"Why not?" demanded Duke.

226

"You might think I made it up. You might even figure I'd lie to you, just to scare you out of your boots. Suppose you ask her." Bolt nodded toward Molly. "Ask her what else, besides her baggage, was in the wagon under that canvas."

Duke asked her promptly and sharply enough.

"You, girl!" he said savagely. "What's all this about? What did you have in the wagon?"

"It was a sick man," said Molly. "It was one of Daddy's men. It was Ben Shuckton. We were taking him to the doctor."

There was a hush after that. Duke and every other Morgan was doing some bull's-eye thinking. If this happened to be true, if Ben Shuckton lying there in the wagon had heard and seen, and if he had reported all he knew in Red Luck — well, Bolt wasn't wrong and Rance hadn't been wrong before him when pretty much the same words had been spoken: "The drunk Morgans did a damn fool thing to-night."

Duke's gaze, narrowed and speculative, returned to Bolt Haveril.

"That's what you meant, huh?" he asked. "You meant there was a man in the wagon and that he has got to Red Luck and shot his mouth off?"

"Two cowboys heard the shots," said Bolt. "Bud Clark and Sam Harper, they were. They took Shuckton on into town. Shuckton told a good many folks." He looked fleetingly at little Molly; when he turned back to address Duke his words were really meant for her; he hoped they'd carry her some hope, some gladness. He said: "Among others, Shuckton told a young feller named Steve Kendal. You'd think, from the way Steve took on, that maybe he planned to do something about it."

For a time, two or three minutes of heavy silence, Duke didn't have a word to say, and though others stirred restlessly and there was a quick queer play of expressions on their faces, none of them spoke. Here was a matter up to Duke Morgan. They knew that. They knew too they'd better give him his time.

He spoke up at last.

"Budge," he said, "get busy. There's apt to be hell popping. Send a man down the Valley with word. Get men hid out in the brush, watching all three gates. Start things rolling. Then you come back here to me."

"That's the stuff, Duke!" cried Budge heartily, and jerked the door open.

He stopped there, though, listening. The others also froze into whatever positions were theirs as the new sound beat on their ears: It was the swift staccato hammering of horses' hoofs, coming up from the lower end of the Valley. More than one rider, surely, and coming fast.

This, and what happened immediately next, was but the prelude to an entrance. But it happened to be an entrance that pretty well rocked the human element of Dark Valley to its foundations. The only person in the room who didn't go rigid with apprehension when the thing was understood was Molly. But then she didn't know what the others knew.

When a man, one of the Morgans from the lower end of the Valley, came running in and ran straight to Duke, saying something in his ear, Duke stiffened like a man shot.

"The hell you say!" he roared and jumped up and turned toward the door, watching it as one might if he knew something was coming in on him and didn't know whether it was a man-eating tiger or the soft melting lady of his dreams. Duke, with eyes glued on the door, must have been saying to himself:

"Yes, I'm out on a limb like this feller says. But right now! Now!" His big fists rolled up into brutal mallets. "Right now I smash somebody down!"

Then the entrance. They heard outside the second running horse, heard it slide to a standstill, heard the pleasantly musical jingle of spurs when impatient boots struck earth. The rider came in just stepping across the threshold and stopping there.

He was dark and slim and young; he was about Bolt Haveril's height and build. His roving eyes were very black and just now as wicked as sin. He had a small black moustache. His mouth twitched as he looked the room over; there was a faint sneer on his ripe, full lips, and the ends of his moustache went up. Doing so, they revealed a tiny white scar; it was like the thin thread of a little new moon.

"Well?" thundered Duke. "And who the hell are you?"

The newcomer wore the biggest black hat in the room; there was a broad band about it heavy with silver *conchas*. He lifted his eyebrows; he looked like a man at a masquerade who had gone to impersonate the devil.

"Me, Señor?" He spoke liquidly, like the Mexican he looked. "Nobody but only Juan Estrada de Talvez y Morada." He bowed and was infernally graceful doing so. "Your good amigo, Señor — Don Diablo from the Border."

CHAPTER
TWENTY

Bolt Haveril's heart stopped beating. Then, making up for its momentary lapse as he drew a deep breath into his lungs, it started up again, racing like mad. He knew Don Diablo when he saw him; he alone of all here knew him. He had cause to know him well. And he hadn't needed those few words of introduction to tell him that Bolt Haveril, like Duke Morgan, was out on a limb. To see Don Diablo here, never looking more the devil than he was, brought him his moment of upset — brought him, in fact, what was right next door to consternation. He obeyed an impulse and let his hand drop down to the butt of his gun.

Then he realized that Duke was speaking. He had missed Duke's first few words, but he heard, ". . . at the South Gate, huh? You told them who you were, and they let you in and brought you straight up here?"

"Sure," said Juan Morada. "*Seguro.* When I come to a gate I say, 'Open up!' and it always opens up, Señor."

"What do you want?" said Duke, cold and calculating now, a Duke who was using his head, thinking true to the line.

"Can you ask?" exclaimed Morada, and opened his palms and lifted the thin black lines of his brows.

"You're damn right, I can ask," Duke told him. "There's lots of other things I can ask, too."

Others were thinking pretty much as Duke was thinking: Here were two men, one calling himself Bolt Haveril, from Texas; the other saying, "Me, I'm Juan Morada." Get them together this way, in the same room, they did not look very much alike. Both were tall and both were dark, however; and a thin black line of moustache shadowed each man's lips — and there was that scar, a thin white crescent, which on one was like a mirrored image of the other's. Not alike, no; yet, from a printed description, such as a sheriff's office would send out, either might have been Don Diablo.

"So you're Juan Morada, are you?" said Duke, and stared again at the newcomer.

"*Seguro,*" said Morada. "Sure. Me, I'm Juan Morada."

"Then tell me something," said Duke. "Who the merry hell is this other fellow?" He jerked his thumb in Bolt Haveril's general direction.

Morada really saw Bolt then for the first time. His brows went up and his nose came down; his eyes distended like the eyes of a horse about to run away, then the lids squeezed almost shut, just giving the glint of glistening black malevolency.

"Aha!" said Morada. "So he is here, no? That's what I heard, it's what I hoped! — Who is this *hombre?*" he exclaimed, swinging back toward Duke. "If you like to know, Señor, you come the right place when you ask me who it is! He is the man who sticks the nose in when it is not a business of his. He is the man who

232

plays me dirt and plays you dirt too when he runs out on me, taking that keed, Bob Morgan, along with him. He is a man that if I don't kill pretty damn quick it is because I drop down dead first. He is a ranchero from Texas down close to the border, and maybe down there he is a deputy sheriff, too, and his name is Bolt Haveril. That's what, Señor!"

Duke Morgan didn't say a word. He didn't jump up to his feet. He just sat there and blinked. He had started trying to get his head clear, himself sober. He held on tight now, holding himself back, growing cooler and calmer as he watched for pitfalls underfoot.

As for Bolt Haveril, for the moment he was no better than a derelict lost in a heavy fog with no compass to steer by and no rudder, with the boom of the surf somewhere — one couldn't tell where — on the rocks. He might fight this thing out; he might drop Morada and, with luck, Duke. But there'd be a swift end to Bolt Haveril — and there'd be no better, though it might be a slower, fate for Lady.

Yet he managed a smile, one quite naturally enigmatic, since not even he knew what he was thinking; he wasn't exactly thinking yet. Just feeling, sensing — groping in his fog. He did note the look on Duke's face, one of a blind groping to match his own; and he did see Lady. A quick eager brightness swept across her face; it made her eyes luminous, it even tipped up the corners of her mouth. She was glad! Glad to have someone else, any stranger, say, "He is not Don Diablo; he is what he has said he was all along, a

233

rancher from Texas, Bolt Haveril!" She didn't look beyond that; she hadn't had time yet.

Bolt wore that protective smile of his as long as he could, and kept still — and, again like Duke Morgan — did his level best to get his thoughts in order. Here, it seemed, was the end; the end of the limb —

The smile came off but only to give place to his sudden laughter. Man, it was funny! For even yet Duke didn't know, not a Morgan of them all knew which of the two dark, lean and unexplained newcomers before them was the much publicised Don Diablo of the border. Even now, after what Morada had just said to Duke, Duke wasn't sure of anything. Doggone it all, Duke didn't *know!*

And so Bolt laughed; and Duke could have killed him then with all the joy in life, and was strongly tempted to — But, hang it, he had to make sure what this was all about!

"Funny, ain't it?" he said ponderously. "Funny as hell, ain't it?"

"By golly, Duke, it *is* funny!" said Bolt, and wiped his eyes with a thumb knuckle.

"Sure," said Duke. "Only you might tell me what is the joke, anyhow. I don't see nobody else laughing. Only just you — Bolt Haveril, from Texas!"

"The joke, Duke? Man, it's you! You're so rattled that a kindhearted feller could almost be sorry for you. Say, Duke, it would pay you to go look in a looking-glass. Honest. What's funny? Why, your mug, Duke, all puzzled like that! Right now you don't know

234

which one of us is Johnny Devil Morada, and you'd rather know that than anything on earth!"

"I reckon I know now," said Duke. "Yes, I reckon I know. You said all along, didn't you, that you was Bolt Haveril? And I just made it up in my own head you was Juan Morada. Now Juan Morada himself comes along, and he says who he is and who you are. Yes, I reckon I know now, Haveril."

"Don't you wish you did know, Duke," chuckled Bolt. "Don't you just wish you could be sure! Happens it might make a whale of a lot of difference to you whether you guess right or wrong to-night."

"You said all the time you wasn't Juan Morada," said Duke. "You said right along you was Bolt Haveril. Well, this feller says the same thing. And he says he is Morada."

"Sure, I told you I was a Texas rancher named Haveril," said Bolt and grinned at him. "You wouldn't believe me though. You thought, just because I was riding a certain red stud horse, and because I happened to have some gold pieces with your mark on 'em, and because a sheriff or two was chasing me, that I was Morada! Got all that out of your head now, Duke?"

No, Duke hadn't really got any of that out of his head; confusingly he still retained it and had acquired some other puzzles along with it.

"One of you fellers is Morada," he said slowly. "The other is a fake. What the game is, I don't know right now. But pretty soon I'm going to know. And when I do know — Well, one of you fellers is going to wish he was somewheres else."

He turned then to Morada. He said brusquely:

"You! You got anything to say? What about the horse and what about the gold pieces I sent down to Juan Morada, with my mark on 'em?"

Morada answered, first with a high-shouldered shrug and a crooked smile, then with the terse statement:

"This *hombre* cut into the play when I wasn't looking for him. He shot me out of the saddle and rode off with my horses and with what I had in my saddlebags."

"I'll get to the bottom of this somehow," said Duke. "I'll get the low-down on both you fellers. What the hell do I know about either of you right now? Not a damn thing. But I'll get to know, if I have to chop you into mincemeat."

He looked at Bolt a long while, studying him; then he looked just as steadily and piercingly at Juan Morada. Under his breath he muttered something; not all the words were audible but his thought was clear enough: ". . . both with a scar like that, huh? — didn't just happen — some sort of a game —"

Suddenly he slewed about, facing Budge Morgan who still stood at the door; Budge hadn't stirred since Morada made his entrance.

"Budge," said Duke, "I guess you better step along. Get a gun in the hand of every man, woman and ten-year-old kid in the Valley. I can't figger this thing yet, but all hell's on the rampage to-night or I miss my guess. Get busy, Budge."

"You're damn right, Duke," snapped Budge, and went out on a run.

236

Budge had not taken off his spurs; as he ran down the steps to his horse they could hear the clank and jingle of the heavy long-pronged rowels and chains. Then as the sounds were dying away they seemed to return more clearly, with more of silvery chime and music. And then they knew that as Budge was going away Barnaby was coming.

Barnaby ran up the steps and to the door and stopped just inside, his bells quieted as he leaned on his long crooked staff and sent those darkly brilliant eyes of his travelling from face to face. He was laughing softly, all to himself.

"Hello, Barnaby," said Duke.

"Hello, Duke," said Barnaby, and kept on with the subdued, silent laughter.

"You're not wet like this feller here," said Duke, and jerked his thumb once more in Bolt's direction. "Look at him drip, Barnaby. Looks like he'd fell in the river, don't it?"

Barnaby's quiet mirth seemed more delighted than ever. He nodded his head a dozen times, making the ragged black hair fall forward over his thin face, snapping it back again with a toss.

"We had fun, we had lots of fun!" said a happy Barnaby.

"Did you?" said Duke. "That's fine. Just who had all the fun, Barnaby?"

"We did, us three!"

"You three?" said Duke, milder than ever, since he knew Barnaby so very well. "That would be you and who else?"

237

"Why, Johnny and Stag and me!" cried Barnaby merrily. "We had fun, didn't we, Johnny? They won the first part of the game when they came up with us and found Lady, but after that we won, didn't we? We're here now, all three of us, and they don't know — Duke don't know! — how we got here!"

Obviously he was addressing Bolt Haveril. Yet Duke, bound on making sure of any small detail that might come in handy, said: "Johnny? Who are you talking about? What Johnny?"

Barnaby pointed to Bolt.

"We're friends and I call him Johnny now," he explained. "His real name is Juan Morada and some folks say he is Don Diablo and a bandit and a killer. But that's all a mistake; he is a good man. I know."

"Of course he's a good man," agreed Duke, and asked, "and you're sure who he is, Barnaby? That he is Juan Morada?"

"Of course he is, Duke," the boy laughed. "He just pretended he was someone else; it was a game and he was fooling you when he told you he was named Bolt Haveril."

The real Juan Morada, forced to guess what this was all about, glowered at Barnaby and muttered "*Tonto!* Is the boy a fool then?"

"Not a fool, just crazy," growled Duke. "Not a fool though by a damn sight."

And as for Bolt — he had talked with Barnaby by the hour as they plodded through the woods, trying to make him understand — he was suddenly grateful that no words of his had been able to dislodge a conviction

238

which, once implanted in the mad youth's brain, was there for all time. Here was a bit more mystification for Duke, here a thin hope that somehow out of that uncertainty there might grow that lucky Chance for which every man in desperate straits watches with such stubborn and hawk-eyed eagerness. Then all of a sudden it was Barnaby himself who pricked the fragile new bubble of hope.

"Duke, you're the crazy one!" he cried. "Me, I'm smart; Barnaby is as smart as a deer or a wild turkey or an eagle or an old timber wolf; and you're not so very smart at all, Duke. You're the crazy one, I tell you! Listen! You want to know if this man is Juan Morada or not? You want to be sure? You won't just believe me, but you want someone who knows to tell you? Well, there is someone who can tell — Wait, I'll bring her!"

He would have darted out of the door then, but Duke yelled him back, and Morg Blount standing next to him snared him by the arm in full flight.

"Maybe you're right, Barnaby," said Duke. "Maybe you're right about everything. Just the same, tell me where you're going. Who is this she that knows Juan Morada?"

"Didn't I say you didn't have any sense, Duke?" exclaimed the boy petulantly, wriggling in Blount's grasp. "Morada's a Mexican, ain't he? He came from down on the border, didn't he? Who's your wife and where did she come from? It's poor little Teresita I'm talking about. She knows!"

"Hell," said Duke disgustedly. "How could she know? It's been over twenty years since she came up here — she was only a kid, fifteen years old — she —"

"She knows!" cried Barnaby. "She knows, I tell you!"

"The damfool boy ought to have been drowned when he was a pup," growled Duke.

"Throw him out, Morg!"

Then Sid broke in on the discussion, saying excitedly:

"Duke! Damfool as he is, Barnaby's right! She does know! When this feller was here the other day," and he thumbed toward Bolt, "she didn't know who he was supposed to be until late that night. You went over to Pocket Gully; you left me here; I was watching him —"

"You let him get away," said Duke. But Sid overlooked that, running on swiftly:

"I had a talk with her. She said: 'Tomorrow morning I will talk with him. I knew all the Moradas down there; my brother married a Morada girl and my sister married one of the Morada's cousins. I was going to marry a Morada myself!' That's what she told me, Duke. Barnaby's right. She'll know for sure!" "Go get her!" thundered Duke.

CHAPTER
TWENTY-ONE

Bolt Haveril was able to take a quick, silent step backward without drawing attention; that brought him up with the log wall at his back; comforting feeling. He stole a glance at Lady, saw the anxiety in her eyes as she began to think of what it was going to mean to him, and therefore to her, when the definite disclosure was made. He tried to flash her a signal, yet realized how impossible that would be. If he could only prepare her to break and run the instant trouble started . . . He saw Molly clinging so desperately to her unexpected new friend and read what was written so plainly on her white face, and thought grimly: "If I don't drop Duke in his tracks to-night, Steve Kendal will!" He thought too, "If Duke only guessed that Steve is right out there now, using all his will power to keep from crooking his finger to the trigger!"

Juan Morada, arrogant through habit and supercilious through nature, was talking. He was saying:

". . . and so you need somebody to tell you? And this woman, she is your wife, no? And she has lived on the border?"

"By God, it would be a funny thing!" said Duke. His eyes flicked back and forth between the two lean, dark men with their hard, tell-nothing eyes and their small pointed black moustaches — and their twin crescent scars. He considered the alertness which marked them both; alike in that, they were, too. Ready, those two devils, to go for their guns at the drop of the hat.

Duke pulled his own gun out of its oily black holster and rested it on the table before him, his hand feeling the fit of the worn butt, his big forefinger flirting with the trigger. Then, while his eyes kept flashing back and forth like a cat's watching two rat-holes at the same time, he answered Morada.

"Sure, Teresa was a border girl. I brought her up here when she was fifteen. Let's see; Sid's about twenty now, so that was more than twenty years ago. Think she might know you — Morada?"

"What was her name?" asked Morada. "Teresa? There are many fish in the seas and many birds in the trees and many Teresas in Mexico."

"Her name?" mumbled Duke. By thunder, he had forgotten!

Of them all, Sid was the only one who knew.

"She was Teresa Refugio Estrada," he said.

"She was fifteen. She was going to dance at La Luna Amarilla. Duke rode down with a crowd; he grabbed her and brought her up here. She had many friends —"

Juan Morada began to laugh softly. Lady shivered; she thought, "If a tiger could ever laugh, it would laugh like that!"

"Like you said, Señor Morgan," said Morada, and lightly touched up the points of his moustache, sharpening them one after the other, "maybe it is going to be funny! The little Estrada one danced down in my Nacional so long ago? You see, Señor, when you look at me, a young man, very strong and handsome? Sure for sure! But I am going to tell you some secrets: I am a *leetle* more than thirty years old, Señor! So you see? I was maybe ten when some wild gringos came riding like devils through Nacional — and carried away La Teresita Estrada! People don't forget these things, eh, Señor? Down in Nacional they talk about it yet."

Bolt was trying to plan but couldn't. He'd never make it alive half-way to the door; there was no window he could dive headlong through without carrying along with him a dozen bullets in his body. He could get Duke Morgan — he could get Morada, maybe — Steve would nail Rance and maybe another man or two —

But what good would all that do? It didn't lift Lady Morgan out of Dark Valley; it didn't save that tender blue-eyed baby thing, Molly —

"If I simply got the drop on Duke," he thought. "A quick flip of the gun does it. Freeze him on to his bench — say, 'Duke, pull your men off, or you're cold turkey — ' Well, — we-ell, maybe — if there wasn't any other way, if no other Chance popped its head up —"

"Go see what the hell's going on," said Duke to the man nearest the door, Baylis. "Barnaby went out on the run; he'd ought to have brought her back by this time."

Baylis hurried out. On the steps he collided with Barnaby returning. Close behind Mad Barnaby, limping and hobbling along, came a small, slight, bent figure like a child's, hidden under a big Spanish shawl.

When Teresa entered she gave even Duke a bit of a start. Small and dark, crooked and venomous, never did a woman look more like a witch — her eyes — big eyes which looked small and narrow and slanting — so did her black arcs of brows come down and so did their lids close like casements arranged to shut the light out, to imprison the noxious dark within.

She gazed sullenly at Duke and didn't say a word. Her eyes, so filled with hate, spoke for her: "You sent for me. I knew you would make me come if I didn't come willingly. Now what do you want? Tell me and let me go."

"We've got company to-night, Tess," said Duke.

She made no rejoinder, she didn't seem interested, she didn't even glance around the room to see who that company might be.

"Ever hear of a man named Juan Morada?" Duke asked. "He's from the border down near Nacional near Cajob where you used to live. Ever hear of him?"

Promptly, swiftly as though to get it over with, she replied:

"Morada? There were many Moradas near my home. Juan?" Her bony shoulders be spoke her indifference in a Mexican shrug under her black Spanish shawl. "Juan Moradas in Mexico are like John Smiths in your country."

"Pull your stabbing eyes off me," said Duke angrily, "and look at the two men here. Which one is Juan Morada? Do you know?"

"Do I care!" she cried spitefully. "You are in some sort of trouble; you ask me to help you! Why should I help you, Duke Morgan?"

"You do what I tell you! I'll kill you —"

She laughed at his threat; she even pulled her shawl back from her bosom, revealing the bare throat which used to be so round and smooth and lovely.

"Do I care?" she said again, asking him now a question that could have but one answer. "With a knife or with a bullet, Duke Morgan, do I care? Have I fallen in love with life then?"

"Damn you!" said Duke. Then with both big hands spread out on the table, the gun between them ignored for the moment, he leaned toward her. He said, as though the thought had just come to him, as perhaps it had, chewing it over in his own mind as he spoke it slowly:

"How'd you like to go back home, Tess? Back to your own place, your own people — to have me let you go free — for always?"

A flash came up into her dark eyes. She hid it hurriedly, shutting down her eyelids, but he saw it and leaned back, laughing at her.

"Look 'em over," he said. "Pick me the right man, the one that is Juan Morada, and I'll let you go."

She turned from him then and regarded all the faces in the room, very attentive faces, most of the men's just eager with interest, Lady's and Molly's pale and drawn and frightened — then the two dark faces of the two strangers, stern, blanker than others, one of them, Bolt's, pretty grim.

Teresa, holding centre stage, appeared of a mind to hold it indefinitely. Her own face was blank, her eyes went back and forth between the two, back and forth.

Then presently she shrugged; then she regarded them again in that queerly intent way; then she frowned.

Duke, grown impatient, bellowed at her out of the rippleless silence:

"Dammit, you don't know!"

She turned slowly and smiled at him like a little weazened witch of a sphinx.

"Yes, Duke, I know!"

"Then tell me! Do you think I've got all night —"

"If I tell you," she asked coolly, "how are you going to be sure I didn't make a mistake? Twenty years is a long time. It has been more than twenty years since I saw Juan Morada. So how will you be sure?"

"If you're sure," he said, frowning and uncertain yet making the best of it, "if you're dead sure, I can tell. And —"

"You're a great big fool!" she scoffed at him. "Now I will tell you, because I want to go back to my people and you have promised. Maybe you are just lying to me; maybe you will let me go. Anyhow, I will tell you. But first I am going to tell you a story —"

"To hell with your story! I'm in a hurry — there are other things on my mind to-night —"

"A very short story," she said, unruffled by his storming at her. "Then you will know that, even after so many years, I haven't made a mistake. You see, we Estradas lived on a little rancho near El Cajon; and on the other side of Nacional lived the Moradas. And among us Estradas were some nice young pretty girls; and there were big, handsome boys among the Moradas. So you know what would happen. And I had

246

a sister, bigger than me, Valencia. And Arturo Morada would come all the time to see her, and sometimes his little brother Juan would come too. And one time there was a big fight, Arturo Morada and another man, Esteben Munoz, and Arturo's little brother Juan, too — and the one to get hurt worst of all was Juanito. And that is my little story!"

"What the hell?" cried Duke, mystified.

Again she laughed at him; again she said, "You are a great big fool! A knife leaves a scar —"

"They've both got scars! That's the hell of it!"

"By the mouth? That is nothing. A man can scratch himself there with the fingernail and get a scar like that! But in that fight it wasn't just fingernail scars they left! Make these two open up their shirts over the chest. One of them — *and that will be Juan Morada* — will have a long scar there! Ah! I know! And it will be — Now I will tell you which man it is!"

As quick as a flash she whirled, three rapid steps carried her to her man. She tapped him on the chest.

"This one is Juan Morada," she said. "You will see!"

It was Bolt Haveril whom she had singled out.

What was more, across his chest was revealed an old scar, half a dozen inches long.

There was no scar on Morada's chest.

CHAPTER
TWENTY-TWO

No one was more astonished than Bolt Haveril himself. Why the woman had elected him to the rôle of Don Diablo — and how she could possibly know he had that scar on his chest — it simply didn't make sense and so, for the moment, muddled and confused him.

Juan Morada, across the room, was roaring and pitching and cursing until he was black in the face, swearing the woman had invented the whole story, the names even. Two or three men held him; it was they who had torn his fancy shirt open across his chest.

Him, and what he was saying, Bolt let go without even mental comment. His interest centred elsewhere. Lady was looking at him with an expression on her face which told him, more eloquently than any mere words could have done, of the tumult within her soul. She had never quite *known* who he was. There had been the moments when she had held that she was sure that he was Bolt Haveril, Texas rancher and a friend. On top of those moments were those others when she had told herself she was sure that he was that devilish and cold-blooded killer, Don Diablo of the border.

And now?

If anyone here should know, that one was Teresa. And she had said so convincingly, "This one is Juan Morada!" And she had said, "There is a long white scar, an old scar, on his chest!" Lady's own eyes, incredulous at first and then widening with a new fear that ran a wide gamut, saw the scar.

Still, she would not believe it! This was Bolt Haveril, her friend and her brother Bob's, the finest, most splendid of men. Breathless, she looked up into his face for his swift denial. So many and many a time he had said, soberly — at times drawlingly, at times with that dear quick flash of a smile of his — "Me? I'm Bolt Haveril, from Texas, you know."

And now?

Bolt Haveril, thinking swiftly and true to the line — thinking, "Here, after all, is that one chance I looked for!" didn't even look at her. He looked at Duke — and he began again to laugh!

"Duke, you old son-of-a-gun!" he shouted and stepped across the floor to clap Duke on the shoulder, and then went on laughing.

"Damn you, Morada," muttered a badly puzzled Duke Morgan.

Juan Morada, freed of the several hands upon him, was shouting at them, at Duke, like a man yelling up against the wind.

"This woman lies! Are you the blind-buff-fool that everybody calls you? Me, I am Juan Morada, and this man is the cursed gringo, the double damned Texas who got Bob away from me and —"

Bolt did his own bit of shouting.

"Knock his teeth down his damn throat! Shut him up; string him up if you like; you'll be doing a good job! Why, Duke, can't you make it all out yet? Can't you tell by looking at him that he's some damned U.S. marshal or some wandered-away-from-home ranger? Some sheriff's spy or something like that? Watch him, Duke! — And don't you think it's about time for you and me to get down to brass tacks?"

And, even while he was triumphing over a maddened Morada, and shouting all that, he was thinking: "There's Steve Kendal just outside, Steve looking in and keeping his finger close to the trigger! And all that Steve knows of me is what he's picked up to-night. If he believes what I'm trying to make Duke believe — damn him, he'll plug me first of all!"

Then he remembered Lady Morgan. He swung about upon her. Her eyes were dilated with horror. Again he had made the firm ground crumble beneath her. It was she now who began to cling to Molly.

Suddenly — Lady could stand it no more — she cried out:

"Molly! Come away. Come with me. These men —"

She darted toward the door, Molly running willingly enough with her. No one thought or cared to stop their headlong flight.

"Let 'em go," growled Duke. "They can't go far and when we want 'em we'll have 'em." He surged up to his feet at last, steady and cold sober now; he swept up his old gun from the table, gripping it so hard that his acorn-brown knuckles went white.

"Boys," he said savagely, "from now on we keep our eyes on both these fellers, no matter which one is Morada and which ain't. Cut the first one of 'em down that makes a move that don't seem right; we're taking no more chances."

Lady and Molly shot through the door and were swallowed up by the outside dark. Bolt thought, "They'll scoot to Lady's cabin; they'll lock themselves in; they'll be all right — and if it comes to a fight, they will know how to hide out until it's all over. They'll be all right."

A forgotten Teresa spoke up.

"Duke, you made me a promise. Are you going to keep it? Or was it just another lie from you?"

"Get out of here, you half-bred she-devil," said Duke. "In the morning, if you're alive, you can go and be damned to you."

"You won't let me go now?" she asked, speaking softly and unemotionally.

"Not a gate opens to-night!"

"But here is Juan Morada; let me go with him!"

"And how is he going to go," he demanded shrewdly, "if the gates are shut? Fly?"

"How did he get here? The way he came, that way let us go."

"Morada? I need Morada. I haven't finished with Morada yet!"

Bolt was thinking: "There's no use waiting any longer! The way things have gone, there's only one way to finish this job. Here goes!"

Then he said sharply to Duke Morgan, in fact raising his voice so that he shouted:

"Duke, I've given you a bit of warning tonight, haven't I?"

"You don't have to yell at me, do you?" snapped Duke.

But Bolt did have to yell. He had to make sure that Steve Kendal outside heard and took his cue and got busy! — Or had Steve, thinking of one thing only, already sped away, following Molly?

"I've got to yell to get anything heard in here," shouted Bolt, and prayed that Steve was sticking to his post. "I've warned you that the Outsiders know what you did to Ed Daly and how you stole Molly away. They are on the job to-night, Duke. You never let me finish. I'm not the only man who got into the Valley to-night. And all the Outsiders are waiting for now is a signal from a spy they've sent inside. Once they get that signal — well, you're wiped out, Duke Morgan. There'll be a hundred, maybe five hundred men pour in on you!"

"You lie!" roared Duke. "There's not that many Outsiders would dare try to break in on the Morgans."

Steve Kendal had stuck to his post. Steve was ready.

Already he had scooped up handfuls of dry pine needles; he had made a pile against the sturdy log wall of Duke's house, close to the rear window; he had piled dead branches on top of all that. He had emptied the two quart bottles of coal oil brought for this purpose. He, too, knew that the time had come. And as Bolt's words reached him, Steve had the match in his hands. He ignited the dry, pitchy heap stacked against the dry pitchy wall — and then ran. He ran, not to escape anything, but to overtake the fleeing Molly. For he had seen her and Lady racing down toward the river.

All details of the raid had been meticulously arranged by the two old sheriffs in their conference with Bolt and Steve. They had broken their party up into three; they would come storming in at all three gates, sweeping the valley when they had their signal. That signal was to be a tall column of fire. They'd wait for that exactly one hour after they estimated Bolt and Steve were in the Valley; if the signal didn't come then, well they'd raid just the same. There must have been close to two hundred men of them, and nearly every man knew Ed Daly, yes and Molly, too. And there wasn't a man among them who wouldn't have been as glad of the chance to shoot a Morgan as to kill a rattlesnake coiled to strike at him.

"There's the blaze!" snapped old Dan Westcott, one of the party hidden on the ridge just above North Gate. "Bolt and Steve reckon they need us, boys. Here we go!"

They were ready enough to go, raring to go, but there was one here sticking as close to old Dan as any cockle burr, a seasoned, horse-faced man who had been given his job by Dave Heffinger. Dave was heading the posse down at South Gate; this man was to hold old Dan down by his suspenders.

"We got time aplenty," he called out. "Remember what Dave said, Dan. Wait for him to make the first move down to the South Gate. That's quite a ways off, you know."

Dan Westcott snorted, but held his horses.

"That's right, boys; that's right," he snapped, and sounded as ugly as a savage dog on a chain. "Give old Dave a chance — and just let's hope he ain't blind and he ain't deaf! Shut up!" No one had made a sound, but he yipped at them as though they had. "Get your ears peeled. *Listen!*"

They only waited for him to grow silent so they could listen. A few heavy, silent, breathless moments passed, only a few, though they seemed many. Then they heard what they listened for.

It was heard down in the Valley, too, and every Morgan there, no matter what he was doing, stiffened in his boots. Those at headquarters, Duke and his sons and men with them, had already dashed out of the house as a voice yelled "Fire!" and as they heard the crackle and hiss of flames and even caught the first glimpse of a wan reddish reflection on the inner walls.

"By damn!" roared Duke, and then someone shouted him down, yelling: "Be still! Listen! The bell —"

The bell notes came from a distance, from so far away that with a shift of the night breeze they all but died into silence; then the breeze, drawing up the valley, stiffened, and the sounds were clearer and louder than before.

254

"That's down at South Gate," someone called; and another, right after, said with the timbre of excitement in his voice: "Listen to it! There's hell to pay down there!"

They did listen; the reason they grew briefly so rigid was that they all knew what sort of thing must be meant when a Morgan bell rang like that — with a clanging clamour that even the far distance failed to soften, an iron tongue beating the bronze sides of the bell to emit such a din that the whole Valley echoed with it.

By now a tall red and yellow plume of fire stood high up above Duke's house. But the knot of men standing in its flickering light did not so much as watch it, did not listen to the hiss of its flame. For before the first bell had ceased clanging and clashing out its message, a second bell, one considerably nearer, started ringing no less violently.

"That's Middle Gate!" roared Duke. "That damn Morada told us the truth. We're being raided. There are men at the South Gate, and at the Middle Gate, too. And —"

Then the nearest bell, the one at North Gate, only a few hundred yards away, lifted its brazen voice, and was so fierce and strong in its message that throbbed and rolled along the air to the Morgans that there could not be the least faint hope the other bells had spoken out of turn, that this was any false alarm. At last Dark Valley was being raided by a band of mountain men who were at an end of all patience, who were out to make an end of the Morgans in Morgan Valley.

From afar came a rattle of scattering shots, rifle and pistol shots — from nearer came, like a swelling echo, another rattle of gunfire — from the nearest gate of all, North Gate where Dan Westcott was no longer holding back, burst out not only the crash of gunfire but, topping it, a hurricane of yells like the yipping of a band of lickered-up Apaches on the war trail.

"Kill that Morada feller!" roared Duke. "Kill that other Morada feller too. One of 'em, maybe both, started this on us! Where the hell are they? Burn 'em down — then we take on the gang that thinks it can come in the Valley and raise hell and get out alive! But get them two damn Moradas!"

Those "two damn Moradas" were hard to get.

When the crowd burst out of the Council Room at the first shout of "Fire!" Bolt Haveril had gone along with the strong current but, as he elbowed his way among them through the wide door, he had swiftly stepped to one side while the rest sped on and down the steps. When they turned the corner of the house, headed for the fire itself, he leaped from the porch into the shadows and ran straight on into deeper shadows, headed for the river and Lady's cabin.

And so he wasn't at hand to be shot down at Duke's command, though he wasn't too far away to hear it ring out like the jangling of the nearest bell.

As for Juan Morada, a desperado now desperate with the knowledge that he had come at the wrong hour, he was likewise of no mind to be chopped down in any clean sweep made by the murderous Morgans, and did his own quick bit of sidestepping. He wanted distance between himself and Duke; also he wanted to square the deal with the man who had shot him, imprisoned him, sent him to jail and had come close to hanging him — and seeing the way Bolt Haveril went, he went after him like a dark arrow through the dark.

"Dammit!" a Duke Morgan gone mad was storming, "get them two men! And get them two girls, too! Burn the men down, and to hell with 'em, but don't put a scratch on either Lady or Molly Daly! Bring 'em to me. They're our ace in the hole. *Get Lady and Molly Daly!*"

This deep, dark, cliff-bound valley might have been known as the Valley of Echoes. When a thunderstorm burst over it, it resounded with all the terrific boom of a siege of cannons. To-night rifles and belt guns started up echoes that went drunk on the joy of reverberating sound and kept the small deadly thunder of it going until after the last shot was fired.

Down at South Gate three men of the raiding party were shot before they broke into the Valley. Dave Heffinger led them and took a bullet grazingly through the outer bulge of his gun-arm shoulder, and still led them, yelling back over his shoulder, to some mumbled comment some lukewarm member of his crowd had haltingly voiced: "To hell with the law! We're out to get the Morgans at last. Come ahead, boys."

They came ahead. They were coming ahead, too, at Middle Gate where two men were shot out of their saddles before they broke through. Up at North Gate, closest of all to Duke's house and Valley headquarters, no less than seven of Dan Westcott's party took rifle wounds before they succeeded in smashing the padlock and breaking through.

"Fellers," yelled old Dan, "me, I'm sheriff down to Rincon County and here I am up in Juarez County; and Dave Heffinger, he's sheriff of Juarez, and there he is coming up in Rincon — and that makes the whole damn mess so illegal, unlawful and dead ag'in the law that every man of you has got a right to cut loose and do's he damn pleases. Get them damn Morgans that wiped out Ed Daly and stole his girl; get every man of 'em if you're lucky — but look out you don't knock over Bolt Haveril and Steve Kendal! Watch it, fellers!"

Steve Kendal couldn't see Molly anywhere, but he heard light, swift running steps and dashed along after them. He couldn't call out to her, not yet; so he only ran the harder. He tripped and fell and swore and scrambled up and hardly stopped running during the whole of it. He heard a door slam, Lady's cabin door; and he was so close that he heard the wooden bar drop into place.

Then he made out the black shadowy squat shape of the cabin. He came close, his hand on its wall. There was no light within; he couldn't hear a sound. He waited a moment.

When presently he heard a faint rustling sound, then hushed whispering voices, he called softly:

"Molly! Molly, open the door. Quick!"

Molly, all but fainting in Lady's mothering arms, couldn't even answer. She just clung tighter. But Lady

Morgan, her thoughts as quick as her light-running tread had been, whispered:

"Molly, it's someone calling you! Who could it be?"

"I don't know. Oh, I don't know. There is no one here —"

"Molly!" called Steve a little louder and clearer. "I am here. It is Steve. Hurry; open the door."

A little scream broke from Molly Daly then.

"It's Steve! Steve Kendal! Oh, Steve —"

It was Lady who ran and unbarred the door. She saw, vague against the background of lesser outside dark, the tall lean form of a man. Molly had run to her side and Lady caught her by the hand.

"Who are you?" she asked. "And what —"

"Sh!" he cautioned. "I'm Steve. Molly knows who I am. I came along with Bolt Haveril. We're getting you out of this. Come along. Come quick!"

"Steve!" cried Molly, and jerked free from Lady and threw herself sobbing into young Steve's arms. "Oh, Steve!"

Her second "Steve!" was a gasp, as Steve's arms shut tight about her. Then he remembered Lady and Bolt Haveril's interest in her and all that Bolt had said to him of her, and said hurriedly:

"You, too, Miss Morgan! Hurry; come with us. We're going to get out of this; we've got a chance if we run for it. Before all hell pops. Dammit, hurry!" It would have been better if he hadn't added, "Bolt Haveril will be with us any minute."

For at that Lady, coming through the door, stopped and held back and asked,

"Bolt Haveril? Who is he? Which is he? Is that man — ?"

"I don't know!" Steve blurted out, all eagerness to get away. "I met up with him tonight for the first time. He's the feller that that crooked little old woman said was Juan Morada — I don't know a damn thing about him except —"

"Neither do I!" said Lady. "Teresa said he is Don Diablo. Teresa knows. And —"

"What do we care who he is?" said Steve. He reached out a long arm and caught her by the wrist, jerking her out through the door and along with him and Molly. "All I know is, he's a guy to tie to. If it hadn't been for him — Here they come! Hurry!"

Molly was all eagerness to run with him, to run anywhere. Lady, uncertain, confused and therefore reluctant since she didn't know what new danger she might be plunging into, would have held back. But Steve's hand still gripped her wrist; she found herself running stumblingly through the dark with them. Steve, as though he knew what he was about, led the way upstream, keeping close to the river bank.

Lady tried to warn him, "Not this way —" but didn't finish. For of a sudden Bolt Haveril, hurrying from Morgan's house and hearing them in full flight, bore down upon them.

"That you, Steve? You've got both girls?" In the dark he couldn't be sure of any of them. When Steve answered him, Bolt added: "Come ahead as lively as we can make it. All that shooting over at the gate — that's Dan and his party. And the Morgans have got their backs up; we'll get caught between two crowds shooting wild."

Thereafter Steve gave all his attention to Molly. Lady, released, started to draw back. Bolt, so close to her now that he could put his hand on her shoulder, said urgently:

"We're on our way, Lady! You're going out of this to-night for good and all."

She felt like one standing in the whirling centre of pandemonium: From the gate came shouts, the thunder of horses' hoofs bearing down upon them, and shouts like the whooping of a pack of Indians. From Morgan's big house a tall and swiftly spreading column of fire wavered against the background of pines and firs, and she could see fitfully figures like ants whose nest had been stirred up with a stick, scurrying in all directions.

"Bolt!" she gasped. "Oh, are you Bolt? Or are you — are you what Teresa said you were?"

His hand found hers unerringly in the dark and gave it as hearty a squeeze as she had ever known.

"You bet I'm Bolt! And you're coming with me and in two shakes are going to be as safe as a church —"

They were running again, Steve and Molly a dozen feet ahead, and not one of them heard above the shouting and rifle fire the sound which they should have heard as Juan Morada broke his way through a breast-high thicket to intercept them. He had heard their voices, having followed so closely, and started shooting the instant that he saw them. Steve heard a bullet whistle past his head, and gave Molly a sudden shove that sent her sprawling on the grassy river bank out of the line of Morada's fire.

As Steve made his first instinctive move to protect the girl and then the second toward his holstered gun, Bolt saw the flashes of Morada's shots and answered, swifter than ever before, with his own six-gun repartee. He could shoot quicker and faster and truer than most men — as witness certain holes in certain sheriff's hats. The devil of it just now was that he couldn't see Morada — just his gun flashes. But his instinct was right; he heard a grunt jolted out of the man he had at least winged, then heard a body crashing down in the brush. And after that there were no more shots from Juan Morada.

"Come ahead, Bolt! For God's sake! They're going to head us off!"

That was Steve who, having found Molly struggling to her feet, helped her up and called back to Haveril. Bolt was every whit as eager to step along: This gunfight with Morada, short as it had been, had advertised his and his companions' whereabouts to the Morgans. He heard Duke's shout, and then many running feet: Duke would give an arm right now to get hold of the four of them before the first of the raiders bore down on him.

Bolt, every bit as impatient as Steve to get going, tried to urge Lady along with him. Again she began expostulating, saying:

"Not this way! They'll corner us between the river and the cliff! Don't you hear me? Have you gone crazy?"

262

There was not a second to waste in explanations. Fire had caught the ancient dry roof of the house and was making all around it as bright as day. Out of the widening circle of light the Morgans, with Duke at their fore, were rushing toward them. So Bolt, emulating Steve with Molly, simply caught Lady by the arm and ran, making her run with him.

CHAPTER
TWENTY-THREE

For some years after that night — until after Lady Morgan and her brother Bob, neither of them ever wishing to come this way again, had sold to the "Wild" Camerons — the place was known as Bloody Valley. Perhaps no one man ever did get the details of all that happened during the hour between the moon's brightening the peaks above and at last shining down into a valley lying still and hushed save for the crackling flames and white clouds of smoke from a cabin here and there still burning. More than one white, still face looked up at the moon that night and saw nothing of its splendour.

From the outset Duke Morgan knew that he had come to the end of his high-handed sway; and that it was to be the end of himself he knew too — unless he could get his hands on those two girls and hold them as hostages, setting them like a double shield between himself and the attackers.

Give him Lady Morgan, give him, most of all, Molly Daly, and he'd ride out of this yet, with his head high and a laugh to send back, and with a saddle-bag heavy with gold. A crafty man Duke thought himself, always ready for an emergency no matter how unlikely.

264

Rifle shots far down the valley were as faint as fire crackers; shooting where the raiders surged through the Middle Gate was louder but still far off and no great immediate concern of Duke's. But here through the North Gate came Dan Westcott's wolf pack following that doughty old he-wolf, Dan himself, and they were very decidedly Duke's instant problem. They and those two girls.

The brief duel between Bolt and Morada gave Duke his clue. He saw gun flashes, heard voices and made out the four running figures.

"We've got 'em, boys!" he shouted. "Let the house burn, you fools! Come along, every man of you, and remember what I told you: We want those girls alive and unhurt. We can grab 'em before this gang of Daly's friends gets on top of us."

So Duke and his sons, Baylis and Curly also, and fat Tom Colby, broke into a run, swooping through the timber and brush after the fleeing four. Duke, well at their head, made out that he could come up with his quarry well before the raiders arrived; they hadn't crossed the bridge but had raced on upstream. There under the waterfall, by the deep, froth-churned pool, he'd have them. Not a chance for them to escape him; not with the wild current of the river to cross. They'd lost their heads, said Duke; they should have run to the bridge, taking their chances there instead of plunging into a blind alley.

Sid, at Duke's heels, began clamouring. Recalling how Bolt Haveril had come dripping water into the house, he said anxiously:

"He can swim, Duke. He swum it once already. Look out or we'll lose them yet!"

"If they start swimming, sink 'em," roared Duke and ran on.

Lady Morgan heard their voices, even made out some of their words. Again she strove to make Bolt understand.

"We're running the wrong way!" she cried as he still hurried her along close behind the speeding blurred figures of Steve and his unquestioning Molly. "We can't cross the river up here — the current's too strong, and there are sharp rocks — and the banks are all rock, high and slippery —"

"Lady! Don't talk. Run! We're going clear — if you'll only *run!*"

"Oh, Bolt! *Bolt!*" For he was Bolt to her now in her desperation; she remembered him as he had been toward her during their brief freedom from Dark Valley, and she didn't care who he was or what Teresa said of him or even that when he was identified by that scar as Juan Morada he appeared to admit at last that he was Don Diablo, none other, and proud of it. All that didn't matter now; she clung tighter than ever to his hand.

All rifle and pistol shots nearby suddenly ceased, though there was still the intermittent noise of a battle being fought farther down the Valley. A moment later even the rush of horses' hoofs was hushed; the riders had stopped at the bridge. Out of the hush rose Dan Westcott's voice as cuttingly emphatic as the crack of a blacksnake.

"Hi, Duke Morgan! Hi, all you Morgans!" he yelled. "Better throw down your guns and step out peaceful;

it's the only chance you got. And if you've laid hands on that Daly girl or on my friend Bolt Haveril — yep, or on Lady Morgan or Steve Kendal — you better cut your own throats soon's you start stepping. — Hear me, Morgan?"

"Who do you think you are? What do you want?" shouted Duke. But he didn't slacken his headlong, blundering pace. A moment's parley suited him right down to the ground, provided it held up the other fellows and gave him his chance to pounce on a couple of fugitives whom he meant to have serve him well that night; they'd save him his life or nothing could.

Though the red fire gushed up brighter and stronger from Duke's house, the light along the river banks was fitful and uncertain at best, obstructed by the dark forest growth, smothered by the smoke of the burning. Dan and his followers could merely discern running figures, losing them almost the instant they were glimpsed.

Dan Westcott didn't answer Duke's questioning. Instead, rising in his stirrups the better to peer into the shadows all about him, he shouted at the top of his voice:

"Bolt! Where are you, Bolt? Are you all right?"

And Bolt shouted back at him: "Burn 'em down, Dan! Cross at the bridge and clean up on every Morgan of 'em that don't throw down his gun and quit. Yes, I'm all right. So's Lady and Molly Daly and Steve. On our way, Dan!"

"Glory be!" yipped Dan. And he led the way again, so that a moment later there was a louder thunder of hoofs than ever, iron shoes beating up echoes out of the bridge planks.

Steve snapped back at Bolt: "Dammit, you oughtn't to have yelled like that. Now the Morgans'll be on top of us before —"

"We're almost there, Steve," Bolt returned. "Run, man, run!"

They broke out of the timber into a grassy open space, darting across it with all possible speed. Yet before they had gained the timber again on the far side they heard Duke's shout behind them, knew that he had seen them, heard him and several other men pounding along after them. And Duke and two of his company, those in front with them, Sid and Tom Colby, began shooting as they ran, bent on bringing down the man they still supposed to be Juan Morada.

Molly cried out; Steve, instantly in a terrible anguish, was sure she had been shot. But no; it was just the whistling of bullets all about them that had whipped that outcry from her.

As they gained the cover of the scattering pines Bolt called sharply to Steve: "Go ahead with the girls. Don't wait for me. They're getting too close. I'll hold 'em a minute. You three can make it easy, Steve; it's only twenty-thirty yards farther. I'll follow on."

"We can all make it now!" Steve insisted. "Come ahead, Bolt. No use you should —"

"Do what I tell you!" Bolt cut in and sounded angry. "You promised me, damn you, to do whatever I said. Get going!"

Steve said curtly to Molly, "Come ahead, Molly." And as they started running again he called back to Lady: "You, too! Get a move on. We —"

"Go!" snapped Bolt. "Lady, hurry. It won't be a minute until I —"

"No," she said. "No! I won't budge until you do. You made me leave you once; I won't again. And anyhow — Oh, it's no use! If you're to be killed, well, I'm ready too. There's no use living — no hope of anything —"

"Then, dammit," he stormed at her, "get behind that tree! Give me a minute to stop 'em and — Here they come — *You're asking for it, Duke Morgan!*" he yelled, and started shooting.

Lady didn't run; she didn't even step behind a tree. No matter who or what this young man from Texas might be, he was somehow fine! He had risked his life for her before; he was risking it now — he had been risking it ever since she first laid eyes on him. So she stood close beside him, her head up, her face white, a clammy fear of death on her and yet, along with it, a strange inner glow.

Bolt saw the dark forms of several men, two or three or four breaking through the underbrush, and started shooting. Now was no chance for anything like accuracy. It was too dark for that, so dark that a man could scarcely distinguish another man's form from a tree or weathered boulder. The only thing to do was blaze away, empty a gun, hope to stop those fellows a moment — then break and run for it.

Blazing away, "Luck's with us," he muttered grimly. For he saw a tumbled confused group which made him sure that at least one of his bullets had found its mark and that a man falling had tripped other men so that they tumbled with him. And he heard Lady's hushed voice in response, "God be with us now — or never!"

"Now!" he whispered to her and caught her hand and started running once more. Thus, their ears filled with a din behind them, some small thunder of hoofs still on the bridge as the last horseman crossed, yells and shots from Dan's party, they came upon the river bank where the deep, troubled pool glinted ever so faintly in the starlight.

"Where are Steve and Molly?" panted Lady. "They couldn't go any farther! Oh, they've been shot — we've missed them in the dark. We —"

Later they were to know that Bolt had fleshed two of his six bullets: He had broken Duke Morgan's thigh and had made a cripple of the loud-mouthed Tom Colby. Sid, whom he would have been very glad to have shot, he had missed. And Sid, with all the fox and none of the lion of his father in him, had estimated truly that Bolt had emptied his six-gun. So now, as for a poised instant Bolt and Lady stood alone at the brink of the uneasy pool, Sid burst upon them and even laughed at them, his laughter high pitched with hysteria, and screamed:

"I owe you this, the two of you —" and started shooting.

Bolt threw both arms about Lady and swept her off her feet, hurling himself and her along with him down into the pool. It happened so swiftly and unexpectedly that it left Sid gawking and staring, and Lady Morgan hadn't time to know what was happening until it had happened. Their leap from the bank carried them down and still down — down so deep that she grew sure that they were never again going to rise up into starlight. There was panic in her breast; also there was something else. It wasn't fear. She was done with hope. Her arms grew as tight about Bolt Haveril's body as his were tight about her. For one small deathless fraction of a second she felt glad! When all hope is gone one can grow calm looking death in the face. It was best to die this way. An infinite stillness was about her, never the faintest sound ruffling it. When they rose to the surface they would be riddled with Sid's bullets. Better to drown — in this dear stranger's arms.

So she clung to him tight, tight. She held her breath until she felt her lungs bursting. Another moment —

But she realized that he was far from being as quiescent as she. He jerked one of her arms away, he began striking out lustily, swimming under water. Would the man never admit defeat!

His own lungs bursting, Bolt swam upstream. Had he had another six feet to go, never would he have made it. As it was he could still master the terrifically agonizing instinct to strive to gulp air, and he could still find strength to propel himself and his burden when they came to the pool's rim under the waterfall. In the dark, so pitch dark down here under water, he began groping, clawing at the submerged rocks. Thus he found in time what he sought; found even better than he had thought to find. Already Steve with Molly had travelled this way; Steve hadn't forgotten him; Steve's hands were reaching down to help.

And the most amazed girl in the world, excepting Molly Daly, of course, was drawn up along with Bolt Haveril into that natural tunnel at the upper end of the pool that was Crazy Barnaby's "Secret." Its mouth was only some three feet under the surface but was well hidden under the fluttering curtain of the waterfall. Where Steve and Molly stood the water was not above their knees; when they helped a pretty nearly exhausted Bolt and Lady to stand and move farther up the dark tunnel with them, they had not over a score of steps to go to have done altogether with the pool and its backwash.

If you knew just where to look for it in the dark here — and Bolt knew, having been led to the place by Barnaby — there was a little tin box containing, among other odds and ends of the boy's treasures, both candle ends and matches. In the eerie light of a draught-drawn candle flame these four who had come through to-night's adventure looked at each other — and didn't laugh!

At another time they must have laughed; later Bolt said, "We sure looked like drowned rats!" They pushed the wet hair back from their faces, dabbed the water out of their eyes and regarded one another gravely.

"It's like being dead and born again!" said Lady when she could speak at all.

Pretty blonde little Molly fell to nodding vigorously. Then she bolted into Steve's ready arms and began to sob.

272

"This is Barnaby's secret way?" asked Lady.

"He showed it to me to-night," said Bolt. "Steve and I came this way. — You're safe now, Lady. They can't get at you here; they don't know how Dan and Dave Heffinger and over a hundred of the boys, Molly's dad's friends mostly, are doing a clean-up job in the Valley. You're safe and you're free, Lady. Safe for the rest of your life."

She started to say something but couldn't. She didn't want to start sobbing the way Molly was so frankly doing now on Steve's shirt. But she looked at Bolt Haveril with a pair of eyes which spoke for her. Wan as the light was, wet and dishevelled as she was, her eyes were warm and glowing and so softly bright with gratitude that — well, a gratitude can be so great as almost to be twin to adoration.

"Even if you are Juan Morada —"

"But I'm not. Me, I'm just plain Bolt Haveril. From Texas, you know."

"But Teresa was so sure! And — and that scar on your chest that proved she was right!"

"That was darned funny," said Bolt.

"How," demanded Lady, "could she possibly know about that scar?"

"How could she? She must have guessed — she looks like a witch — it was Barnaby!"

"Barnaby?"

"That boy! Crazy?" Bolt slapped his leg so that the water flew. "Remember that Barnaby and I had a good long time together after we lost you out in the woods. We went swimming. He saw that scar; he even asked me about it. I got it when I was a kid; falling out of a tree a dead branch snagged me and pretty near opened me up. Barnaby must have told Teresa —"

"But why should she — ?"

"I'd say she hates Duke like poison," muttered Bolt. "I saw her look at him."

"Yes, she does. She tried to kill him once."

"Good for her. Well, to-night she planned to let him down into any sort of trouble she could. She must have known right off which of us was Morada; to get her knife into Duke, to make him trust the wrong man, she told him I was Morada. Can you blame her?"

Lady began to understand, to be sure he was right.

"As soon as Duke sent for her," she said, "she made Barnaby tell her what it was all about. Do you remember how long he was gone? Duke started to send someone else for her. She was asking Barnaby questions, trying to work out a sure way to trick Duke into a blunder. And —"

Molly sneezed.

"Here, let's get out of this," said Steve. "We can dry out a bit walking and then — gentlemen, ask me! — won't we dry *riding!* On horses again, going hell-for-leather, getting out of this corner of the earth. Give me a candle, Bolt."

Even with their candles they made slow progress through their tunnel, an ancient waterway worn through some fault in the mountain ten thousand years ago, a place strewn with round stones and boulders, and scooped out everywhere with round holes polished smooth by pebbles and sand particles awash in a strong

274

current of the very long ago. And they had a long way to go, at times crawling on their hands and knees. Once their tunnel swelled into the proportions of a monster cavern; their candlelight showed no ceiling to it. Here was the place where Barnaby always kept a change of clothes; he had his other clothes hidden in the Valley, in a secret place not fifty steps from the pool.

They went on, walking upright most of the rest of the way, Steve with a protecting arm about Molly. Bolt and Lady Morgan holding hands.

"It won't be long now, Lady," said Bolt. "Soon we'll be popping out in a box canyon so steep-walled and so thick with brush that the other end of the tunnel, pretty well filled with rocks and sand, too, could be there another thousand years without anyone finding it. Unless another Barnaby came along."

"Oh, that dear, blessed Barnaby! Do you think he is all right, Bolt?"

"Sure," laughed Bolt. "Trust Barnaby. I'll bet you that we'll hear the jingle of his bells most any time now. Now hold on tight; a hundred yards of harder going, then we're outside. Then all we've got to do is wait for Dan and the rest of the boys; they're to pick us up there, to tell us just how things went in the Valley."

"Listen!" cried Lady.

"What is it?"

"I — I thought I heard Barnaby's bells!"

She couldn't be sure. They went on. But almost immediately she called out again, soft rapture in her voice:

"Look, Bolt! I can see a star!"